GW00385525

17/8
2.11

E

Barcode
PTO

The Landmark Library
No. 21

THE CASE IS ALTERED

FOR

BERNARD BAYES

I

In one of those parts of London which have never been either very smart or very shabby there is a street called Cambodia Crescent. It was built in the latter half of the last century, and the houses are as solid and comfortable looking as most houses built in those days. Some of them are built in pairs, some stand by themselves, with extremely small gardens in front, and while some have been divided into flats and others turned into boarding-houses, most of them have managed to keep an air of dreary respectability. They smell of the past, stale cooking, thwarted hopes, and all the horrors of life at its worst in the bourgeois backwaters of Victorian England. Built at a time when money was plentiful and national arrogance on the increase, these houses reflect the dullness and vulgarity of their builders. Some of them have damp and gloomy basements and they all seem designed to give servants as much work and ill-health as possible. They have the self-righteous air of a selfish and uncultivated person who thinks that he is good and wise, and the ornamentation round the doors, windows and chimneys forms a lasting insult to the beauties of natural stone and careful craftsmanship. Or perhaps one can regard those Gothic details as the pitiable efforts of the spirit to deny the

7

falseness, the vulgarity and pretentiousness of its surroundings, so vilely corrupted by wealth and puritan-
ism. At all events these houses were built to serve the
needs of a class, and in them that class has left a
memorial of itself. Even to-day there are people who
spring directly from that class still lingering on in
Cambodia Crescent, but this is a time of transition,
and a puff or two of the fierce, cleansing winds that
blow out of the future occasionally blow even among
these grey walls and rattle the windows. It is not
simply that the *Daily Herald* is delivered at several
houses which used to receive nothing but *The Times*
or the *Morning Post*, but new ideas, new aspirations,
and new kinds of people are beginning to live and
move in them. And between the old ideas and the
new there is confusion. Looking along Cambodia
Crescent, you would see an image of material order
and security. The street is clean, the policeman keeps
it safe, the drains are in order, the postman delivers
the letters regularly, the lamps are lighted at the
proper time. But if you could look clearly through
the walls of the houses you would see that material
order is accompanied by spiritual disorder, and in
this way Cambodia Crescent is a microcosm of our
time and our race.

One of the houses, number 45 to be exact, was in-
habited for years by a lawyer and his family. It then
stood empty for a long time with a large notice-
board outside saying that it was to let. Nobody seemed
inclined to occupy it, and it gradually fell into some

disrepair, when Mrs. Fernandez caught sight of it from the top of a bus, and at once decided that it would do for her purpose, which was to establish herself as a landlady. A handsome and lively young Jewess, with ambition but no money, and with a semi-invalid husband and young child dependent on her, she had just reached one of those critical moments which are so frequent in the lives of the improvident. Her husband, who could be described as a person of no particular occupation, had been out of work for some time, and his savings were nearly all spent, while her own relations were either unable or unwilling to help her, because they disapproved of her husband and resented the independence of her nature. With the support of Mrs. Gambitt, she at once made arrangements to take the house.

Mrs. Gambitt, who was her best friend, had had a somewhat varied career. At one time she had helped to run a teashop, but like most teashops it left its proprietors with little but debts and a tendency to varicose veins incurred by too much standing about. At another time she had begun training as a masseuse, but she had given it up because the manageress had a down on her—or so Mrs. Gambitt thought; at all events, although she had paid her fees in advance, she left abruptly. At another time she had been engaged to a man, a commercial traveller. During a long engagement he made a great deal of purely circumstantial love to her, and when she eventually married him he failed to sleep with her and went off with her savings. Her first impulse was to sue him for divorce or theft, but she was unable to trace him and afraid of publicity. Her unhappy experience had at least one good result—it gave her, although falsely, the status of a married woman, and thus saved her from the contempt which women feel for virgins. And besides, when married women sometimes confided to her some of the most intimate details of their married life (women being less modest than men in this respect), Mrs. Gambitt, although she couldn't do likewise, had learnt how to nod knowingly and put a world of feeling into a "yes" or "no," and how to hint, as well, at experiences she had never experienced. After her disappointment in marriage and a few minor misfortunes that followed, she had been left a small legacy, so she decided to live "like a lady" for a year or two while keeping a look-out for a new occupation or another man. She became genteel, constipated and irritable, kept a fat dog and dabbled in the occult, living meanwhile in a boarding-house where she gave herself airs and got herself disliked. It was there that she first met Mrs. Fernandez, together with her husband and child.

God alone knows what it is that sometimes draws the most unlikely people together, but within a few weeks a real intimacy was formed between the two women. Mrs. Gambitt had her virtues, but she was no enchantress. She was not well made, and very thin. Her features were homely. Her complexion,

owing partly to her habits of smoking, eating a great
many sweet things, and taking no exercise, was
muddy. Her voice, hands, feet and movements were
none of them graceful. Her expression was sulky and
her manner assured, but in her eyes there was a
kindness that had never fulfilled itself, and now
sought to do so upon the person of Mrs. Fernandez.

Paul Fernandez was at first inclined to disapprove
of his wife's new friend, but when he understood that
Mrs. Gambitt not only professed an affection for her,
but was actually going to put up the money for the
new venture by which they were all supposed to be
going to make a living, his manner completely
changed, and Mrs. Gambitt became the only other
person in the world, besides his wife and child, to
whom he spoke amiably. Whatever state he might be
in now (and it was clear to anybody that the man's
health was unsound) he had in his time been a fairly
shrewd and successful man, and was not slow to
recognise in Mrs. Gambitt a godsend. She had appeared just at the moment when his resources were
at an end, a circumstance which had caused him
even more than the anxiety which might be expected
in a man with a wife and child to support and no
means to support them. He was much older than his
wife, and had only been married to her a few years.
Even when they had first met he had been in the
early stages of the physical state he was in now, and
yet had been able to attract and win her, in spite
of the fact that handsome young Jewesses of good

character do not usually fail to find suitable husbands. Imagine his ecstasy, finding first that he could attract her, then that he could get her, then that he could keep her. Imagine the dawning of his anxiety lest after all he might not be able to keep her, lest he might lose her, and so lose the whole centre of his life—for he loved her deeply and fiercely, as he had loved no other woman in his life, with the all-consuming passion of a man who feels not only the loss of his youth but a threat of complete physical decay and even of death hanging over him. In the game of life he felt her to be not only his last, but his only chance, and if he lost her, he felt he would lose everything.

If there was one thing he couldn't bear, it was to see his wife talking to any other man. He could hardly bear her out of his sight, and when she was absent he was haunted by images of her in the company of other men. It was not that he actually disbelieved in her faithfulness, but his experience of women—not the best sort of women, perhaps—had taught him how easily they are tempted by material and especially sexual advantages. He was not afraid so much that his wife would forsake him of her own accord, but that some man richer, younger and more attractive than himself might lure her away from him. In secret terror, coughing now and then from his unsound lungs through a cloud of cigarette smoke (it was a vile brand of cigarettes that he smoked), he watched intently to see if his wife took any notice of other men, and then even more apprehensively to see if those men paid any casual attention to her. Whether noticing or imagining that they did, the tendency to jealousy already nascent in him began to develop, and he began to indulge his own passion for her to the point of perversity, in the hope of making more sure of her.

His fears were greatly increased when his money began to come to an end. His business connections had become fewer in recent years, and as for friends, he had none. The only man who might now have been able to help him was one he had quarrelled with some time previously over an agreement of partnership which he considered to have been violated, and the quarrel had not been and could not now be made up. Fernandez' obsession with his wife had for some time made him extraordinarily indifferent both to the outside world and to his own material interests, and his neglect of these, combined with his shattered health, now left him not only without friends who could help him, but without even the means of helping himself. He had no regular trade or profession, and, even if he had had one, would no longer have been fit to practise it. He had lived from hand to mouth, sometimes well-to-do and sometimes starving, but something had always "turned up" at critical times. At one time a performer on the variety stage, he had kept a hotel in Australia, assisted a ship's chandler in Port Said, been concerned in the film trade, acted as a shady

kind of "dealer" in London, and even, for he was of
a mechanical turn of mind, patented an almost useless invention—a collapsible lamp for use on aero-
planes. It was one of his grievances against the world,
a common one amongst inventors, that he had derived no benefit from his invention, and he had a
suspicion, from something he had once read in the
newspapers, that this very invention was being
widely used by the government of the United States.
He had now reached a condition where this invention was almost the only topic, apart from his wife
and child, about which he could carry on anything
like a conversation.

With his money dwindling, he had become a prey
to anxiety, and slept badly, sitting up in bed and
smoking innumerable cigarettes. The other inhabitants of the boarding-house complained of his cough
and also of his appearance and manners, his bloodshot eyes and dirty nails, while they indulged in all
sorts of gossip about him, and his wife, and his wife's
new friend Mrs. Gambitt. Their complaints turned
into rejoicings when they heard that all three were
to leave, accompanied of course by the child, and
they all hoped that somebody more respectable and
more amiable would take their places, though it
must be admitted that they liked and said they were
sorry for Mrs. Fernandez and the child, wondered
"however she could have married him" and "whatever would become of poor little Rosy with a father
like that."

Between the time when Mrs. Fernandez, riding down Cambodia Crescent on the top of a bus, first caught sight of number 45, and the time when, with Mrs. Gambitt's aid, she was ready to move into the house, a change had come over both women, as well as over Fernandez. They had plenty to do, plans to make and business to transact, a new interest in life, a pleasant sense of friendly co-operation, and the prospect of a chance of making a small but steady and not too arduous living—and all this was good for them, and made them take a more cheerful view of things. Mrs. Gambitt, who had at first taken a dislike to Fernandez almost as strong as the affection she felt for his wife, had been melted by his unexpected politeness to her, and even felt strangely fascinated by what was male and saturnine in his nature. Her chief worry was about money and the need of making a little go a long way at first. When they moved in one brilliant summer morning, very little had been done to the house in the way of repairs and decoration, and it was at once plain that a considerable sum would have to be spent on necessities. While Mrs. Gambitt was wholly occupied with the economic side of things, Mrs. Fernandez found time to worry about her husband, for the removal of any immediate anxiety about their livelihood seemed to leave him more obsessed than ever before with his passionate feelings towards her, and while she delighted in his ardour she began to feel a little nervous about it. Only the child Rosy was untouched by these adult cares. In fact, she was in raptures of excitement about her new home, and celebrated her entry into it by spending most of her time opening and shutting the doors, making her voice echo in the empty rooms, and rushing up and down the stairs. As the staircase was uncarpeted, she was able to make a splendid volume of noise by stamping her feet and running the point of Mrs. Gambitt's umbrella along the bannisters.

Mrs. Fernandez, though not in the least aggressive or pretentious, was a woman of somewhat large ideas, and the splendour of her imagination sometimes led others captive. When, for example, Mrs. Gambitt had spoken of employing a maid-of-all-work, Mrs. Fernandez declared that she had already set her heart on engaging a manservant. Mrs. Gambitt doubted whether any man would be willing to do most of the work of the house single-handed (for she herself had become too much of a "lady" to be willing to do any but the lightest and most casual housework), and still more whether he would be willing to keep interrupting his work in order to slip into a black coat and answer the front door bell. But Mrs. Fernandez was sure that a man could be found, because so many people were out of work. ("Brutes!" cried Mrs. Gambitt, "they prefer to rot on the dole rather than do a decent job of work in a good home, the parasites!") At any rate, a manservant they must have, for it would give "tone" to the house. When Mrs. Gambitt heard this, she at once gave in, for she would never have thought of it herself, and as one who was coming more and more to believe in "tone," she could not but agree. It will be guessed that Mrs. Gambitt belonged to that numerous and depressing class of women who are not exactly of the kind known as decayed gentlewomen, but whose chief aim in life is to be taken for decayed gentlewomen.

A man, a respectable and capable man, who was prepared to undertake most of the work in the house for an absurdly small wage and his keep, was easily found—so easily, in fact, that Mrs. Gambitt was suspicious from the first, and said there must be something wrong with him. But Mrs. Fernandez, who engaged him, was delighted both with the man's looks and his character. It was true that he had had no experience of quite this kind of work before, but still he seemed more than willing to attempt it. His name was Albert Empringham. He was a small, alert, fresh-complexioned man with grey hair and rather a puzzled expression on his face, as though he couldn't quite make out why life had treated him quite the way it had, or what it was likely to do to him next. It was not that he had had a particularly rough time, but that he had found life full of surprises. If you looked carefully at his hands you could see that they were the hands of a craftsman, and, in fact, he had as a young man been apprenticed to a marquetry worker. Just when he had become really skilful, had set up on his own, and was on the point of establishing a steady and lucrative little business,

B

the War broke out and nobody bought any more marquetry work. Like most men in those days, Empringham wanted to join His Majesty's forces, but failed to pass the physical examination and was obliged to look about for a job. The first one he could find was that of a waiter in a quiet, old-fashioned hotel in a very central position, and there he remained for nearly fifteen years. At the end of that time the site of the hotel was sold for rebuilding purposes, and the staff was dismissed. Empringham had been able to put a bit of money by, but it was by no means as much as he could have wished, and he felt bound to seek another job. Mrs. Fernandez' advertisement caught his eye, Mrs. Fernandez herself came up to his standards, and although the situation had obvious disadvantages, he undertook to fill it. He rather liked the idea of being in at the beginning of the adventure, and Mrs. Fernandez cleverly managed to give him something like a sense of partnership in it, promising him that if or when it was a success he should have a substantial rise in his wages.

Among the disadvantages which sprang to his notice when he came to live at 45 Cambodia Crescent, one of the chief was Mrs. Gambitt. Empringham was himself a genuine and unpretentious man; he had at once taken to Mrs. Fernandez, finding her to be the same; his long experience of hotel life and his natural shrewdness had given him a very nice sense of human nature, and especially of the finer shades of gentility, and when he found out that Mrs. Gambitt was pretending to be better than she really was (which he found out as soon as he set eyes on her), and in addition that she was inclined to be disagreeable in the process, he at once took a dislike to her. He was by no means philosophical enough to allow for the numerous misfortunes and disappointments in Mrs. Gambitt's life, or to see that her pretentiousness was only assumed to try and make up for her unhappiness; he simply judged her as the world always judges the unsuccessful—unfavourably.

Within a few days of taking over the house, Mrs. Fernandez had the pleasure of seeing three lodgers installed in it. One of them was an acquaintance of Mrs. Gambitt's, a Mrs. Petherham-Porter, a middle-aged woman whom people wrongly said had been abandoned some years previously by her husband. She had just enough money to live on, nothing particular to do, nothing in particular to look back on and nothing in particular to look forward to. She had no relations except a stepson in South America. A lonely woman, with few resources either inside or outside herself, she seldom left her room after she had settled down in it, insisted on looking after it herself, and would scarcely allow anyone to enter it. When she went out, she locked the door behind her, though she owned nothing of any but sentimental value. Her only regular visitor from the first was Mrs. Gambitt, for whom in the afternoons she provided strong tea and sweet cakes, and whom she talked to in confidence. Otherwise her habits were frugal and solitary. No meals were taken in to her, and it was known that she had peculiar views about diet.

Empringham felt some curiosity about her, and wondered if she were not one of those old misers one reads about in the papers, where they are called "rich recluses," and who are found dead with holes in their stockings, rats in their cupboards, and an enormous bank balance. "She gives me a cold look whenever I see her," he said, in describing her, on his first evening out, to his married sister, "and I don't believe she's quite right in the head." And indeed he was perhaps not altogether wrong, for Mrs. Petherham-Porter had come to regard people with disfavour unless they were professed spiritualists. "She's getting very psychic," Empringham overheard Mrs. Gambitt telling Mrs. Fernandez one day, "more so than ever." In fact, Mrs. Porter took some interest in observing her neighbours, sometimes by gazing into a crystal and sometimes by the really more direct method of gazing through the keyhole of their room. On one occasion Empringham caught her in the act. She didn't hear him approach, so he just waited with his hands on his hips till she should see him. When she had had an eyeful of the rather limited view through the keyhole, she straightened herself and turned round, and seeing Empringham standing behind her, gave a guilty start.

"Are you looking for anything, madam?" he asked ironically.

When she recovered herself, she gave him what he would have called a cold look, made no answer, and went back to her own room. But the glance she gave him had something helpless in it, which almost made him regret for a moment that he had found her out.

The room into which she had been peeping—or trying to peep, for, indeed, she had seen little except part of the back of a chair and two leaves of an aspidistra—was occupied by a married couple, the two other original or foundation lodgers. They had been persuaded to live here by Mrs. Fernandez' cousin, who worked in the same office as the man, rather a seedy-looking individual called Rudd. Rudd was a Londoner. Between thirty and forty, he was not very tall and not very cheerful, had a prominent Adam's-apple, a mouth full of false teeth, and a good deal of trouble with his digestion. He stuttered, wore spectacles, had parents at Streatham whom he helped to support, and spent much time solving cross-word puzzles in the hopes of winning a prize. Needless to say, he never won a prize. He always had tickets in the Irish, the Calcutta, and other sweeps, always dreamt that he had drawn a winning number, and was continually nagged at by his wife, a fluffy, fretful, disappointed young woman, for not having done so.

Such, then, was the general position at 45 Cambodia Crescent soon after its opening. That fairly large and untidy-looking house was expected to provide employment and prospects for Albert Empring-

ham, a living for the decaying Fernandez, his wife
and daughter; it was expected to enable Mrs.
Gambitt to keep her dignity, to house Mrs. Petherham-Porter and Mr. and Mrs. Rudd in some degree
of comfort, and prospectively a number of other
people besides. How far the house responded to the
demands put upon it will be made plain in the
succeeding chapters.

II

ONE afternoon, about three weeks after Mrs. Fernandez had moved into the house, a lady, no longer young, and neatly but not at all well dressed, was making her way along the street and looking up at the numbers on the houses. You could see to look at her that she was not rich, but that she believed in order and cleanliness and kindness, and although she might have lost that assurance which the possession of money brings with it, she had a natural dignity or authority in her manner and movements which evidently enabled her to face the world. Her very umbrella, a long, slender, old-fashioned thing with a curved silver handle, was a kind of index to her character.

When she arrived in front of number 45, she put a lorgnon to her eye and looked the house up and down, just as though it were an animal or a piece of furniture which she had some intention of buying but suspected of weak points. The slightly dilapidated façade and the garden, ragged and sombre compared with its neighbours, caused a faint expression of distaste to pass over her face. For a moment she hesitated, as if in doubt whether it was really worth her while to take any further notice of number 45, but with a sigh she walked deliberately up the

steps and rang the bell. She felt rather apprehensive
and even a little frightened as she waited for an
answer, but nobody could possibly have guessed this
from her exterior.

"Damn," said Albert Empringham, "that front
door bell again! You don't get a moment's peace in
this place."

And he put down the plate he was washing, dried
his hands on a dish-cloth, slipped into his black coat,
and hurried along the hall with the characteristic
gait of the small and active middle-aged man that
he was. When he opened the door and saw the unknown lady waiting on the threshold he was able,
from long years of self-control, to preserve a grave
absence of expression on his face while making a
quick but careful judgment of her. As he himself
would have said, he knew a lady when he saw one,
and he was ready to be respectful to her. As for the
lady in question, she was agreeably surprised to see
such a respectable-looking manservant at the door,
instead of the slatternly maid she had expected.

"Good afternoon," she said. "I came about an
advertisement I saw in the paper. I wanted to inquire
about some rooms."

"Yes, madam. Will you please step this way?"

She stepped that way, and found herself in the
hall, which was still entirely bare of carpets, furniture or pictures, and was just going to comment
on its appearance, when she caught sight of the
child Rosy Fernandez, who was tracing a pattern

on the lowest stair with her first finger and some spittle.

"Well, little one, and how are you?" she said affably, inclining slightly over the child, like a queen over an orphan, her scanty jewellery tinkling a little, and her cheap stays creaking.

"I'm not a little one," said the child scornfully. "Everybody says I'm very big for my age."

"Dear me," said the visitor. "How very precocious."

"Old-fashioned, she is," Empringham explained.

"And what is your name, my dear?"

"What's yours?" said Rosy.

"You tell me yours first," said the lady, determined to be kind, "then I'll tell you mine."

"My name's Rosy Fernandez," said the child importantly, "and I'm nearly six and a half."

"That *is* nice, isn't it?"

"Now you tell me your name," said Rosy archly.

"My name is Constantia Brixworth."

"That's a silly name! How old are you?"

Here Empringham tactfully intervened.

"Get along, Rosy," he said. "Where's your mummy?"

"A silly name," cried Rosy exultantly. "Silly, silly, silly!"

But just at that moment her mother appeared at the top of the stairs, and Empringham said:

"A lady to see you, Mrs. Fernandez, about some rooms."

Miss Brixworth noticed that he didn't say "madam" to Mrs. Fernandez as he had done to her. Looking up at Mrs. Fernandez, who came tripping down the stairs, young, hopeful and cheerful, she had another agreeable surprise, for the outside of the house had led her to expect the usual dowdy landlady.

"Good afternoon," she repeated. "I came about some rooms."

Even if Miss Brixworth had not been able to see at once that Mrs. Fernandez was a Jewess, it would very soon have been easy to tell that she was one, by the way she began over-emphasising her partiality to bacon for breakfast.

"And you would be requiring breakfast?" Mrs. Fernandez queried. "Just an ordinary breakfast, I suppose, coffee and bacon and so on? Don't you think a couple of rashers ideal? With an egg and a tomato or two? Oh, there's nothing to beat it!"

They were standing in an empty room on the first floor, and so full of vitality was Mrs. Fernandez that you might have said that she was the only decoration the room needed and that she seemed at the same time to fill it with warmth and light. Miss Brixworth felt a little fluttered and greatly charmed. The voice of Mrs. Fernandez, so warm and vibrant, gave a full-bloodedness to the most casual remark, and afforded a ringing contrast to the lax and mincing speech of the average Englishwoman. Though the day was dull and there was no carpet on the stairs Mrs. Fernandez moved with a swing, showed signs of frankness and good humour, but none of meanness or cunning, was without any question beautiful, and only resembled other landladies in the fact that she took occasion to remark that she was not like other land-ladies. For once the remark was true in almost every sense. And it was clear that she was proud of her appearance without being unduly vain. Her skin was clear, her complexion fresh, her features were regular, her plentiful hair was at once fine and wiry, with a natural crimp in it—she wore it parted in the middle and kept it well brushed and free from any ornament. She gave the impression that she was a person who functioned as a human being is supposed to function, and that she enjoyed it, and with her rolling eyes and animated manner she very soon captivated Miss Brixworth, who looked a little stately and was really a little timid. Whatever the rooms had been like, it would have been very difficult for Miss Brixworth, now that she had seen Mrs. Fernandez, to have avoided taking one of them. Actually they pleased her, these fairly large, solidly built rooms with heavy doors and windows and massive marble fireplaces. Most of them were still unfurnished, though there were signs of a recent attempt at decoration. The bathroom had been equipped with a new geyser, and the wallpapers had obviously been newly hung, their patterns being florid, and designed to give "a rich effect," very much in the Jewish taste. Miss Brix-worth noticed that enamel number plates had been fixed on the doors.

"Of course, you know," said Mrs. Fernandez, "you can't do everything at once, can you? I want to make this place really nice, but it takes time——" And she launched out into a sea of Jewish visions of luxury and comfort far beyond her means. Miss Brixworth interrupted her to say:

"Very well, I'll take this room, provided you can get it furnished for me."

"Oh yes, and have you any idea how long you'll want it for?"

Miss Brixworth looked out of the window at the grey housetops.

"If it suits me," she said, with a sigh, "I might stay a long time." How often she had made the same remark in recent years, and how seldom she had been able to stay long in one place!

"We'll do our best to make you comfortable," said Mrs. Fernandez. "Of course we may have to wait a bit before we get everything as we should like it. I hope we shall have a carpet on the stairs before very long——"

Miss Brixworth didn't say that she didn't care whether there was a carpet on the stairs or not, or that she liked the look of the manservant who had opened the door to her, or that she was glad there was a child in the house, or that she had taken an immediate liking to Mrs. Fernandez, or that she was touched by the way the landlady said "we," inviting her to share the present discomfort for the sake of future ease, or that she could see an eagerness that was a little desperate in Mrs. Fernandez' manner, for although all these things were true, she was a little shy, and always a little distrustful of herself when she took too quick a fancy to people or places. Besides, these lonely, nomadic women get into the way of keeping their feelings to themselves, for want of anybody to confide in. So she simply told Mrs. Fernandez when she expected to arrive, and said good-bye.

No sooner was the front door closed behind Miss Brixworth than Mrs. Fernandez hurried to the kitchen to tell Mrs. Gambitt of her success. But unfortunately she found a dispute going on between Mrs. Gambitt and Empringham, who was saying:

"And I may say I'm not used to being ordered about like that by a woman or anybody else, and I don't mean to begin now. If I'm to work in this house I'll do the work Mrs. Fernandez requires in my own way, and nothing more."

"How dare you speak to me like that?" said Mrs. Gambitt. And so they were going on, while Mrs. Fernandez, instead of walking straight into the room, paused to listen for a moment outside the kitchen door, which had panels of frosted glass. Her heart beat a little quicker with the sudden sense of vexation and anxiety caused by this early dissension in the household. She was about to open the door and enter the room in the rôle of peacemaker when she felt a tug at her skirt. It was Rosy.

"Well, dear, what's the matter?"

"I want a rocking-horse," said Rosy firmly.

"A rocking-horse! Well, you may have one some day."

"But I want one *now*!"

"Well, you can't have one now."

"Why not?"

"Because there's no money to buy one with."

"Hasn't Mrs. Gambitt got some money?"

"No, dear, not to buy rocking horses with."

"Hasn't daddy got any money?"

"No, dear, not now."

"Why not?"

"Never mind, dear."

"Has the new lady got any money?"

"Perhaps she has a little," said Mrs. Fernandez, "but not to buy rocking-horses for little girls with."

"But when I'm a big girl, mummy, will she buy me a rocking horse then?"

"Perhaps, dear, if you're good."

"And when shall I be a big girl?"

"By and by, Rosy. Now run along and don't ask so many questions." Rosy ran along. She ran into a little room, originally meant no doubt to serve as a study or a housekeeper's room, with a window looking out on to the narrow back-garden, but now used by the Fernandez family and Mrs. Gambitt as a sitting-room, and called by them for some reason or other "the office"—probably because they had already formed the habit of sitting in there and wondering how they were going to pay their bills. The day was cloudy and the room was made especially dim by the foliage of a large plane tree which grew in the narrow back-garden. When Rosy went in she found her father sitting by himself. He had a cigarette in his mouth and was bending over a doll of hers which he had been trying to mend, not very successfully, for his hands were shaky. He was always doing odd jobs nowadays, trying to mend things and clean things. This was because he felt secretly ashamed at being in such a dependent position as he was now, and he wanted to try and justify himself and show that he was helping the household. As soon as the child was with her father, whom she resembled, her manner quite changed. She seemed to become in her own childish way as moody and sparing of speech as he was himself. She stood watching him trying to mend the doll, but where most children would at once have had their whole attention occupied by that process, she looked without really seeing, for she was still thinking of the rocking-horse. She didn't pester her father with questions, and he seemed to understand her silence as she stood there brooding, her finger in her mouth. Suddenly he looked up and said:

"What is it, Rosy?"

"I want a rocking-horse," she said.

"You wait," he said, "and you'll get it one day." And then, seeing his wife come into the room, he added: "Takes after me, Rosy does. If she means to have a thing, she'll have it."

"Don't go putting ideas into her head," said Mrs.

Fernandez. "Paul, do you know what Natalie said to Empringham just now? She said, 'I know what it'll come to,' she said, 'either you'll have to leave this house or I shall.' I don't know why she finds fault with him so, I'm sure."

She stopped abruptly, as she heard Mrs. Gambitt coming into the room behind her. Mrs. Gambitt's face looked peaked and sulky in the murky afternoon light, which had a greenish tinge from the leafage outside.

"If only servants knew their place!" she said in a hard voice, and going to a cupboard she took out a box of dates and began eating them. She liked eating, she liked eating sweet things, and she specially liked eating dates, and spitting out the slim, sticky stones into her hand. She saw Mrs. Fernandez pass her hand over her forehead, pushing back her hair.

"What's the matter, Beryl?" she said. "Got a headache? Tired?" She leant forward, with her mouth full, to kiss her.

"No," said Mrs. Fernandez, "I was thinking I'm glad we've got this Miss Brixworth coming. If we only let one more room after that we'll keep going nicely. . . ."

Now when Miss Brixworth left Cambodia Crescent she hurried round to see her only intimate friend, Miss Frances Haymer, who was expecting her. And although she saw Miss Haymer very often, and although Miss Haymer was a distant relation of hers, she was always a little afraid of her, for Miss Haymer had a knowledge of the world and a vigorous manner which she herself entirely lacked. Miss Haymer was usually confined to the house by a rheumatic affection of the leg, and this reacted on her temper in such a way that her servants seldom stayed long with her. Miss Brixworth, too, was often used as a scapegoat and made to bear the burden of her friend's meditations on life in general. But Miss Brixworth enjoyed being scolded almost as much as Miss Haymer enjoyed scolding her, simply because she knew, beyond all doubt, that Miss Haymer was really very fond of her, and in the gradual wreckage of their lives (for Miss Haymer had also come down in the world) the two women helped to keep each other afloat.

The contrast in their appearance was remarkable. The neatness and modesty of Miss Brixworth was just perceptibly flavoured with elegance; Miss Haymer, on the other hand, was fantastic and flamboyant, and invariably attracted attention, which always made Miss Brixworth feel uncomfortable. When she went out, Miss Haymer used a stick with a rubber end, and tottered along on heels that were rather too high, supporting, like some caryatid, a large, old-fashioned hat, decorated with a bird or two and some fruit, as in her heyday. She wore too much jewellery, and moved with a mixture of difficulty and dignity, gesticulating as she talked, so it was no wonder that people often turned to stare at her. To look at her you would say that when she went to bed her toilet must be almost a dissolution; so carefully got up each

morning, she must end the day by an equally careful disintegration, almost a dismemberment; the
removal of hat, wig and shoes would at once take
cubits off her stature; out would come teeth, off
bracelets and stays, and with the removal of that
perennial velvet band, down would tumble a cascade
of chins. Heaven alone knew what supports and
safety-pins, screws, straps, skewers and stanchions
might not hold the old girl together. Perhaps she took
all to pieces, like one of those ready-made houses with
every section numbered; perhaps after the arduous
day she went all limp, and folded herself up and put
herself away in a drawer, quietly going to bed in her
bones. . . .

A generation ago the name of Miss Frances
Haymer was quite well known. Travel in remote
regions has become a commonplace in recent years,
but in the days when it was uncommon for women,
and especially young unmarried women, to travel
alone in obscure countries, there was nobody more
enterprising than Miss Frances Haymer. Away she
went to places nobody knew anything about, and
back she came to write books which "everybody"
read, and to lecture not only in London but at Bath,
Bournemouth and Torquay, and in public halls as
well as drawing-rooms. People admired her, were
afraid of her, and believed everything she told them,
for she looked so confident and energetic that one
couldn't imagine that she was speaking anything but
the truth, and besides, her geniality helped to make

her views convincing. One of the greatest lady travellers of her day, she had gradually fallen into obscurity. She had grown old with a good deal of bravura, and although she now lived in a small flat with only one servant she had managed to preserve a great many souvenirs of her travels, signed photographs and bric-à-brac, together with her independent and autocratic manner.

Sometimes the two friends would take an outing in Hyde Park, when the weather and Miss Haymer's leg permitted, and the sunlight would catch those large, double-jointed hands, formerly capable but now arthritic, which Miss Haymer used to wave about in the air as she talked. Or it would light up the large, gaunt face, rather elaborately made up. The eyes, between dark lids and pouches, seemed as cold as a parrot's and as malicious as a crocodile's; the nose was large and heavily powdered; the seamy cheeks were wild-rose colour, and a little darker in the seams; the large, reddened mouth was shadowed by an almost imperceptible moustache; and a pair of massive Burmese earrings tinkled, like the bells of some barbaric temple, on each side of the head. And when the man came round to collect the chair money, Miss Haymer would look at him with a firmness that made him quail—very much, in fact, as she had looked at keepers of Mongolian *khans* in the late eighties, with an expression that seemed to say, "If I want a night's lodging, my man, I mean to have it." One doesn't practise an intimidating manner for nearly

seventy summers for nothing. If you take up Miss
Haymer's once celebrated books, *Beyond Baluchistan*
and *Back to Bactria*, you find that intimidation was
her passport—she always asked for things as though
she were conferring a favour by merely asking. The
most refractory yak would yield milk at sight of her,
kvass flowed like water, and difficulties of all kinds
folded their tents like the less hardy of the local
inhabitants and silently stole away. The head-
hunters of Formosa complimented her at first on her
head by saying that they would like to hunt it, but
they were soon made to realise that it was no Aunt
Sally who had visited their shores, for she took two
of their own heads and, instead of hunting them,
knocked them quietly but firmly together. She had
never thought much of the human race, but as she
got older and saw how easily hypnotised and in-
timidated it was, she thought even less of it. But if
you really got to know Miss Haymer you found that
under her stiff corsage beat the kindest of hearts, and
that the skirted grenadier was sometimes as spon-
taneous as a child. Miss Brixworth sometimes felt a
slight pang of envy mingling with her admiration for
her friend.

"You have such magnetism," she sighed.

"Rubbish, Connie," said Miss Haymer. "I know
how to manage people, and you don't."

The contrast between them was never plainer than
on those rare occasions when they set out together to
visit a museum or a picture gallery. Constantia Brix-

worth, in black cotton stockings and an old fur tippet, would lean forward and peer through her lorgnon at each canvas as though she were looking for finger-prints, but as her sight was nearly perfect and her knowledge of painting strictly limited, her behaviour could only be put down to enthusiasm and curiosity. "You can't possibly see it from there!" Frances Haymer would exclaim from under one of her two remarkable hats, and she would stride back from the walls with her head on one side, leaning heavily on her rubber-ended stick, usually backing into some unsuspecting group of bystanders, and uttering some forceful expression of approval or dislike.

About both of them there was undoubtedly something heroic, a "Nelson touch" in the way they gradually approached their end, determined to go down with all their flags flying. They understood pretty clearly that they were left over from the past, that nobody had much use now for the ideas they had been brought up to believe in, but they hardly complained at all about their isolation, their diminishing incomes, or the poor outlook for their future. But while Miss Brixworth had little to glorify her approaching old age, Miss Haymer had not yet parted with most of her jewellery. The more her flesh withered on her bones the deeper she rifled her jewel-box to load herself with the last treasures of her race. She would have sympathised, no doubt, with that Eastern poet who left certain letter-like packets to be burned with his corpse, packets which, at his cremation, burst out in all directions as Roman candles, Catherine wheels, and rockets showering emeralds and rubies on the astonished heads of the undertakers. Miss Brixworth to some extent consoled herself for the scantiness of her clothes and ornaments by cultivating a passion for cleanliness. "I don't expect luxuries," she would say, "but I will not be dirty. When one is old one cannot expect to be pretty, but one absolutely must be *soignée*." But the pleasure she took in order and hygiene was not limited to her person. No dust ever settled in those bed-sitting-rooms that she lived in, she would accept no Treasury notes from her bank but brand-new ones, and the little coin that came her way she actually scrubbed with soda or soap and a nail-brush in very hot water with just a dash of Jeyes' fluid. At times, however, cleanliness failed to console her, and she couldn't help thinking of Miss Haymer's adornments. Although she knew that Miss Haymer would lend or give her almost anything she asked for, she never liked to ask, while Miss Haymer, ruthless as she was in some ways, was too delicate to allow herself to make any suggestion that Miss Brixworth lacked anything. But on one occasion, when they were out of doors together and the sun was shining, Miss Brixworth couldn't help exclaiming:

"My dear Fanny, do you realise what you've got on this morning? You really *can't* wear three brooches at once!"

"Can't I? But I *am* wearing them. You never remember, Connie, that I'm very fond of good jewellery." And she added impulsively, "Just to show you *how* fond, I'm going to pick out the best of these and give it to you."

And she suited the action to the word with as much ceremony as a sovereign taking an order off his own breast to pin it on that of a beloved subject. Miss Brixworth blushed with pleasure, and tried to utter a stammering protest, but her friend silenced her with a look and a word. And there was no doubt that she must be obeyed.

"And now," said Miss Haymer in that dry yet juicy voice of hers, "and now, Connie, what about these new rooms of yours in Cambodia Crescent?"

She knew perfectly well that her friend could only have taken one room, but still she said "rooms."

"A Jewess, Connie, I think you said? Very wise of you I should say, and likely to be much more human than the average landlady."

"That's just how she struck me," said Miss Brixworth, "and she has a very pretty little child and a most respectable-looking manservant."

"Well, I shall look forward to hearing all about them. I know I can rely on your curiosity to find out all the essentials."

Miss Brixworth knew that this was true, and she knew also that Miss Haymer would express some downright opinions on whatever she was told, for, going back, no doubt, to the lecturing habits of her younger days, she tended more and more to lay down

the law. Protected so long by the advantages of
birth, money, experience, and a natural arrogance,
it was a wonder that she hadn't developed into a
more unpleasant character. But perhaps the reduced
circumstances in which she had found herself since
the War had brought the natural warmth of her
heart to the rescue of her better qualities. When her
opinions were wrong she could only with difficulty
be induced to abandon them, for she was obstinate
and didn't like being contradicted, but as they were
usually based on common sense and some knowledge
of the world, Miss Brixworth was already rather
curious to know what her friend would think about
the people at 45 Cambodia Crescent.

III

Two people were standing on the pavement opposite the house. One of them was a young man in a rather worn blue serge suit and a bowler hat, the other a girl of about his own age who seemed to be wearing her best clothes. It was early in the evening, and summer being on the wane, the light was beginning to fail. Streams of people going home from work were crossing the road some fifty yards away, for at right angles to Cambodia Crescent was a busy shopping street. At one corner was a large and expensive shop for women's clothes, which seemed rather out of place in that part of London, but which had been built at a time when the surroundings were richer, and had prospered ever since. As a rule, hardly anything was displayed in the windows beyond a blouse, a hat and a necklace, perhaps, on which the prices were never marked; two gorgeous commissionaires took care of the customers and their cars; and a notice over the door said nothing except *Pélagie: Robes and Modes.* As you went past you caught a glimpse of luxurious saloons with many mirrors and thick carpets; or perhaps through an open window you could see a crowd of young dressmakers at work; or you might meet half a dozen elegant and painted young women who worked there as mannequins coming, as now, out of one of the side doors.

The young woman now standing on the pavement in Cambodia Crescent was employed at Pélagie's, but not as a saleswoman, nor as a dressmaker, nor as a mannequin. She was employed in the kitchen (for Pélagie's is one of those prosperous and up-to-date firms which take proper care of their employees, and provide them with good cheap meals, just as with sports grounds and other amenities), and that was why she was able to get out earlier than many others who drew much higher wages. Once the tea-things had been washed up she was free to go. It was nice of course to be able to get out early, but she was far from satisfied with her position, and would far rather have been a dressmaker or a mannequin—though she knew she could never aspire to be a mannequin, for she wasn't pretty or graceful enough, and knew that she would never be able to assume, under any circumstances, that assured and sinuous way of moving, so full of affected languor and sensuous grace, which is customary in the mannequin's profession.

"The girls are just coming out," she said, looking towards Pélagie's. She hoped that some of them might see her with her young man, but unfortunately the light was failing, they were too far away, and also too much occupied with themselves even to glance down Cambodia Crescent.

"Yes," he said, "but look, Amy, that's the house."

He nodded his head towards number 45 on the other side of the road. There were lights in the rooms occupied by Mrs. Petherham-Porter and by Mr. and Mrs. Rudd. From that occupied by the Rudds, which was on the ground floor, came the sound of a gramophone.

"Oo, is that the house?" said the young woman.

"Well, why not? D'you think it's too good for me?"

"No, it's not that."

"Well, what is it then?"

"Oh, Eric, I was only thinking it'll be so expensive."

"No, only two bob more than I've been paying in the other place, if you want to know. I'll be on the top floor of course."

She stood, with her head a little on one side, gazing across the road. Her companion couldn't see her face. All he could see was her dark-red felt hat with its little paste ornament in the shape of a swallow. It was the hat she had always worn so far when walking out with him. Just at that moment a cool wind blew down the street, carrying before it along the pavement a fine alluvium of dust. Amy shivered, and said:

"I know it's silly of me, but I somehow wish you weren't going there."

"Why? What d'you mean?"

"I don't know, Eric. It just gives me a queer feeling. I can't explain."

"You're dreaming," he said, without taking his

eyes off the house. Mrs. Porter appeared in silhouette at her window, drawing the curtains.

"Of course it's a good address," Amy admitted.

"Oh, I don't care much about that, but I'm glad it's not a boarding-house. I know I couldn't stand a boarding-house. Everybody wanting to know everybody else's business, and all that."

"Why?" she said. "Have you got any secrets?"

"I like to go my own way," he said. They began to walk away in the direction of a bus that would take them to Kensington Gardens, where they had decided to go and benefit by the fine weather instead of going to a cinema. And they walked in silence. This silence of theirs must be explained a little. Perhaps the best way to describe it is to say that they hadn't known each other long, and that, although there existed between them a deep and secret trust and affection, they weren't able to put it into words. They had in fact something of that bashful pride and awkward reserve so common among the English, but their very awkwardness made them seem all the more touching to those who knew them—that is to say, to the young man's aunt and uncle and the young woman's mother.

Eric Alston, who hadn't been very long in London, worked as an assistant in a fruiterer's shop only a few hundred yards from Pélagie's. He often attracted the eyes of customers, for he was tall and slender, easy in his movements, wore a clean white coat, and had a very fresh complexion, as if his cheeks were reflecting a rosy glow from the apples and peaches which it was his work to sell. He had come to London from Crotchester, a country town in the Southern Midlands, soon after his widowed mother had taken her second husband, a man with children of his own. He had run no risk of not agreeing with his stepfather, for he had seen very little of him, and whenever they did meet, they got on passably well together. Coming up to London to earn his living, he had gone to live with an aunt and uncle, the aunt being his mother's sister. The aunt and uncle were childless and quite glad to take care of Alston for a time. They were supposed to keep an eye on him, to know something of his affairs, and to see that he didn't go astray. But from the first they didn't find him easy to understand. He seemed steady in his work and well-behaved, but independent, and they couldn't win his confidence at all. His aunt was inclined to worry about him, for she had a strong sense of responsibility, but her husband said, "Leave the lad to himself, and let him find his own feet." She said she wondered whether he *could* do that without a little help; she was afraid his mother had rather spoilt him and hadn't taught him to be self-reliant enough.

"What he wants," said her husband, "is a nice, decent young girl to spend his evenings with. He doesn't seem to be quite like other lads, or like I was at his age. Why, I couldn't leave the girls alone at his age. But he doesn't seem to worry much about them, or about anybody else either."

"The sort of girl I should like him to know is that girl of Mrs. Pascall's. She works at Pélagie's. I wonder if we could bring Eric and Amy together? They might take a fancy to each other."

"You've got a hope! That quiet little thing? Oh, she's not the sort at all. She's too shy. What he wants is a lively young woman who'll take him out of himself a bit."

But Alston's aunt stuck to her intention, spoke to the girl's mother about it, found Mrs. Pascall in favour of a good understanding between the two young people, and arranged with her that they should meet. Alston wasn't a boy who could easily be forced into doing things he didn't want to do, but he didn't make any resistance when he realised that he was being manœuvred into associating with Amy Pascall. He was young, and knew little either of the world or of himself. He was lonely, and he felt that public opinion—as represented by his aunt and uncle, by his relations at Crotchester, by Mrs. Pascall and Amy herself, by his associates in the shop where he worked and other casual acquaintances, by "everybody," in fact, as well as by his own conception of how a young man of his sort was supposed to behave—public opinion required him to pay attention to a girl, so why not Amy Pascall? Not exactly the beginning of a passionate courtship, perhaps, but Alston was far from cold. He was English, and therefore middle-class, and so without either the easy natural instincts of the peasant or the carelessness of the aristocrat. In other countries people are more generally aware of bodily joys, but he began seeing Amy as if it was a duty.

The encouragement of the aunt and the mother did little at first to quicken the progress of the affair, although the two young people were sent off together to the cinema, and so on. Mrs. Pascall invited Alston to her house, and treated him as one of the family, got him to mend the wireless, and sometimes very pointedly left him alone with her daughter. She began to think highly of Alston, found him steady and good-tempered, and told his aunt so. But her admiration for him was nothing by the side of Amy's.

Amy Pascall was the sort of young woman that the world easily overlooks. She was quiet in her manner and not in the least distinguished-looking. She was shy and inexperienced, and she made no parade of her merits. It wasn't until her hat was off and her fair, wavy hair could be seen that one realised that she was attractive, and it wasn't until her eyes met yours that you saw that they were as lustrous as moonstones, and that in their depths lurked curiosity, tenderness and faithfulness. People always liked her because they found her gentle and unassuming, but as she didn't show off at all, either in her dress or her behaviour, nobody had ever taken much notice of her. When she was out with Alston she noticed that people looked first at him, then at her, and she began to take pride, first in him, then in her affection for him, then in herself. She waited for some sign of his feelings, but his response was slow. When they were together he never so much as took her arm, and when they talked it was never about his or her thoughts and feelings, but about casual, everyday matters. Once when he asked her to tell him about the other girls at Pélagie's, she was almost reduced to tears, and she wondered sadly if it was any good their going on seeing each other. Once or twice her mother, suspecting that all was not well, tried to question her about Alston, but Amy's pride and her love for Alston forced her to make out that everything was all right and to hide her fears. But quick as she was to detect the least warmth of impulse on Alston's part, she didn't understand him as well as she thought, and didn't realise how fond of her, in his heart of hearts, he was becoming.

And then one warm evening when they were returning home on the top of a bus, something happened which drove Alston to an expression of what he felt. There was nobody else on the top of the bus except a young couple who were sitting a few seats in front of them and making love as if they were quite alone. The young man had his arms round the young woman and kept squeezing her so that she could scarcely breathe. Each time he squeezed her he pushed her hat on one side, and each time she pointed out what he had done he laughed, kissed her vigorously, and hugged her so hard that the same thing happened again. But sometimes there was a less boisterous interval when he would slip his hand inside her blouse, and she, with her head on his shoulder and her eyes shut, would kiss repeatedly his cheek, his neck and the lobe of his ear with delighted, fluttering kisses. So near this scene, obliged to watch it, and indeed fascinated by it, both Amy and Alston felt excited, but neither said anything. She stole a glance at him, but he didn't return it, and she couldn't read his thoughts in his face. If only he had turned to her with a wink or a smile she would have felt so reassured, so happy, but he made no sign, and she looked gloomily out at the passing trees and houses. But the force of example was too strong for him. He suddenly caught hold of her with an unpractised hand and kissed her for the first time, on the mouth, with all the awkward eagerness of inexperience. And that night she went to bed happy, knowing that his slowly awakening protectiveness had turned into love. . . .

After staying some months with his uncle and aunt, during which he once or twice went down to Crotchester for a week-end, Alston had moved into lodgings, and now, after several more months, had decided to move again. He told nobody of this decision until he had actually settled the details of his move, and nobody could quite understand it.

"I can't make it out," said his uncle. "You're quite comfortable where you are, you're well looked after, you're within easy reach of your work, and then all of a sudden off you go. And you supposed to be so steady, too. I can't make you out at all."

"Well," said Alston's aunt before he could answer, "I dare say the boy just wants a change, and that's all there is to it."

D

And that, in fact, was about the only way in which Alston could account to himself for his behaviour. It so happened that Mrs. Fernandez, after advertising several times in the newspapers, thought she might as well spread her net more widely. In Parthenon Street, the street of shops near Cambodia Crescent, on the opposite corner to Pélagie's, there was a tobacconist and newsagent's shop with a glass frame outside containing a number of local advertisements, for the display of which the advertisers paid a small fee to the shopkeeper. Mrs. Fernandez had added her advertisement to the number, and it was there that Alston had seen it, and, partly on impulse and partly because he was dissatisfied with his lodgings at that time, had decided to answer it.

He had been rather uneasy when first approaching the front door of 45 Cambodia Crescent, for the house was grander-looking than any he had ever lived in. Luckily it hadn't been Empringham or Mrs. Gambitt who first opened the door to him, for either of them might have been rather grand with him, seeing that he didn't perhaps quite come up to the requirements of their high social standards. It was Mrs. Fernandez herself who had appeared, and with her usual enthusiasm and warmth of heart she had at once made him feel at home. Within five minutes of first meeting him she had got him to take a little room on the top floor, and had made an impression on him which was not likely to fade easily. And indeed, on this evening when he stood with Amy looking at the front of the house, it was not Amy that he was thinking about, nor the house itself, so much as Mrs. Fernandez. And poor Amy, seeing him so thoughtful, wondered, as she so often had before, whether he hadn't got something on his mind.

"I believe he's ambitious," she confided to her mother. "Socially ambitious, I mean. I mean to say, it's a very good address and all that, and a big house —you should see it! Anyway," she blurted out, "I sometimes believe he thinks I'm not good enough for him!"

And with that she burst into tears. Her mother tried in vain to console her, and later went to consult Alston's aunt.

"Well, you know my wishes," said that lady, "but I can assure you, Mrs. Pascall, I know very little more about the boy than you do yourself. A mystery to me he's always been, and I'm afraid as he gets older he'll go more his own way than ever. One thing I'm sure of, and that is that he's a good fellow at heart."

And while the two women were trying to reassure each other and the anxious Amy, Alston was moving into 45 Cambodia Crescent.

He arrived at a moment when Mrs. Fernandez was somewhat distracted. In the first place, she was more than usually anxious about her husband's health. Besides, his manner had sometimes lately been quite odd. Happening to meet the inoffensive Mr. Rudd one day in the hall, he was quite rude to him, so that

she had to go in afterwards and apologise. Certainly
Mr. Rudd took it very nicely. But there were other
anxieties. The friction between Mrs. Gambitt and
Empringham was on the increase. The two were now
scarcely on speaking terms, and as they were continually in each other's presence, this didn't make
the house any easier to run. In any case, there were
already certain bills to be met, and they could only
be met with Mrs. Gambitt's money, the production
of which depended on Mrs. Gambitt's goodwill. So
it seemed as though Empringham (whom Mrs.
Fernandez liked and was proud of employing, a
person of good character and a willing servant)—it
seemed as though Empringham would have to be
sacrificed to Mrs. Gambitt's peevishness. If only
Natalie wouldn't eat so much, Mrs. Fernandez
couldn't help thinking, and if only she would go out
a bit more into the fresh air, surely her temper would
be a bit sweeter, and everything would become easier
—but it was no use wishing. . . .

And now a room had had to be furnished for Miss
Brixworth, who was expected to move in within the
next day or two, and apart from the worry of that
there was the expense, for she was obviously a person
used to good things. Meanwhile Rosy had been
somewhat neglected, and had got into the habit of
going by herself to play in the attic upstairs, and
heaven knew what the child was up to up there. And
now, on the top of everything, here was the new
lodger, Mr. Alston, coming in, and things must be

got ready for him. Really, it was too much, especially
as she seemed to be the only person who approved
of Mr. Alston—although nobody but herself had yet
seen him. Mrs. Gambitt felt an instinctive contempt
for the obscure young male ("a shop boy!") who
had taken the smallest and cheapest room in the
house, and expressed her doubts as to whether he
was exactly a suitable lodger, murmuring something
about references. However, when Mrs. Fernandez
reminded her that the room had remained empty
ever since they had taken over the house, and that
it might very well have remained so indefinitely, she
softened considerably. Fernandez was less easily persuaded. He asked question after question about
Alston.

"How old is he?" was one of the first.

"How should I know?" said Mrs. Fernandez.
"Between twenty and twenty-three, I suppose."

"And is he good-looking?"

"What a funny question," said Mrs. Fernandez
innocently. "I can't really say that I noticed his
looks."

Her husband looked closely at her while she said
this, but she met his gaze directly, and nobody could
have appeared more frank.

"What does he do?"

"I believe," she said, "that he works in a shop."

"Oh, does he?"

"He told me so."

"What kind of a shop?"

"A fruiterer's, I think he said."

"You seem to know a lot about him."

"I hardly know more than you do."

"Well, why should he want to come and live here? Why doesn't he go and live with his family or go into a boarding-house? That's what young men like that usually do."

"Well, how should I know?" said Mrs. Fernandez, and left it at that.

Then there was Empringham to be considered. She didn't expect him to be too pleased about the extra work which the arrival of two new lodgers would mean for him, but he said that he would be very pleased to wait on Miss Brixworth, for he had taken "quite a fancy" to her, and as for the young man, well, young men didn't usually give much trouble, especially when they were out at work all day.

The news of course reached every one in the house. Mrs. Gambitt told Mrs. Petherham-Porter, and Mrs. Fernandez herself told Mrs. Rudd that the house was filling up nicely. On the following day Alston duly moved in, and on the day after that, with rather more pomp and circumstance, Miss Brixworth did likewise. The two had this in common, that they brought with them all their worldly possessions, but whereas Alston's were contained in two suitcases, Miss Brixworth's, the precious residue of a lifetime, were somewhat more elaborate, and included a handsome chair, some books and pictures, and a number of odds and ends.

IV

As might have been expected, Miss Brixworth at once took as much of a liking to Empringham as he had taken to her. Directly she arrived, he offered to help her to arrange her things, and they were soon deeply engaged in conversation. Miss Brixworth, although shy, was inquisitive, and Empringham, polite as he was, was ready to talk, so before very long she knew a good deal about the house and its inhabitants. She knew her friend Miss Haymer would ask her a great many questions, so she took pains to inform herself carefully. What impressed her most, perhaps, was Empringham's dislike of Mrs. Gambitt, and at the same time she was a little puzzled as to why Mrs. Fernandez should like that individual.

"The reason why she and Mrs. Fernandez are so thick," said Empringham, "and why they're always together, is because Mrs. Gambitt holds the purse-strings. She's mean, you know—wouldn't give you the tail off a dead mouse. It's usually the way, isn't it, the nice people in this world have no money and the moneyed ones aren't nice. But it seems to me that it's Mrs. Gambitt that sticks to Mrs. Fernandez and not Mrs. Fernandez that sticks to her. She's afraid, if you ask me, of Mrs. Fernandez spending too much."

"You're not very fond of Mrs. Gambitt, Empringham, are you?"

"No, madam, I'm not. I'm not used to people like that."

She asked him what he did before he came to Cambodia Crescent, and before very long he had given her a rough outline of his life.

"And what about the future?" she said. "You aren't thinking of marrying and settling down?"

"No, madam."

"But you won't always stay on here or do this sort of thing?"

"I hope not," said Empringham. "To tell you the truth, I've always thought that I'd like to start a little sort of restaurant place all on me own. In fact, I've been planning it for some time. Putting a little by, you know, from time to time. And as a matter of fact, I've got all the fittings ready."

"The fittings?"

"Well, you see, it's like this. I've got a friend who's a carpenter by trade, and he's always let me use his shop. So I used to go there at week-ends and play about a bit. As I told you, I can do a bit of marquetry, served my apprenticeship and all that. So I've just got ready all the fittings for my little restaurant— shelves, counter, cupboards, you know, and so on— all in nice inlay work. There they are, you see, all finished some time ago, all stored there in my friend's shop, ready for the time when I'm ready to start my little place, which I mean to do as soon as I've got a

bit more money together. A nasty turn I had a month
or two ago, I can tell you, when I dreamt one night
that all my work was burnt up in a fire and I was too
late to save it. I rang up first thing in the morning to
find out if everything was all right, and you can guess
how glad I was when I heard that there hadn't been
a fire at all."

It was with a sense of adventure that Miss Brixworth listened to all this. Old she might be, but she
wasn't so old that she had lost her appetite for life.
She looked forward to knowing the other people in
the house, or at least to learning something more
about them. Her landlady was of course the first she
got to know at all. Mrs. Fernandez, accompanied by
Rosy, paid her a call after breakfast the next morning,
in order to ask if everything was all right, and took
occasion to admire some of Miss Brixworth's few
possessions, an attention which pleased their owner.
Mrs. Fernandez was impressed because Rosy, who
seldom took to people at first, seemed to take at once
to Miss Brixworth.

Miss Brixworth had arranged to have her breakfast
brought to her every morning. As for other meals, she
would prepare light ones herself for economy's sake,
would often eat with Miss Haymer, and occasionally
at a restaurant. The first time she saw Miss Haymer
after moving to Cambodia Crescent, she had to
answer a great many questions.

"Mrs. Gambitt I haven't had a good look at yet,"
she said, "but Mrs. Fernandez came in to see me this

morning. I liked her from the very beginning. I like the child. I like the manservant."

"You're so impulsive, Connie," said Miss Haymer.

"And Mrs. Fernandez particularly admired some of my things—my tortoise-shell box, my pair of Chinese vases, my paper knife, and my pictures—she looked at each in turn. I dare say she was surprised to find that I had such good things when I've scarcely got a pair of shoes fit to put on. 'Oh, I do love good things!' she said."

"Of course she does, my dear. She's a Jewess, and the Jews always like good things. And what's more, they know that when one has champagne tastes and a lager-beer income, the only thing is to do without necessaries and buy luxuries. That's the only way to make poverty endurable. I remember when I was in the Southern States of America being taken to see some black people who had a grand piano, a harmonium, and a small organ in their one-roomed house, but only one cup and saucer. That's the way to be happy! . . . But tell me, do you suppose that Fernandez and his family are quite without means? Do they depend entirely on this Mrs. Gambitt?"

"So I understand, Fanny, from Empringham."

"Funny," said Miss Haymer. "The Jews usually look after each other. . . . Of course it's not unnatural that Mrs. Gambitt should be more fond of Mrs. Fernandez than Mrs. Fernandez is of her. After all, Mrs. Fernandez has both a husband and a child, and from what you say, Connie, is devoted to both.

I shall certainly look forward to hearing your impressions of Mrs. Gambitt."

It was some days, however, before Miss Brixworth saw Mrs. Gambitt again, for the latter was inclined to be unsociable—also, she was particularly afraid of Miss Brixworth, whom she knew by instinct to be a real "lady," which she herself was only pretending to be. Empringham understood, and took a malicious delight in this. Miss Brixworth also understood. She differed from the typical decayed gentlewoman of a generation ago, who was only an exile from the advantages of money, love and kinship, in that her very class was rapidly ceasing to exist. She found herself not merely exiled, but isolated. And this gave her a curiously resigned and detached point of view, and freed her from the bitterness which the earlier type so often felt. Although she would never have thought of putting it into so many words, Miss Brixworth understood that she was the victim of a revolution. With her trinkets, her memories, and her faded manners, she resembled a Russian *emigrée*, but she had this advantage, that she cherished few illusions about the resurrection of a dying system. She knew there could be no return to the past.

Mrs. Gambitt was unyielding in the dislike she felt for Miss Brixworth, although she had scarcely set eyes on her so far. Her position in the house had become something like one that has sometimes arisen in oriental history—a bogus empress, though dreadfully annoyed by the appearance of a genuine one, is determined to keep up a separate court, just to show that she is as good as she thinks herself. Certainly since Miss Brixworth's arrival, Mrs. Gambitt, whether in the kitchen with Empringham or at tea with Mrs. Porter, was more than ever inclined to give herself airs.

Meanwhile Rosy had continued to attach herself to Miss Brixworth. She was no longer scornful, as she had been when she first saw her. On the contrary, her main ambition seemed to be to get to know her better, and after Miss Brixworth had shown her a picture-book one afternoon and entertained her to tea, she could talk of nothing else. She came to regard Miss Brixworth as a person who could and would provide any delight one asked for. For instance, Rosy had long had an ambition to see the Round Pond, about which she had been told, but neither her mother nor Mrs. Gambitt would ever take her there —they were always "too busy." Her father would no doubt have taken her, but he seldom went out of the house nowadays. And now she had scarcely mentioned the Round Pond to Miss Brixworth when she found herself standing at the very edge of it, the blue water sparkling under a light breeze, the toy boats with their white or coloured sails gliding this way and that, and an old woman feeding the sea-gulls from a paper bag. She came home radiant. But her appetite for pleasure was insatiable, and the next morning she presented herself at Miss Brixworth's door.

"Well, Rosy," said Miss Brixworth, "and what can I do for you?"

"I want some jelly."

"What?"

"I said, I want some jelly."

"That's all very well, my dear, but where can I get jelly from? Why don't you ask your mother or Mrs. Gambitt?"

Rosy took refuge from her disappointment at this attitude in an appeal to reason.

"Don't be silly," she said.

"Well, look," said Miss Brixworth, "I'll tell you what I'll do. I'll buy you some jelly, and you shall have it to-morrow."

"I don't want it to-morrow. I want it now."

"Well, you can't have it now, my child. Jelly doesn't simply *happen*. You have to wait for it. It has to set."

"What do you mean, set?"

"It has to get hard, Rosy."

"I don't want a hard jelly. I want a soft one."

"Well, if you'll wait till to-morrow you shall have a soft one. Pink or yellow?"

"I prefer wine jelly," said Rosy grandly. "A soft one."

"Well, come and see me to-morrow, and you shall help me to make it."

"No, you make it and I'll eat it."

"I'll be damned if I do," said Miss Brixworth under her breath (as she thought), but still, when she went out she bought a small packet of jelly, and having prepared it, left it in a cool place to set. And the next morning she had the pleasure of giving it to Rosy, who ate it with lingering pleasure and much rolling of the eyes.

"I love it," she said, looking exactly like her father as she spoke.

"So I see," said Miss Brixworth. Whereupon the child ran out on to the landing and called to her mother:

"Mummy, mummy, I'm full of jelly."

"What?"

"Wine jelly," said Rosy, licking her lips.

"What, has Miss Brixworth been spoiling you again?"

Mrs. Fernandez hastened to knock at Miss Brixworth's door in order to thank her, and after a short conversation turned to go.

"Come along, Rosy," she said. The child was giving a last lick to the spoon, and made no effort to obey.

"Rosy, come along!"

Rosy looked up with large eyes.

"I'll be damned if I do," she said.

"Good heavens, what a way to talk! Goodness knows where she gets it from!"

"Odd, isn't it," said Miss Brixworth, "the things they pick up? Good-bye, Rosy."

"Give Miss Brixworth a kiss and say thank you for the lovely jelly, Rosy."

"Thank you for the lovely jelly," said Rosy casually, and strolled with the utmost self-possession out of the room and down the stairs, as though the whole world was full of jelly which could just be had for the asking. And while she was going downstairs the marvellous thought struck her that Miss Brixworth, who had almost instantaneously produced a visit to the Round Pond and a wine jelly, might even produce with equal ease a rocking horse. But she said nothing.

When her first bill was made out, Miss Brixworth smiled to see that her room was referred to as *Suite No. 5*—evidently yet one more example of that Jewish impulse towards grandeur so noticeable in Mrs. Fernandez, and in this case a luxury that cost nothing. Before paying the bill she showed it to Miss Haymer, who said:

"Poor thing! But just what you'd expect. *'Suite No. 5*!' That goes exactly with the showy wallpapers you told me about, and the love of good things."

"And Empringham," said Miss Brixworth.

"Exactly, Connie. It's absurd to keep a man-servant in a house of that sort, though I must say I prefer men to women as servants. So much more docile. . . . As for your Mrs. Fernandez, I dare say if she had the money she'd run that place very comfortably. But it'll be a long time before she does have the money, I should say. What strange creatures the Jews are!"

"She's very worried about her husband," said Miss Brixworth. "I hear she's thinking of getting a doctor for him."

"Ah, what'll that lead to, I wonder?" said Miss

Haymer. "Connie, I can't help feeling that you've settled in rather a funny house."

Mrs. Fernandez had already had the doctor to see her husband. As soon as she had made up her mind to call him, Fernandez had gone against her. He threatened to make a scene, and finding that he couldn't shake her decision, grew sulky. When the doctor arrived he refused to answer his questions and kept on saying that he was all right. The doctor, who was young and rather inexperienced, tried to act the strong man.

"By going against me like this," he told Fernandez, "you're not only making a fool of yourself but you're acting selfishly. Anybody can see you're a sick man, but how can I tell exactly what's wrong with you if you won't give me a chance to examine you? What you don't understand, and what you ought to be made to understand, is that your wife here, and others perhaps who are fond of you, are anxious to know what's wrong with you so that they can help you. Don't you see that they'll be much more anxious if they don't know what's wrong with you, and see you steadily getting worse out of sheer obstinacy?"

Now this line was perhaps the worst that could have been taken with Fernandez. First of all, he had got it firmly into his head that no doctor could do him any good. Next, he resented the fact that this doctor was young, and was on the point of believing that the doctor and Mrs. Fernandez were either conspiring against him or would be tempted to do so.

Then finally, like so many people who are not quite balanced, he wanted to be, and believed that he could be, a law to himself. It is only a step from that to the anti-social dream-world of the madman, who lives in a trance or frenzy of his own, which is for him so absolutely right that he is unable to bear any kind of interference or contradiction. Fernandez, unsettled by ill-health and misfortune, was tending more and more to surrender to an unfounded jealousy where his wife was concerned. And now, when the doctor dared to call him a fool and to question the rightness of his understanding, and that actually in the presence of his wife, Fernandez trembled, and clenched his hands.

"I suppose you're not a Christian Scientist, are you?" said the doctor, with a sneer. He was by no means a disagreeable young man, and was not in the habit of sneering, but he thought that by changing his tactics he might be able to laugh Fernandez out of his opposition.

"No," said Fernandez, in a surprisingly quiet and controlled voice, "I'm not a Christian Scientist. And I must tell you that my wife had no authority to bring you here. When I want a doctor I can send for a doctor. So now I think you'd better get out of this."

He took a cigarette and lighted it with a hand that was still trembling. Mrs. Fernandez stood by with tears in her eyes and fear in her heart. The doctor looked from one to the other.

E

"You'll regret this," he said to Fernandez in a quiet voice.

"Don't threaten me!" said Fernandez.

"Oh, Paul——!" cried his wife restrainingly.

"Be quiet!" he cried, turning roughly on her.

The doctor was alarmed. He picked up a stethoscope which he had produced in the hope of encouraging Fernandez to submit to an examination—though actually it had had a precisely contrary effect—and put it away in his little bag. As he fastened the locks, he looked gravely up at Fernandez.

"I'm not going to argue with you," he said, "but you're behaving in a very foolish way."

Fernandez made no answer, but stood by, waiting for him to go. When the doctor took up his hat and gloves, Mrs. Fernandez opened the door and followed him out in order to show him downstairs. Fernandez went half-way down the stairs after them and waited for his wife to come back again. He saw her pause to exchange a few words with the doctor at the front door, and grew pale with fury.

"I'm sorry," said Mrs. Fernandez (the words were inaudible to her husband), "to have given you so much trouble for nothing, but my husband——"

"And I'm sorry that I can do nothing for you, Mrs. Fernandez, until you can persuade him to be a bit more reasonable. Good morning."

"Beryl!" cried Fernandez from the stairs, even before the front door was shut.

His wife turned anxiously to meet him. He didn't

utter a word till they were back in their room again.

"What were you saying to him?"

"What do you mean? I was just showing him out."

"Ah, you're like him; you think you can deceive me, don't you? 'Making a fool of myself,' am I? But do you think I'm going to let you be alone with *him*? Not if I know it! Just think of all the nice plans you might make together! 'Let's get him certified! Let's poison him! Let's give him a sleeping draught, so that we can have some fun together!' "

His wife had never heard him speak like this before, and was horrified.

"You don't know what you're saying," she said.

The sudden pallor of her face brought a dark and dazzling lustre into her eyes. Fernandez caught hold of her wrist in an exceedingly tight grip: he was strong, but his strength was nervous rather than muscular. The tendons and purplish veins stood out on his wrist, and there was a wild and determined expression on his face. Suddenly he twisted her arm, twisted it behind her back, and the pain caught her so sharply that for an instant she thought her arm would be broken. She closed her eyes and was just opening her mouth to cry out when he fastened his upon it, and, catching her in his arms, lifted her bodily off the floor on to the bed, covering her face with frantic kisses.

V

ALSTON was sitting one evening at the window of his little room on the top floor. He had returned from work about half an hour previously, and now, his chin on his hand and his elbow on the window-sill, was gazing at a sports car which had been standing by the pavement on the opposite side of the road for at least a quarter of an hour. The car was unattended, and belonged to a youngish woman of independent means. It was brand-new, painted in two colours, dark brown and light brown, with its chromium-plated fittings all gleaming and shining, and every line of it seeming to speak of speed. He couldn't take his eyes off it, and would have given anything to own it or just to be able to go down and get into it and feel the controls under his hand, to start it up, and to drive off, gliding easily through the traffic to the joy of beholders, and so out of London, out along one of the great arterial roads into the country, where you can just step on the accelerator and eat up the miles while the wind shrieks past your ears. . . . For Alston was not so much in love with Amy, or with himself, or with anybody or anything in particular, as he was in love with power, a strange sense of power that he had never fully felt, but had only experienced in odd moments, as once in childhood

when tobogganing down a steep hill, or when shooting sparrows with an air-gun, or once when he and
another boy had gone one quiet summer's evening
and by throwing stones had smashed every single
pane of glass in a certain empty house. Even now he
sometimes recollected those glorious minutes—the
smooth grey stones the size of small plums, the queer
thud as they struck the mark, the tinkle of breaking
glass that immediately followed, and the irregular,
dark, satisfying emptiness that remained in the
window-frames. Then again at home, when he was
growing up, he had been able to keep a motor-bike
for a time, and a few chances had occurred of going
all out along some straight and empty road until he
was drunk with his own speed. That intense joy had
been spoilt by his being run in and fined, and soon
afterwards he had had to give up the bike because he
couldn't afford to keep it going. But there were other
ways in which he had felt similar pleasures since then.
Once at a film with a scene of smashing, a comic
film—husband and wife throwing crockery at each
other, wood splitting, iron falling on wood, glass
smashing, curtains torn from rods, jugs broken over
heads, ink spilt on sheets—when everybody was
laughing at this happy home, where all their own
latent lust to destroy was given in to, Alston didn't
laugh. Amy felt his thigh tauten nervously under her
hand, which lay on it clasped in his, he sat bolt upright and seemed about to get up, and when she
glanced timidly up at him she saw his eager profile,

his eyes gleaming, his lips parted, and even heard
him chuckle, not with laughter, but with a sort of
animal delight, as if he was enjoying a secret or was
just going to eat something good or get into bed with
somebody, and she was frightened and excited at the
same time. Afterwards (and it was very seldom that
he made any particular comment on the films they
saw) he said, "It was grand, Amy. That's the sort of
picture I like." And she had agreed with him, not
daring to go against him. But because he hadn't
laughed, she was afraid.

At the films, in his dreams, from scraps of conversation, childish recollections, or paragraphs in the
newspapers, fleeting visions obsessed him of scenes of
violence—dynamite, the lighting of fuses, flags and
cries of warning, a whole cliff face cracking, leaning
outwards, collapsing in a flying cloud of dust and
debris; a factory chimney blown up, cracking, sag-
ging, plunging to nothing through a shower of bricks
and sparks; flying in a bomber, judging the moment
to release the bombs just before flying over the target,
then puffs of smoke far below, first here, then there;
a train rushing out into space where a bridge had
been, the delicious fraction of a second before the
jointed, twisting fall, the fearful hissing of steam and
fire and water; train wrecking by rock or bomb;
motors skidding over cliffs, into other motors or
houses, scattering pedestrians, or crushing the bones
of a bicycle against a concrete wall, the scraping of
buckled metal and the crunch of splintered glass;

typhoons, tidal waves, fires, earthquakes, sleepers thrown out of bed, trees dragged shrieking like man-drakes from a stony soil, telegraph poles snapping, fused wires and showers of violet sparks; guns of all sorts, the revolvers of gunmen, the stutter of machine guns, the boom of cannon; speed-boats; window-slashers; the race for the Schneider Cup; a case of wilful destruction by a youth in a compartment on an express train. . . .

These two instincts in Alston, the wish to smash and the wish to speed, were really one and the same. There is a nihilist in every man, and it is the mark of the nihilist to seek an easy and intense ecstasy of a particular kind without counting the consequences. In its expression this nihilism is paradoxical, for it seems that it makes a man wish to impress the world around him with his own importance, and at the same time to lose himself in that world. Sometimes this nihilism is a mark of innocence. To-day, when so many people seem to be living secure and out-wardly orderly and respectable lives, you find these well-behaved people getting thrilled by proxy, as it were. They don't go to boxing matches or bull-fights to quench their thirst for thrills; they read novels or see films of crime and detection, and you will hear them speak jokingly of "a good murder," meaning that they have really enjoyed an account of gruesome events because the gruesome, which is one of the necessary ingredients of life, is almost entirely lacking in their own lives. For Alston, leading a life in many ways static, constrained and monotonous, there was a real need to see what had stood firm suddenly fall, to annihilate, if possible, some solid thing, animate or inanimate, or else, in a new sports car, painted dark brown and light brown and with all its new fittings shining, to annihilate distance, to lose himself and the world and time and space, and yet to assert himself, at a speed of fifty, sixty or seventy miles an hour, or more if possible—as much more as possible. . . .

Just before he had left school some years before, at a time when the newspapers were rather short of news, an absurd fuss had been made over some small trouble caused by a handful of noisy English communists who were said to be in the pay of the Soviet, and who had attempted to provoke discontent and sedition in the army and navy. Every day there was some fresh "grave charge" or "Red sensation," the word "treason" was used in leading articles, and Alston's schoolmaster, a patriotic soul, used the story as an object lesson to show the errors of all creeds but the one he taught, which was a kind of smug and old-fashioned jingoism. Whereupon Alston and a young friend of his, who both disliked their teacher, came to the conclusion that they must become communists. They hadn't the faintest idea what a communist was, except that it was a person who had something to do with Russia and was therefore wicked—but probably, by differing from their schoolmaster, deliciously wicked. With the wish to oppose the schoolmaster by siding with his enemies and the sense of illicit excitement that came from doing so, there arose at the same time the instinct for conspiracy, the need to devote themselves to a "cause." Small minds in petty surroundings always occupy themselves with plots and intrigues, but a certain creative energy coming to life in Alston gave his adventure a glamour it would otherwise have lacked. To this adventure he and his friend gave themselves as keenly as they had previously given themselves to making mud pies, playing soldiers, bird's-nesting, or spinning tops. They found it hard to think of a way to help the "cause." They neither had nor could obtain arms or money, but they could whisper and wink, they made invisible ink with the juice of an onion and sent secret messages in code, and finally even decided to cut some telegraph wires that led to a military aerodrome near where they lived. The whole plan was made—how they were to steal some pliers from a garage, conceal a ladder in a certain spot, and so on—but it was never carried out, and before long they forgot all about it.

There was one thing Alston never forgot, and that was the memory of his father. His idea of his father was different from the reality, because it was made on heroic lines, and his father had been quite an ordinary person, a policeman in fact—not that policemen are prevented by their profession from being extraordinary, but Alston's father was quite an ordinary policeman. Ordinary except in one way. He was a very good swimmer, and this made the whole

basis of his son's idea of him after he was dead. When
Alston was very small his father had won a special
medal for rescuing a boy from drowning, and had at
the same time been given a certificate and an address.
This had made a great impression on the child. On
the mantelpiece at home there stood a photograph of
his father wearing this medal, and on either side of the
photograph there were silver cups and other medals
all won as swimming prizes. Even after Mrs. Alston's
second marriage these things had stayed where they
were, and she still kept them brightly polished and
carefully arranged, just as in eastern countries house-
holders tend an altar dedicated to the family dead.
She had brought her son up to reverence his father's
memory, and certain things that he himself remembered enriched his admiration even more than the
silver cups, photographs and other relics. He distinctly remembered the way his father dived and how
he swam a long way under water, his figure and
movements curiously distorted. He remembered how
he looked when he came out of the water, the black
hair on his head and chest oddly straightened, his strong
body outlined by the wet black bathing-suit that
clung to it, and how he laughed, and refused a cigarette, saying, "Got to think of my wind, or I'd swim
like a stone." There was something impressive about
Alston's father, in spite of his easy good-humour.
Perhaps it was simply that the habit of maintaining
order, combined with his natural dignity and physical
well-being, had invested him with a real authority.

THE CASE IS ALTERED

At the same time there was nobody more capable of tenderness, and he adored his child.

But none of Alston's own memories of his father fascinated him so much as a story which his mother had told him many a time after his father's death— that incredible event which had been celebrated with white flowers and black horses, which had seemed as important as something that shakes the whole scheme of life. It was a story of her honeymoon, which had been spent with relations in the Scilly Isles. On one of the islands there is a large cave whose floor is of water, which extends into an unknown darkness. One day they had gone to visit this cave, and the local men who rowed them there said that nobody had ever penetrated its depths. Alston's father was anxious to explore it, and when they were all standing just inside the entrance, he suddenly surprised everybody by stripping, and putting in his mouth a small electric torch which they had brought with them, he waded into the water and without once looking back swam away into the darkness. The boatmen called after him to be careful not to go too far, and his bride, who was at first proud of his daring, began to be nervous. One of the men took out his watch to see how long the swimmer was gone. Not a sound could be heard except the sound of the sea outside the cave, and the young woman was soon in a state of terror. After twenty-five minutes, when she had made up her mind that she would never see her man again and was quite ready to collapse, a distant splashing was heard, a wavering light appeared, and there he was. In a moment he stood beside her, wet and panting, and laughed as he opened his right hand to show to the astonished boatmen and his agitated and ecstatic young wife a little sand which he had collected on the far side of the cave and had kept as a proof that he had been there. It was said that no man had ever dared to make such a swim before, and no boat had ever attempted it, because in places the roof of the cave came so low over the water that it only just allowed room for a man's head.

This story, then, stood in Alston's mind for all that was glorious in his father and in life itself. To go where nobody else had ever been, to do what nobody else had ever done, to return naked out of an unknown darkness with a handful of sand—if that sand had been diamonds it couldn't have sparkled more brilliantly in the child's imagination. And although he couldn't have expressed it clearly to himself, that handful of sand was a kind of symbol of his own desire to snatch something rare out of the heart of life and to say, "There! That's a proof that I've been where nobody has ever been before!" But so far he had never found a proper outlet for his personality, his undeveloped ambition and energy.

What he would have excelled and been happy in was hunting. There all his craving for speed and destruction might have been satisfied, and with it the need for quick calculation, skill, and risking his life. To make a plan secretly; to carry it out as swiftly as possible, aware all the time of imminent danger; to bring it to a successful conclusion by destroying somebody or something, partly for some definite purpose but mainly for the sheer love of the doing—that was really how nature had meant him to function. Is it any wonder that he was left leaning on his window-sill and gazing in a day-dream at the sports car which he longed to control, considering idly how he could get hold of it, imagining himself going downstairs, walking across the road, getting into the car and driving off . . .? Of course it was all impossible.

If only his father had been alive! The weaker side of his character needed somebody he could at once trust and look up to, somebody he could respect and obey, but someone who would be kind to him, somebody strong, cheerful and sure of himself. Alston was uncomfortably aware of his own diffidence. There was nobody in his life who made him feel sure of himself. All of them, including his mother, including even Amy, made him feel unsure of himself, lonely, and, because lonely, in a way rather vain. He was not given to introspection, but was inclined to a vague moodiness, and his love for Amy didn't prevent him from feeling at times unhappy, lonely and bored. If only there were somebody like his father——

He got up vaguely from where he was sitting and crossed the room to find a cigarette, and just at that moment was surprised to hear a knock at the door. He started, as if he were guilty of something.

"Come in!" he said then.

The door opened, revealing Empringham.

"Oh, you *are* here," he said, with a hint of disapproval in his voice. "Had your tea yet?"

"Not yet. Why?" said Alston.

"There's a lady on the floor below, Miss Brixworth her name is, asked me to tell you that you can come and have tea with her, if you like."

"How do you mean? I don't know her. What does she want?"

"How should I know?" said Empringham.

Alston followed him uneasily downstairs, combing his hair with a little pocket comb as he went. He wondered what he was letting himself in for.

"How old is she?" he asked.

But Empringham didn't answer. Instead, he knocked at Miss Brixworth's door and then opened it, nodding to Alston to go in. As if he was walking in his sleep, Alston went in, and heard the door close behind him.

"Ah, here you are," said Miss Brixworth nervously. "I wondered if you'd had your tea. I thought you might perhaps care to come and have it with me instead of our both sitting up and eating by ourselves. Do sit down, won't you?"

It is hardly necessary to say that this strange meeting between two shy and completely different people, who would never have dreamt of it themselves, was the work of Miss Frances Haymer.

"Get hold of him, Connie," she had said; "ask him to tea or something. You're much too stuck-up and stand-offish. It's no good using your grand Edwardian manners in a house like that. You must be a bit more democratic. Besides, you'll be less lonely, and we shall be able to find out some more about the people in the house. I must say I'm just dying with curiosity, and you're rather a poor spy, you don't give me much information."

"But, Fanny," Miss Brixworth had protested, "am I to get to know this young man, whom I've never set eyes on and am quite afraid of, simply to provide a little gossip for you?"

"Partly," said Miss Haymer, "and partly for your own good."

"You can't expect me to alter much at my age."

"I do expect you to. Now do as I ask you. It won't do any harm, at any rate. And if you don't like him you needn't see him again."

So now here was Miss Brixworth face to face with Alston, both of them feeling awkward, but she not showing it much.

"You don't mind my asking you like this, do you?" she said.

"Oh no," said Alston.

"I'm afraid it's not very interesting for you to come and see an old woman like me, but it's very kind of you to come and keep me company like this. London is so full of lonely people, isn't it? But I don't know why I should think you were a lonely person. I suppose it was just that I thought this sort of house is not much of a place for a young man like you."

He was sitting very stiffly in his chair and listening politely. She longed to say, "You mustn't sit *quite* so near the edge of your chair, or you might fall off," but she didn't know how he would take it. So she went on as before:

"You haven't been in this house very long, have you? But of course nobody has. How do you like being here?"

"Oh, all right," he said.

"Well, I call it rather unusual. I've been in several places somewhat like this, but never in one *quite* like this. Have you?"

"No. This is my first experience of this kind of place. But it's better than a boarding-house."

"Oh, much! I find it rather adventurous. In a place like this you feel almost anything might happen."

"Yes."

"But tell me, Mr. Alston, what made you come here? Did you perhaps know some of the people in the house——?"

"Oh no, I answered an advertisement, and then I saw Mrs. Fernandez——"

"Ah yes, so did I, and of course it was mainly on her account that we decided to come and live here, wasn't it? Such a nice woman—I do so agree with you."

Was she laughing at him? No, he thought not, still pleased because she had just called him "Mr.," which nobody had ever done to him before in his life. She seemed to understand him. She knew that he admired Mrs. Fernandez. He wondered what he ought to say next. Miss Brixworth saved him by saying:

"I don't know what you generally have for your tea, but I thought of making an omelette. I rather fancy myself at making omelettes. Can you do them?"

"No," he said, feeling very uncomfortable. He was not at all sure what an omelette was.

"Anyway, if I break the eggs," she said, "you can beat them up for me, while I get on with something else, can't you?"

"Yes," he said, and as soon as he began to beat up the eggs he felt more at ease, just as she had hoped he would. Absurd of Fanny to call me stuck-up, she thought, as if I hadn't had to do with people of the lower classes before. And she thought of how she had entertained poor people and visited them and of how she had helped in hospitals during the War, and how full of class-consciousness she had always been, never able to make any real personal contact with those people, although she really thought in her heart of hearts how much nicer they often were than people of her own class.

"Well, now, you'd better watch me," she said. "Next time you come to tea with me you'll have to have a shot at it yourself."

He watched her making the omelette. She in the making, he in the watching, forgot their awkwardness.

F

"To return to what we were saying just now," she said. "I must confess that I'm sometimes a bit bored by myself. That's why I think it's so good of you to pay me a visit like this. But I dare say you're sometimes in the same boat yourself. I know they say that young people don't get lonely, but I think they do sometimes."

"Oh, they do," he said.

"There we are!" said Miss Brixworth, turning the omelette out on to a dish. If we've nothing else in common, she said to herself, I expect we're both hungry.

"What do you generally do about tea?" she said aloud.

"Well, sometimes I just have a bit of something out. Or I go to my uncle's."

"Well, don't forget you can come and have tea with me whenever you like. Only let me know beforehand, so that I can get something in. I'm going to ask Mrs. Fernandez in sometimes, but I dare say you won't mind if you find her here too."

"Oh no," said Alston.

"Do you know any of the other people in the house?"

"No. Only the man——"

"Empringham? Such a good sort, isn't he?"

Alston said nothing. He didn't like Empringham because Empringham plainly didn't like him. Empringham disliked waiting on anybody of his own class, and somebody young at that. Besides, the extra flight of stairs to the floor on which Alston and Mrs. Gambitt lived always left him short-winded.

"Fernandez is such a mystery to me," said Miss Brixworth. "Have you seen him at all?"

"Never set eyes on him yet," said Alston.

"I believe he never leaves their bedroom, or only leaves it when there's nobody much about."

"Yes."

"By the way, I never asked you whether you're used to having tea at this time—I mean a sort of high tea like this?"

"Oh yes," said Alston.

"You see, I've only been doing it for a few months myself. When I had more money I used to have an ordinary afternoon tea and late dinner, but now the case is rather altered. . . ."

When he left her it was getting dark. There was no light on the stairs, so he groped his way up, wondering whether the light in his own room was in order. It had wanted attention and he had spoken about it to Mrs. Fernandez, who had promised that it should be seen to. As he went into the room, he saw a man actually doing the work by the light of a candle. He thought for a moment that it must be the electrician, but realised almost immediately that it was Fernandez. In the light thrown upwards by the candle the landlord looked almost terrible.

"Just trying to mend your light," he muttered as he caught sight of Alston.

He stood there, looking down at the work he was

doing on the table, where a pair of pliers and some coils of wire were lying. A cigarette was stuck to his lip, and he coughed, with a spasmodic, painful cough. His movements were laboured and slovenly. He hadn't at all the air of a man who knew what he was doing. As for his face, it was the reverse of what is called an "open" face. The expression was shifty but set—set in shiftiness, as it were—the hair was scanty, the eyeballs were discoloured, the cheeks sunk and unshaven, the teeth few and bad, and the whole complexion was that of a mortally sick man.

"Can't manage it now," he said, gathering up his things. "I'll leave you the candle."

And looking sharply at Alston, he shuffled out of the room.

Alston was just getting ready to go out when he heard a knock at the door, and Mrs. Fernandez came in, closing it carefully behind her. She seemed agitated, a little pale, and her appearance was more striking than ever in the candlelight. Alston felt surprised.

"I'm afraid Mr. Fernandez was trying to mend that fitting," she said in a low and hurried voice, "and I'm sure he hasn't been successful. I wanted to send for the man, but he wouldn't let me."

"Wouldn't let you?"

"Yes," she said, "he thought he could do it better himself."

"Well, I'd be glad if it could be fixed up to-morrow. It's a bit awkward by candlelight."

He was astonished when he saw clearly that her eyes were filling with tears. He was just going to ask her what was the matter, but he checked himself, afraid of provoking a scene. But she suddenly began talking rather rapidly and cheerfully about her plans in regard to the house. She wanted to make sure that Alston shouldn't think of leaving because everything wasn't exactly shipshape yet or because little things, like this electric fitting, were apt to go wrong. For although she could see that he wasn't of quite such a high class as she could have wished (she had thought vaguely of actors, authors, or some other kind of professional gentleman occupying her rooms), yet he seemed a decent, kind, respectable sort of young man, of the sort who would be likely to pay the rent regularly. She liked him for being cheerful and well-spoken, and for the sadness which his cheerfulness seemed to hide. She liked him for being so young and innocent (as she thought), and she liked him because she felt sure that he had a bit of devil in him too. She hoped he would stay in the house a long time. She sometimes looked forward to the time when she would be able to boast how long her lodgers stayed with her. That would show anybody who might doubt it that she was not like other landladies. . . .

"You can't do everything at once," she said confidentially, "but I hope we shall have a carpet on the stairs before very long."

While she talked, she wanted, and yet didn't want, to get round again to the topic of her husband, as though it was one that half pleased and half displeased her.

"You see," she said, "it isn't as if Mr. Fernandez could really do much to help us to get things going. He's not really well enough."

"No, he doesn't look it," said Alston.

"He isn't. He's a great anxiety to me. Sometimes, you know, he's just a little—uncertain."

"Yes," said Alston, wondering exactly what she meant. But before he was any the wiser Mrs. Fernandez, forcing for once the brilliant smile that was usually natural to her, said she must go, and left him to his thoughts.

She was surprised that evening to find her husband unusually cheerful. He played a lot with the child and made her laugh.

"You seem very pleased with life, Paul," she said.

"He *is* lively, isn't he?" said Mrs. Gambitt, watching Fernandez carrying Rosy round the room on his shoulder.

"Cough's been better," said Fernandez, without looking at either of the women as he spoke.

"You oughtn't to smoke so much," said Mrs. Gambitt.

"Makes no difference," he said. The improvement in his temper wasn't due to his cough or the number of cigarettes he had smoked during the day. It was due to a conclusion he had come to about Alston. Up till now he had been suspicious of him. Glancing through door or window he had seen him entering or leaving the house, and the sight of Alston's slender figure and youthful movements had woken anger in his heart. He was always ready to suspect the worst, and had looked black when the younger man's name occurred in conversation once or twice while his wife and Mrs. Gambitt were doing the accounts. Mrs. Gambitt had noticed this and had been careful to let fall some remark about Alston's walking out regularly with a young woman. At this Fernandez had smiled inwardly, thinking it only a trick to put him off the scent. But now that he had seen Alston face to face he felt reassured. Not by any process of reasoning, but by instinct, he felt that he had nothing to fear from him. His face was not the face of a seducer. Whatever Alston might wish to possess or enjoy absolutely, Fernandez felt sure that it wasn't his wife. And indeed, the emotion which Mrs. Fernandez had aroused in Alston's breast was not, although he wondered at her beauty and wished to be with her, a sexual one. . . .

"Mr. Fernandez seems so elusive that I sometimes wonder if he really exists," said Miss Brixworth. "Do *you* ever see him, Empringham?"

"Now and then, madam, but he keeps very much to himself."

"I imagine he's an invalid from what Mrs. Fernandez tells me, and I've sometimes heard a husky, graveyard cough in the distance which I suppose must be his."

"It's those terrible smokes of his," said Empring-ham, "that accounts for *that*."

"But what's he like to look at?"

"He looks a wreck of a man, but I bet he's got a lot of life in him," said Empringham. "A bit queer, I should say. Like the child."

"Like Rosy!" exclaimed Miss Brixworth. "Oh, but I don't think she's queer, Empringham. . . . At least, no queerer than most children."

"I hope you're right, madam, but she's a little too old-fashioned for me. I never saw such a child, and like father, like daughter, as they say."

She made up her mind that whenever she saw Rosy she would watch the child carefully for signs of oddness.

VI

"TELL me he's lazy,
Tell me he's low—"

sang a deep negro voice on the Rudds' gramophone.
The record was rather worn, for it was one of Mrs.
Rudd's favourites. A kind of hissing and sputtering
accompanied the song, and at frequent and regular
intervals there was a harsh sound caused by the
needle jumping over a crack in the record. There was
also a sound and smell of frying sausages.

"Tell me I'm crazy,
Maybe I know—"

At this point Mrs. Rudd herself joined in. Her
voice was girlish but a trifle shrill.

"When he goes away
That's a rainy day,
And when he comes back again—
Tra-la-la-la-la!"

Her husband was sitting at the table where he
was engaged in a newspaper competition called *Are
You a Judge of Dress?* Spread out before him were
seven photographs of the same mannequin in seven
different suits of beach pyjamas and the same picture-
hat. These had to be placed in the correct order of

merit, a feat which, it seemed, would entitle the competitor to two thousand pounds. Rudd, hesitating between pyjamas that laced up at the side and pyjamas with a gigantic butterfly embroidered on the hip, looked up over his spectacles.

"For Christ's sake stop that row!" he said.

"I shan't," said his wife.

"You will," he said, making a move towards the gramophone, but his wife snatched the frying-pan off the fire and stepped nimbly between him and the machine. Each time he made a move to stop the motor she thrust the frying-pan out at him. It was naturally extremely hot, and the contents were still sizzling merrily, so he dared not touch it and could not get past it. He looked so silly in his helpless rage, with his awkward movements, his receding chin and ill-shaven Adam's-apple, that his wife began to taunt him.

"Oh, you cave-man!" she cried. "Don't come near me or I'll burn you! If I want to play a tune I'll play it, see? Oh, you masterful man!"

The gramophone, slowing down, began to utter the most dreadful grinding howl, which acted as a goad upon the already maddened Rudd. He made another move, and again she stopped him.

"Yes," she said, "do you know how long it is since you——?"

"Since I what?" he retorted, watching the record stop revolving.

"You know very well what I mean! Do you know

how long it is, I say? A nice one you are, aren't you!"

She was so indignant by now that she had forgotten that she was on the defensive, or she may have thought that as the gramophone had stopped her husband wouldn't want to touch it: however, he caught her unawares by the arm, and made a dash for the gramophone, but in doing so tilted up the frying-pan, and the contents fell out. Not only did the gravy fall on to the carpet, but Rudd's spectacles fell into the gravy, and as he bent forward to rescue them he stepped on one of the sausages and squashed it flat.

"Now I hope you're satisfied, you great clumsy fool," said his wife, as she stooped to pick up another one in her fingers. Holding it up in the light, she found it was covered with ashes. "And what have I told you about dropping ashes all over the floor? Oh, I could just cry!"

She just cried. Rudd cleaned the gravy off his glasses, and blew his nose, forgetting that his handkerchief was all wet with gravy. And suddenly, just outside in the road, a barrel-organ began to play, and a voice could be heard singing, "*Tell me he's lazy, tell me he's low. . . .*" Rudd swore violently. As if his married life were not wretched enough without having this wretched chorus to accompany it, indoors and out!

But dissension at 45 Cambodia Crescent was by no means confined to the Rudd family. The same evening a fearful scene was going on in the kitchen. The hostility which had from the first shown itself between Empringham and Mrs. Gambitt had gradually increased, but for many days now they hadn't even spoken to each other. Their accumulated rage suddenly broke out. Mrs. Fernandez had "just popped out" to buy one or two necessaries which she had forgotten to get earlier in the day. Her husband had only consented to her going on condition that she returned in five minutes, and now, upstairs in the bedroom, he was tortured by the wildest suspicions. No doubt she had gone to meet the doctor, or that handsome young milkman who came round in the mornings and had such pleasant, such far too pleasant manners, or perhaps there was some man in a shop that he didn't even know about? Always under the necessity now of having to fidget with something, he took up a pair of scissors and began cutting his nails with a trembling and bony hand, the back of which appeared quite dark, with its dry, discoloured skin, prominent purplish veins, and a profusion of overgrown black hairs. Rosy was playing on the floor at his feet, and talking to herself. She was playing a game in which a teddy bear which was supposed to be married to a doll continually told his wife that she went out far too much. "Don't be so silly, Teddy," the doll was made to reply; "who do you think will do the shopping if I don't?"

Mrs. Fernandez was back, as she had promised she would be, in five minutes. But during that time much had happened. Empringham, enjoying a quiet pipe in the kitchen, had suddenly become aware that there was somebody else in the room. Turning slowly round, for he had a touch of sciatica, whom should he have seen but Mrs. Gambitt, standing and watching him, with her hands on her hips and righteous indignation on her face? He said nothing, took a deliberate puff at his pipe, and blew out a thin slow stream of smoke towards the ceiling.

"Look!" said Mrs. Gambitt, pointing to a pile of five or six dirty plates.

"Well?" said Empringham.

"I suppose you don't *mean* to do any washing-up to-day," she said, in a tone of voice that was meant to be sarcastic.

"Oh," said Empringham, his anger rising so quickly that he couldn't speak.

"Well, are you going to wash those things up or not?"

"Look here, Mrs. Gambitt, let me give you a piece of advice. I advise you to mind your own business."

"How dare you speak to me like that!"

"Well, then, go away while there's still time, because if you stay, I dare say we shall have a row."

"A row, indeed! Why don't you do your work properly?"

"I'm not taking any orders from you," said Empringham, puffing furiously at his pipe. "It's Mrs. Fernandez I'm working for, and if she's displeased with me, she's quite able to tell me so."

"We'll see about that," said Mrs. Gambitt, "before very long."

"Oh, forget it," said Empringham. Mrs. Gambitt became livid.

"You'll do what I tell you or you'll get out of this house!"

"If it came to that," said Empringham slowly and emphatically, choosing his words as carefully as he always did, "I shouldn't hesitate to leave, for I'd see you in hell before I'd take any orders from a woman like you. Do you know what's the matter with you? You haven't got enough work to do. And a woman like you isn't fit to give orders to people. You ought to be taking them, that's what you ought to do. But *I*'d be sorry to employ you, I can tell you. It's only some freak of nature that's got you into the position you're in now, where you've got nothing to do but give yourself airs and pretend to be what you're not."

Mrs. Gambitt was not unnaturally furious. The truth is seldom palatable.

"I'll make you pay for this!" she said, her somewhat decayed teeth positively chattering with rage. She began backing towards the door, and Empringham made a feint of pursuing her. She darted out, slamming it behind her.

On the other side of it she ran straight into Mrs. Fernandez, just back from shopping.

"Why, Natalie, whatever's the matter?" cried Mrs. Fernandez.

"Come in here," said Mrs. Gambitt, leading the way into the office.

"Wait, I must just go and tell Paul that I'm back," said Mrs. Fernandez, running upstairs.

When she came down again Mrs. Gambitt was standing facing the door and smoking a cigarette.

"That fellow must go," said Mrs. Gambitt in a harsh voice which she thought was like that of one of the proud heroines in the novels which she sometimes read.

"What fellow?" said Mrs. Fernandez, knowing perfectly well.

"That Empringham! That *servant*!"

"Oh dear, what has he done now?"

"I've told you again and again about him, Beryl. I can't put up with it any longer. He must leave or I shall, and it must be him."

"But what has happened?"

"Happened! He's so *insolent*!"

"But I'm sure he's not an ill-natured man," said Mrs. Fernandez. "Don't you think if you were to try leaving him alone——?"

"No, Beryl. You must get rid of him."

"And then?"

"You'll have to get that Irish boy we heard of instead."

"And perhaps the same thing'll happen all over again," Mrs. Fernandez couldn't help saying. She didn't at all like the idea of an "Irish boy" taking the place of the capable and respectable, the dignified

Empringham. But she knew she would have to give way.

"No," said Mrs. Gambitt. "I'll see that he's taught to know his place from the start."

"Oh, how can I do it, Natalie? How can I tell Empringham that I'm not satisfied with him, when he's such a good servant?"

"I suppose you're satisfied that he should go on insulting me? But you needn't worry; I'll see that he goes."

She said this in a hard voice, but she had hardly said it when she burst into tears, she was so sorry for herself and the insult she imagined she had received. And Mrs. Fernandez was so upset by her friend's being upset that she clasped her in her arms and they mingled their tears in a united torrent of self-pity.

When they separated Mrs. Gambitt went upstairs to relieve her feelings still further with Mrs. Porter, while Mrs. Fernandez sighed, shook back her splendid hair from her forehead, and went into the kitchen. When Empringham saw her he said he was very sorry for what had happened, but he couldn't put up with Mrs. Gambitt any longer.

"I'm very sorry too," said Mrs. Fernandez, "for I shall be sorry to lose you, and so will Rosy, and so, I'm sure, will Miss Brixworth. Oh dear, such is life!"

In the morning Empringham knocked at Miss Brixworth's door.

"If I'm not disturbing you, madam, can I speak to you for a few moments?"

"Come in, Empringham."

"It's that Mrs. Gambitt——"

"Ah."

"That woman's not fit for human society!"

"She's not much to look at, I must say, but is she so bad as all that? I'm afraid she's getting on your nerves, Empringham."

"Well, it's not going on, madam. I'm leaving."

"You're leaving!"

"It had to be one of us," he said, "and it has to be me."

He explained why.

"And where will you go?" said Miss Brixworth. "Will you be able to start your little restaurant at last?"

"No, madam, I haven't enough put by as yet."

"Oh dear, then what will you do?"

"Well, I have a married sister who's just starting a poultry farm down Aylesbury way, and I think I'll go in shares with them, and see if I can't make a bit that way."

"Oh, Empringham, I wouldn't do business with relations. That's seldom wise. And I'm sure poultry farms never pay."

"Oh, once they begin to lay——"

"If only I had as much money now as I had even five years ago," said Miss Brixworth, "I would willingly have helped you to start your little restaurant. But things have changed——"

"I'm sure I'm ever so obliged to you," he said. "I'll never forget your kindness, madam."

G

"It's a shame to be poor," she said musingly. "I know I'm lucky compared to lots of people. But things are so uncertain for us all nowadays. . . . And who's going to do your work when you're gone, Empringham?"

"It seems they've got someone already. A young Irish chap, I hear he is. I wonder if he'll stick it as long as I have. I wish him joy of it, anyway." He chuckled.

"Oh," said Miss Brixworth, "something has just occurred to me. Supposing, Empringham, that you could get another job in London, would you take it?"

"That depends——"

"I was just thinking it's just possible I could get you a position with a friend of mine. I'll inquire. You'd better leave me your address, and I'll let you know."

Miss Brixworth was thinking of Miss Haymer, who was dissatisfied with her maid of all work, and had said several times lately that she preferred men to women as servants. She determined to speak to her on the subject at the first opportunity.

"I must say I'm sorry to lose him," said Mrs. Fernandez after Empringham's departure. "Gave a tone to the house, didn't he? But there was nothing for it——"

"I'm afraid the fault must have been more Mrs. Gambitt's than his," said Miss Brixworth.

"Well, you may be right, Miss Brixworth; "but I

must say I don't like to hear anything against Mrs. Gambitt, for without her we couldn't carry on here at all."

"A pity."

"I'm getting a new man. He's not so experienced, but I think he'll soon learn. And I mean to have a girl in, two or three days a week, to give a hand with things, so I'm sure we'll be all right."

"Yes," said Miss Brixworth, "I expect so. But you're losing a treasure in Empringham. I'm afraid Mrs. Gambitt can't be very good at managing people. I hope you won't allow her to upset the new man in the same way."

Mrs. Fernandez looked at her with large, appealing eyes, as if begging her to say no more.

"Of course I know it's difficult for you," Miss Brixworth said quickly.

"Financially, you see——" said Mrs. Fernandez.

"Yes, I see."

"And she's a very good friend to us."

"I'm glad."

"So we have to try and make the best of things. Oh, Miss Brixworth, you're so sympathetic!"

"I know you have plenty of worries, and I hope they'll get less."

The gratitude in Mrs. Fernandez' face faded out and anxiety took its place.

"And there's my husband," she said. "He's been so funny lately, and I'm worried about the effect he'll have on poor little Rosy."

"Don't worry so much."

"Oh, there's always something to worry about in a house like this. And now Mrs. Gambitt's been given a dog, and I wonder how it'll behave itself."

As that afternoon was fine and sunny, Miss Brixworth, after lunching with Miss Haymer, persuaded her friend to go out with her. So Miss Haymer, leaning heavily upon Miss Brixworth with one hand and as heavily upon her rubber-ended walking-stick with the other, made a difficult and grunting progress into Kensington Gardens, where they sat down to watch the children playing round them and the first leaves falling from the trees. Miss Haymer was at first somewhat out of breath, but when she recovered she said:

"And what news from 45 Cambodia Crescent?"

Miss Brixworth was longing to tell her all about Empringham (indeed, she would have done so before, had not Miss Haymer been very talkative all through lunch), but now she thought she had better lead up to the subject gradually.

"Mrs. Gambitt has been given a dog," she said. "Such a sweet little thing."

This was not a good opening. Miss Haymer was not fond of dogs.

"How could a dog possibly be sweet?" she said.

"Oh, I thought you'd lost your old prejudice against them! I love them, as you know. I sometimes feel I ought to keep one myself."

"What, in London! I must say I greatly prefer cats.

They're so independent and mysterious, so elegant.
Oh, these old women and their dogs! Connie, it's
disgusting. I may be an old woman, but at least I
don't have myself lugged about by a gross, overfed,
flabby dog. . . . You know why the English are so
fond of dogs, don't you? It's because they're so like
themselves. Dogs are simply full of public-school
spirit and cheerful stupidity and false pride—all the
things the English admire so much in themselves. And
then look, when one is abroad, and one sees two
English people meeting for the first time in some out-
landish spot. Watch them circling round and round
each other with a growl and an angry but inquisitive stare, trying to find if they're of the same breed
or rather class. Watch the careful top-and-bottom
sniffing to see if the stranger is a friend or an enemy.
What could be more doggy than all that? And then
the War—an unthinking cheerfulness, a blind faithfulness, hard fighting, tail-wagging at the end, and
then two minutes' silence, with the head on the paws.
. . . And just because dogs are what they call 'plucky'
people will overlook all their filthy habits, and the
same people love to tell you that dogs are 'so clever,'
just because they can tell the difference between the
smell of their owners and the smell of other people
you would otherwise think were indistinguishable
from them."

"Fanny, what a tirade!" said Miss Brixworth. "I
think you're most unjust."

"Oh, but I could say a lot more," said Miss

Haymer. "They smell, they have fleas, they're greedy, they make sudden noises."

"Well, so do human beings."

"Not nice human beings."

"Nor do nice dogs, Fanny. And they're often much more faithful and affectionate and better companions than human beings."

"That's not saying much," said Miss Haymer. "And if it's true, it's no doubt because they're often more kindly treated than human beings. If you like them, I'll try and admit that dogs may be very nice, because I like you. I once knew a man in Morocco who said scorpions were the most faithful and affectionate little creatures, and I'm pretty sure he said they were intelligent, too. And he was a very nice man. . . . But I must say, what annoys me is that dogs always like me. It's most galling."

"They're probably better judges of you," said Miss Brixworth, "than you are of them."

Miss Haymer grunted, then she said:

"No, it's all very well, Connie; look at that woman over there fussing over that vile little mongrel. It's disgusting! She wants a man or a child. It's unhealthy, it's repulsive."

Miss Brixworth put up her lorgnon and looked in the direction where Miss Haymer was pointing with her stick, its rubber end fastening on the landscape like a huge tentacle.

"She's actually kissing it," said Miss Haymer.

"Why, it's Mrs. Gambitt!" cried Miss Brixworth.

"My dear, what an awful-looking woman! What on earth does she dress like that for? Why doesn't she learn how to put her clothes on? And she's as thin as a scarecrow!"

"Take a good look at her, Fanny; there's something I want to tell you about her."

"Well?"

"Well, there's been an awful row."

"And——?"

"And that woman has obliged Empringham to leave us."

Miss Brixworth explained what had happened.

"Ah, well, what do you expect?" said Miss Haymer. "People like that never know how to treat servants. You can see to look at her that she's really of the servant class herself, and so is quite unfit to manage others."

"How angry she would be if she could hear you!"

"Oh, I dare say. The truth's an uncomfortable thing. By the way, what's Empringham going to do now?"

"Well, Fanny, that's just what I was going to speak about. I was wondering if you'd like to take him on yourself?" Miss Brixworth was a little nervous at the possible effect that this bold suggestion might have on her friend, but she needn't have been, for Miss Haymer thought the idea a reasonable one, and said she would at least be willing to interview Empringham. Her maid was under notice, and she saw no reason why she shouldn't employ a manservant instead. Miss Brixworth therefore wrote to Empringham, and the upshot was that Miss Haymer agreed to engage him. Miss Brixworth was pleased, feeling that she had done them both a good turn, but at the same time she rather regretted that Miss Haymer, instead of herself, would now receive Empringham's confidence. She got over this by transferring the interest she had shown in him to Alston and the new manservant.

VII

THE new manservant's name was Carol, but whether this was surname or Christian name never became clear, for everybody at 45 Cambodia Crescent knew him as Carol from the first. He came from the south of Ireland, but brought with him a suggestion of the warmth and strangeness of the Mediterranean. He had some drops of Spanish blood in him perhaps, or simply that touch of magic which you find now and again in people whose blood derives from districts where southerners, the Greeks or the Phoenicians, have touched our shores, as in Wales, Cornwall or Dorset. He hadn't been very long in London, and there was a pleasant brogue in his speech. His face was rather ugly, but naughty and lively. If at times he looked rather worried, he had a cheerful temper which could only be ruffled by real or imagined assaults on his dignity. His dark hair continually fell over his eyes while he talked, and whenever he pushed it back it at once fell forward again. This was rather symbolical of his nature, which was to accept the inevitable: it was as if he knew that you may try occasionally and shove Fate away, but Fate will be throwing its shadow over your eyes again the very next minute. He also had a habit of licking his lips, which were thick and red, and while you were talking to him you found yourself involuntarily watching his mouth and waiting for the tip of his tongue to appear.

He quickly became a favourite with Mrs. Fernandez and Miss Brixworth, the enthusiasts of the house, but Mrs. Gambitt looked down on him on principle, as he was a "servant." Carol was fond of girls, and he was disappointed to find that there weren't any under the roof with him. Mrs. Rudd was the only one that seemed to have any sex appeal, he told Alston, but "if she's got 'it' she can keep it, so far as I'm concerned," he said. "They say women are like religions, and that if you can't say something nice about them it's safer to say nothing, but I must say it's not so easy to be nice about the women in this house. They want this, and they want that, and they want the other, and most of them don't know what they want at all, and if they did they wouldn't be able to get it."

But if he disapproved of the people he had to wait on, he took a lively interest in their behaviour. He was soon pretty well aware of most of what went on in the house, and one afternoon, only a week after his arrival, he made the fascinating discovery (which he later communicated to Alston) that Mr. and Mrs. Fernandez had spent over two hours together in the bathroom. This excited his imagination very much. But he was already up against the severity of Mrs. Gambitt, and he complained of it to Miss Brixworth.

"And then," he added, "she tries to make out that nothing's good enough for her. She's not used to living like this, she says, and things are not what they used to be. Oh, it's terrible, Miss Brixworth." Miss Brixworth couldn't help wincing, because Carol called her by name instead of calling her "madam" as Empringham had always done, and she sighed, feeling that she was sinking lower in the social scale and yet knowing that it would be pretentious to correct him.

"People that's always grumbling about the times," Carol went on, "these hard times, and what a terrible age we live in, and all that—they're mostly people that are a bit too sorry for themselves, and don't know a good thing when they've got it."

I wonder if he means that for me, she thought.

"But sometimes, Carol," she said, "it's because they're old. There's some excuse for being sorry for yourself when you're old. Look at a person like Mrs. Porter, now. I don't suppose *she*'s got very much to live for."

"Perhaps not, Miss Brixworth, but 'a year or two ago,' Mrs. Gambitt said to me, 'no servant would ever have dreamed of leaving a breakfast tray in a bedroom until eleven o'clock.' 'Perhaps not,' I said, 'but no servant ever had more work to do than I have. And I can't take your tray yet,' I said, 'there's Miss Brixworth upstairs to be seen to.' Oh, she looked daggers at me then!"

"I dare say she has never had anybody to wait on her before she came here," said Miss Brixworth, who couldn't help feeling mildly triumphant at having become as much an open favourite with Carol as she had been with Empringham. And she was not incapable of feeling pleasure at being able to score off another woman, especially when that woman was Mrs. Gambitt.

She had always made it a rule to be amiable but not familiar with landladies, but when she found that Mrs. Fernandez was beginning to form the habit of dropping in now and then to talk to her, she didn't discourage her. At first she thought Mrs. Fernandez came to see her just because she wanted to keep on good terms with her. But she soon came to other conclusions. Mrs. Fernandez possibly liked her for her own sake, but seemed to have something on her mind. Was it possible that she didn't find Mrs. Gambitt a perfect confidante? Whatever the matter was, Miss Brixworth felt sure that it had something to do with the relationship between Mrs. Fernandez and her husband. Yet Mrs. Fernandez said little about him, except perhaps that he was often out of sorts, and that she had accordingly to take full charge of the house. Miss Brixworth was sympathetic and tactful, and speculated vaguely about the Fernandezes without feeling much the wiser. And then Carol introduced the subject.

"I can't make out what she sees in him," he said. "It beats me."

"I must confess," said Miss Brixworth, "that I don't understand it either. It seems to me that Fernandez is not only much older than his wife, but an invalid, repulsive to look at and disagreeeable in his behaviour."

"You're right," said Carol, "but he's not so much of an invalid as he makes out. And he's terribly jealous of her. The other day, when she wanted to have the man here to do the electric light, he refused to let her, and got worked up, hinting, you know—— If he sees her talking to the milkman there's the devil to pay. And this very morning it was the postman he almost chased away from the very door. When she goes out shopping he stands at the window watching for her to come back, and if she's gone more than a few minutes he doesn't know what to do. Terrible, it is. But he worships that child."

"And why do you think she puts up with all this?"

"Och, you never know with women," said Carol, looking very wise. "I suppose she likes him."

But here their conversation ended abruptly, for Mrs. Gambitt's voice could be heard calling indignantly for Carol. . . .

"Oh, I was going to tell you about Mrs. Fernandez," said Miss Brixworth to Miss Haymer when she next saw her.

"Well?"

"Well, it's about her husband."

"*What* is about her husband?" Miss Haymer cried impatiently. "Do try and say what you mean!"

"Well, do give me time, Fanny."

"Go on, then."

"Now I can't remember what I was going to say."

"How stupid, Connie."

"Oh yes. I was going to say that she appears to be in love with her husband and afraid of him at the same time."

"Quite likely," said Miss Haymer sharply. "But why is she afraid of him?"

"He's getting more and more jealous of her, it seems."

"Hm!" said Miss Haymer. "She ought to feel flattered. She ought to congratulate herself. There's many a woman would give anything for a jealous husband. She's lucky to be loved."

"But I'm afraid, Fanny, that his jealousy's rather extreme. It's becoming a sort of mania."

"Oh, is it? How d'you know?"

"I've gathered it."

"Oh, you've gathered it, have you? Well, after all, she's made her bed and she's got to lie on it. And don't forget that she's a Jewess. When you can't understand her behaviour say to yourself, 'Well, she's a Jewess.' It saves thinking, and what's more, you'll probably be right. She probably *does* behave like this just because she's a Jewess."

Miss Haymer was here nearer the truth than she knew. And in her Jewishness Mrs. Fernandez was typical of the spirit of modern life, which is Jewish, feminine, and paradoxical. The little movements of her life were like the large movements of the world we live in—a world which, for better or worse, centres everything in sex and material things, a world that thinks of everything in terms of capitalism and communism, a world without great artists but full of cravings to be "artistic," a world without religion in fact, a world which seeks negation instead of the godlike, desires death, perhaps, rather than life.

And the paradox of her loving Fernandez even while she feared him was only a tiny illustration of the paradoxical nature of her race. You can never make out whether the Jews want to be aristocrats or socialists. Half-way between East and West, they may be somewhere near the truth, if the truth really lies in paradox. Jesus Christ was the greatest and most para-doxical of the Jews. He had the most aristocratic nature imaginable, and yet he lived with the lowest of the low. He was unique, and yet expressed himself in terms of what is ordinary and universal. . . .

Being Jewish, Mrs. Fernandez had an extraordinary gift for contriving both to have her cake and eat it. You get men like Heine and Proust, men who managed to enjoy life thoroughly and yet saw through it, who took pleasure in just those people and things about which they were most malicious and ironical. Jews kiss and kill at the same time, just as a sports-man may feel a real affection for the game he slaughters. The Jew to-day comes to us with the world in his hand like a gamekeeper carrying a partridge which he has shot. "Dear little thing, isn't it?" he says, stroking the satiny brown feathers with his rough hand. And he really means it. The bird doesn't stop being a dear little thing just because it's dead. It would still be a dear little thing put in a hat for ornament or a dish for food. The bear and the boa constrictor hug their victims to death, and the ichneumon fly chooses the fattest caterpillar to lay its eggs in.

And then Russia! The dictatorship of the proletariat is a Jewish idea. What a contradiction in terms, what a fantastic paradox! An aristocracy which shall include everybody—how very Jewish! And yet it's not such a bad idea after all, it's not so unlike Christianity, itself a collection of Jewish riddles, Asiatic conundrums—the Virgin Birth, the Trinity, and so on. How rich are the ideas, and movements of ideas, with which the Jews have been associated! And how meaningless the individual without the race of which he is the epitome! The beauty and character of Mrs. Fernandez were not quickly and easily bred. . . .

"She's a good, unselfish woman," said Miss Brixworth, "and there's no doubt that she loves him."

"Connie," said Miss Haymer, "do you believe that love is an unselfish thing?"

Miss Brixworth felt that she did, but she was afraid to say so.

"Well," said Miss Haymer," if you do you're wrong. 'Nothing is so selfless,' you hear people say, 'as the love of a mother for her child.' But how can a feeling be selfless into which one's whole self is poured?"

"Greater love hath no man——" said Miss Brixworth sententiously.

"Ah, that's all very well," said Miss Haymer, "but if you make sacrifices to ensure the happiness of somebody you love, isn't it only because their happiness is almost identical with yours?"

"Perhaps, Fanny. But isn't it unselfish to give things up for other people?"

"The trouble with you, my dear, is that you're too soft-hearted."

Miss Brixworth made no answer.

"The point about love," Miss Haymer went on, speaking as if with the authority of one who knew, "is that it's a terribly dangerous thing. Yes, it's dangerous, it's always dangerous. Didn't the Greeks understand that better than anybody? What clear thinkers they were! They saw that love, whether between lovers, or brothers and sisters, or people of the same sex, or children and parents, or husbands and wives, is a thing absolutely beyond human control, a thing which can easily land you in a mess. Look at Medea, and Phaedra, and so on."

"Yes," said Miss Brixworth, whose education had been concerned more with Judaea than Greece, and who wasn't at all sure who Medea and Phaedra were or what they did.

"Or look at this case in the paper," Miss Haymer went on. "A handsome and amiable and apparently quite normal young chauffeur falls in love with a little girl of six, the child of his employers, who apparently don't for some time understand the strength of his feelings. When they at last realise how

H

the child and the servant are obsessed with each other, they protest, but it's too late. The young man takes the child away and they die together in a gas-filled room."

"It's horrible!" cried Miss Brixworth.

"Unusual, unfortunate if you like, Fanny, but why horrible?"

"It's absurd to talk of love in the case of a child of that age."

"Is it, though? I don't agree at all. The coquettishness of little girls is extraordinary."

"But coquettishness isn't love."

"Ah," said Miss Haymer, "but just think of your own feelings as a child. Didn't you centre your whole being in people and adore them passionately with a love which, just because it was so unconscious and uncritical and immature, was real and strong? I know I did. Now you just watch that child of the Fernandezes and see if you can't imagine how she might inherit from a father like that quite intense feelings. Empringham tells me that she's very precocious."

"He told me the same thing, but I think she's just a little darling. I can't believe it's right, Fanny, to believe that children aren't innocent."

Miss Haymer shrugged her shoulders impatiently.

"Empringham's not a fool," she said. "And from the account he gives me of Mrs. Fernandez and her husband, I don't like the outlook at all."

"How do you mean?"

"*Ça finira mal.*"

"I think Empringham's a bit of an alarmist. Fernandez is an invalid, Fanny, and he'll probably die before long. I don't know what she'll do then, poor thing."

"She's a fool to live with him," said Miss Haymer. "Oh, if I could only get hold of her, I'd give her a good talking to." As she spoke she prodded vigorously at a dead twig with her stick.

"But you don't know her, Fanny."

"Oh, don't worry, I don't mean to interfere. Only somebody ought to point out to the woman that she's playing with edged tools—not that that would make any difference, though."

"She adores him. And there's the child, which they both adore. How could she leave him?"

"Oh, the child! Well, don't be surprised if it all ends badly. . . . But really, I suppose nobody ought to interfere in such matters."

"But, Fanny——"

"Wait, what right has anybody to interfere in their lives? They may be fools, but I don't suppose they're bigger fools than anybody else. At least they're having a run for their money. No, we ought to leave Mrs. Fernandez alone, and let her find her happiness in her own way. It may all turn out all right and it may not, but in any case it's not our business."

"Fanny, it seems to me you've rather contradicted yourself. First you suggest that they ought to be separated, then that they ought to be left together."

"Well, what of it?" said Miss Haymer. "There are

two sides to every question, and both may be true. It just depends how you look at it. And people who never contradict themselves aren't good for much. Let Mrs. Fernandez go her own way—she'll no doubt be happier in her folly than many people in their prudence. She loves that man to distraction, that's clear, and that's all that matters. It's a duty to love. It's very nice to be loved, but it's much more important to love. Unless she loved somebody, life would probably mean nothing at all to her. . . . And that applies to us as well."

"Yes, I suppose it does," said Miss Brixworth, "but it's getting chilly, and we ought to go in."

Where Miss Haymer was content to reason about Mrs. Fernandez, Mrs. Gambitt was more inclined to protest and implore, for her heart was involved. She loved Mrs. Fernandez. And she was beginning to be seriously disturbed by the behaviour of Fernandez. He had, for instance, just made the most fearful scene with the milkman, a nice, cheerful fellow whom everyone liked and who was a special favourite with Rosy. Suddenly appearing at the door, very early in the morning, Fernandez cried, "You think I don't know what you come here for, but I do!" and so saying, kicked several bottles of milk down the steps and shook a gaunt fist in the milkman's face. The milkman, however, who was an ex-soldier, was not in the least daunted by him, and said:

"Go on, you're balmy. You ought to be in bed at this time of the morning, instead of making a fool of yourself on your own door-step like this. What d'you think you're playing at?"

Ridicule was of course the last thing to have any effect on Fernandez, who thereupon slammed the door in the milkman's face, threatening that if he came again he would kill him. So an arrangement had to be made by which the milk, instead of being delivered at the door, was to be fetched every morning from the dairy, which was in Parthenon Street—the street of shops which ran at right angles to Cambodia Crescent, and had Pélagie's and a cinema as its chief ornaments. But since Mrs. Fernandez, had she gone every morning to fetch the milk, would have been at once suspected by her husband of an intrigue, and since Mrs. Gambitt was too proud to fetch it, this task fell upon the already rather overworked Carol, who didn't fail to curse about Fernandez for having made it necessary.

Fernandez, who had once had as much common sense as could have been expected in a man with hardly any sense of humour, was now not only totally unable to laugh at himself, but indeed seldom smiled at all, except perhaps when playing with his child or making love to his wife—and in each case the smile was the sign of an emotion almost purely physical. More openly violent and suspicious than ever before, Fernandez was gradually being overcome by the powers of darkness that were assailing his soul. He could scarcely bear his wife out of his sight, opened every letter that came to the house addressed to her, thinking that even a bill or a receipt might be used to convey some secret message of love, and when a most grotesque incident occurred, he remained absolutely unmoved by it.

The incident in question was this. Mrs. Petherham-Porter had, in common with Mrs. Gambitt, an interest in the occult. This she combined with some degree of curiosity about more everyday matters, and she never hesitated, when the chance offered, to use one to supplement the other. She seldom undertook to tell anybody's fortune, or to read their characters by palmistry or handwriting, without having first tried to find out something about them. She thus gained prestige by telling you something about yourself which you couldn't possibly have expected her to know. Besides, she loved other people's business because she had so little of her own, and liked nothing better than a nice juicy bit of gossip, particularly if she had started it herself. But she was neither cruel nor mischievous—she was harmless, easily hypnotised and not always discreet.

Now Mrs. Gambitt was always telling her the latest news about Mr. and Mrs. Fernandez, and this interested her so much that she longed to supplement what she learned from Mrs. Gambitt with what she could learn for herself. Unfortunately the wall of the Fernandez' bedroom, which was next to hers, was so thick that she could hear scarcely anything through it, and certainly no distinct words; but one afternoon, at a time when there was usually nobody about, she cautiously opened her door, put her head out to ensure that she wasn't being watched, and tiptoed to the door of the Fernandez' room, where she took a peep through the keyhole. And there she was, this respectable-looking woman of middle age, standing with her bottom in the air, in just the position in which Empringham had once caught her trying to spy on the Rudds.

The peep revealed nothing except part of a chest of drawers. But a conversation in low tones was undoubtedly going on—such low tones that not a word could be made out. If only Mrs. Porter had known, the talk was not in the least worth hearing, for Mr. and Mrs. Fernandez were only discussing the most trivial domestic matter. But she felt sure that it was something important, and leant against the door with her ear to the keyhole instead of her eye. Now it so happened that just at that moment Fernandez felt a need to go to the lavatory, stepped silently towards the door, and swiftly opened it, causing Mrs. Porter, who was leaning heavily against it, to lose her balance and tumble headlong into the room.

Had she been a man, any man, no doubt Fernandez would have done her some awful violence there and then, but directly he had got over his surprise, he stared vaguely at Mrs. Porter as she began to pick herself up. His wife, on the contrary, rushed forward with an exclamation.

"Oh, Mrs. Porter, I do hope you're not hurt! What a nasty fall! How *did* it happen?"

"Oh! Oh dear!" panted Mrs. Porter, as she was helped to her feet. "I can't *think* what happened! I must have slipped on the landing there just as Mr. Fernandez opened the door. Oh, oh dear!"

"Well, I *am* sorry! Did you hurt yourself? I really must get a carpet for the stairs and landing. They're quite dangerous and slippery like this," said Mrs. Fernandez, though she had guessed at once that Mrs. Porter had been eavesdropping and had been taken by surprise. She tried to help Mrs. Porter to recover from her shock and embarrassment, helped her into her own room again, and as soon as she had left her, burst out laughing. Her husband watched her morosely.

"Oh, can't you see how *funny* it is?" she cried impatiently, but he made no answer, and the child Rosy, who had been playing in the room but had scarcely realised what had happened, looked up and said, "What is it, mummy? What are you laughing at?"

This was too much for Mrs. Fernandez, who was determined to enjoy the joke with somebody. She hurried downstairs to find Mrs. Gambitt, but Mrs. Gambitt happened to be out just then, so she told Carol instead. Carol found her laughter infectious, and his lank black hair fell over his face, so that only one eye was visible, all screwed up with laughter. When Mrs. Fernandez saw this, it made her laugh more than ever, and they both went on laughing till they ached.

But Fernandez, standing on the stairs, paused, with
one hand on the banisters, listening to the merri-
ment downstairs and wearing an intent and inscrutable expression on his face. He loved to hear
his wife laugh, and although he himself could never
make her laugh, he didn't feel jealous of Carol. Both
Mrs. Fernandez and Mrs. Gambitt had commented
on the fact that he wasn't jealous of Carol, who they
thought would inevitably provoke him. Carol himself had noticed his immunity, but he couldn't account
for it. "My turn next," he sometimes said to Alston.
Perhaps Fernandez' indifference could be accounted
for by the fact that when a man is suspicious he
sometimes tends to think so much of remoter pos-
sibilities that he overlooks what is right under his nose
—like a golfer who searches anxiously for a lost ball
in the rough when it is all the time lying quietly on
the fairway—or it may have been simply that Carol,
harum-scarum as he was, had a very frank and dis-
arming manner with Fernandez; a respectful, con-
fidential manner which he had from the first main-
tained towards one who was nominally his master.
Or it may be that if Fernandez at first suspected
Carol's easy popularity with women, the frequent
sight of that comically ugly face had reassured him.
At all events, he at no time showed any sign that he
was jealous of Carol.

The pleasure which he derived from listening to
his wife's laughter as he stood so still on the stairs
was purely a sexual one, for his love for her had

passed all bounds. The pleasures of love are always in proportion to the fears and anxieties of the lover, and the more Fernandez' suspicions had increased the more ardent his love had grown, until at last it might be said of his jealousy and his passion that each was fuel and each was fire; each fed the other, until the flames of desire were always roaring in his ears. Love is always a monomania, but with him it had become a more dangerous one than even Miss Haymer could have suspected. His mood had become that of a man who will set fire to a town to cook himself an egg. Obsessed with his own feelings, he could think of no one else's, and as his passion increased, his wife, growing ever more excited by it, became at the same time ever more alarmed. He had never yet offered her real violence, but just lately he had uttered vague threats against her, swearing that he would like to beat her, to pull her hair, or to throw cold water over her, and while she was still all wet and shivering, to smother her with kisses. . . .

And in those dead hours of the night, when his wife and child were asleep and the whole of London seemed silent, he would sit up in bed, smoking his everlasting cigarette and watching his own enormous shadow, cast by a night-light upon the walls and ceiling, and such dreams, and madder ones besides, continually haunted him. The idea of cruelty (which is only a diseased form of sympathy) was beginning to exercise a fascination over his thoughts. Not content with love, and love fully requited at that, he wanted power as well, he wanted to command more love, a stronger, a more intense kind of intimacy than is humanly possible, and so he began to seek how he might obtain such power. It is for some people a hard lesson to learn, that intimacy can only be based on the knowledge that a complete intimacy is unobtainable; for Fernandez it was impossible. As he wanted more, and as he began to realise unconsciously that what he wanted was impossible to obtain, the more unbalanced did he become, and the more did his resentment against his fellow-men increase. It was no wonder that his wife, alone with Mrs. Gambitt on a fine Sunday when Fernandez had for once gone out for a walk with the child, completely broke down.

"Oh, Natalie," she cried, "whatever am I to do?"

"Be calm," said Mrs. Gambitt, and her voice was quite soft. "And stop crying." In those words was concentrated whatever tenderness there was in her nature.

"I almost wonder sometimes," said Mrs. Fernandez, "whether I oughtn't to leave him."

"Leave him! You ought to turn him out into the street!"

Mrs. Gambitt felt Mrs. Fernandez' body, which she held in her arms, grow taut with protest.

"Oh, you know I could never do that!"

"Is he such a good husband then? A useless, selfish parasite, that's what he is. I don't say he was that when you married him, but that's what he is now. He's no good to you, he's no good to the child, he's no good to the house. If he goes on like this he'll get the house a bad name, he'll wear you to a shadow, and what the child'll grow up like I'm sure I don't know. Why do you put up with him? Don't you see that the more you put up with his nonsense, the more he'll go on with it? And he's begun to come out with the most shocking language lately, for I've heard him myself. You've got quite enough to do without being worried by him, and if you won't get rid of him quietly, there's two things you can do—you can call in the police and get them to give him a good telling-off, in the hopes that that'll do him some good, or you can try and get him certified——"

"Natalie!"

"Well, isn't he behaving just like a madman? Isn't that what he deserves?"

"Oh, I don't know how you can say such things!"

"Well, you seem to forget that I've got more interest in this house than anybody else has, and that I deserve a little consideration."

She would have liked to say, "Beryl, you must get rid of that brute, because I want you all to myself and I'm sure we can get along very well without him," but all she could do was to catch hold of her friend and kiss her clumsily on the cheek, while Mrs. Fernandez, struggling for breath and freedom of movement, gasped out:

"But Natalie—when you talk like that about Paul —don't you realise—how can I make you understand—can't you see—that I *love* him?"

VIII

THE routine of Alston's life was little varied. He didn't dislike his job, except for the fact that it didn't seem to lead anywhere, though he vaguely looked forward to a day when he would set up on his own. It was a clean job, it gave him a living wage, and he got on well with his fellow-workers. When his work was over he returned along Parthenon Street towards Cambodia Crescent, passing some furniture auction rooms, a shop that sold bags and trunks, and the entrance to a small billiard saloon, where he sometimes spent an evening. A few doors beyond that there was a public-house, where he had two or three times been in for a drink with casual acquaintances. That pub had a funny name when you came to think of it. It was called "The Case is Altered," though everybody called it simply "The Case." Inside the bar there was a framed notice hung up which told the story of how the place had got its name. It was originally called "The Three Cranes," but in the eighteenth century a famous highwayman was caught there unawares by a young lord whom he had robbed. "Now, sir," cried the peer as soon as he had made sure of his capture, "it seems the case is altered!"

On the other side of the street was the Parthenon

Cinema, where Alston sometimes went with Amy, and a little further on, just before you turned into Cambodia Crescent, there was Pélagie's, where she worked. He saw her very often. They could go to her mother's or to his aunt's whenever they liked, but when it was fine and warm enough they preferred to stroll about out of doors, and when it was wet, to go to the pictures. When he was away from her, he felt anxious and restless and uncertain about her, and made resolutions to speak more boldly and frankly to her than he had ever done hitherto, but directly he saw her all his doubts seemed to vanish and there didn't seem to be any need to say the things he had meant to say. Besides, it was quite clear that she was devoted to him, and when he and Amy were at her mother's, Mrs. Pascall treated him not only approvingly but affectionately.

The Pascall family didn't consist only of Mrs. Pascall and Amy. There was also a son, Amy's senior by nearly ten years. His portrait, an enlarged photograph, hung in the place of honour over the mantelpiece in Mrs. Pascall's living room. It showed a young man in the uniform of a sailor. He had a lively and energetic face, with regular but rather unusual features. It was a handsome face. The hair was curly, the eyes were large and frank, and the mouth wore an enigmatic, mischievous smile such as can be seen on the faces of primitive Greek statues. For this being, it was clear, both Amy and Mrs. Pascall had an unbounded admiration. They were never tired of talking about him, and Alston gradually formed an idea of what Willy Pascall was like. At school, it appeared, he never did a stroke of work, was always getting into scrapes, and was a shameless little liar besides. Nobody could do anything with him, not even his father, who was then still living. (Mr. Pascall had been killed in the War.) Willy ran away from home three times, and had the most extraordinary adventures on each occasion. Later he joined the Navy, but got out of it before long (was probably turned out of it, Alston thought), and since then had done a whole lot of odd jobs, had worked in a grand hotel, had been a navvy, had taken a small part in a film. . . . At present he was on his way back from Egypt, where he had gone on a cargo boat, as an ordinary seaman. Why? Oh, he said he wanted a change. "He may be wild," said Mrs. Pascall, "and I'd be the first to admit it, but he's just like his father was at his age, always looking for experience, no matter what it is. Why, at one time he was taken up by a very rich gentleman, who took him abroad as his companion, and I don't know what else. He even took him to supper once at the very hotel where he'd been working in the kitchen only a short time before, and there he was, being waited on by the very men that were used to ordering him about. Oh, you should hear Willy telling you about it, Eric. You'd laugh yourself sick. . . . But, of course, he soon got tired of that, and next time we heard of him where was he, Amy? Oh, yes, at Elstree, if you please, acting for the pictures, because they wanted somebody to do a parachute jump, and he said he'd had some experience of that, though, of course, it was the first time he'd ever done any such thing in his life. . . . Well, as I was saying, he may be wild, but I don't believe he's ever done anybody a bad turn in his life, and I believe if he ever settles down, he'll be as good as any man alive, just as his father was before him. And there's one thing, he never comes back from one of his adventures without bringing a present for me and a present for Amy. Goodness knows where he gets the money to do it with. Why, he brought me some beautiful furs once. I've got them still, but of course they're much too good to wear. And he's like that, you know, he doesn't seem to know what it means to want to own things. As soon as he has anything he just gives it away, whether it's money or anything else. Oh, I tell you, our Willy isn't half a handful, is he, Amy?"

It is hardly to be wondered at that the legend of Willy Pascall, so adored by his mother and sister, and, according to them, by the rest of mankind as well, took a firm hold of Alston's imagination. The knowledge that this extraordinary person might walk in without a moment's notice at any time when he was at the Pascalls' made their house even more attractive, and Amy seemed to him all the more wonderful for having such a wonderful brother. But at the same time he was a little afraid that he mightn't make a good impression on Willy Pascall when they eventually met each other face to face, and he would steal an anxious and admiring glance at the photograph over the mantelpiece. . . .

At 45 Cambodia Crescent Miss Brixworth felt a little hurt because he didn't seem over-anxious to share her evening meals with her. Perhaps, she thought, he imagines that I'm offering him charity. So to make him feel more at ease she suggested that he should contribute a share of what they ate, and on the rare days when he had tea with her he would bring back a tin of sardines with him, some eggs, or a cake. He wondered why a person of such a different class from his own should care for his company, and put it down to Miss Brixworth's loneliness. He didn't see clearly that, having gradually lost such power as money brings with it, she was trying to make up for the loss; nor did he understand that a person of more or less aristocratic breeding and character and intelligence is apt to enjoy qualities that are found in a different class.

Miss Haymer, having as a young woman had an unusual amount of luck and enterprise, besides some beauty, had rushed off to mingle with the hill-tribes of Central Asia or the negroes of the Southern States in order to enjoy the excitements of the unfamiliar, of snakes and shamans, harems and haciendas, and to share the lives of flat-nosed nomads and pock-marked sheiks; getting older, she had reverted contentedly to her origins and a world that contained Harrods' and the Times Book Club. But Miss Brix-

I

worth, far less dashing when young, was now, urged
by poverty, by a sense of lost opportunities and by
that uncanny energy that sometimes occurs in ageing
women, trying to get hold of life. She found one
handle in Anglo-Catholicism, and was an active
churchwoman, although she hid the fact completely
from Miss Haymer, fearing to provoke an outburst of
pagan mockery. She had clutched at Empringham,
had lost him, but had found a kind of substitute in
Carol. And now she was concerning herself with
Rosy, with Mrs. Fernandez, and with Alston—who
had the advantage of being male. He found her quite
sympathetic and not too inquisitive, and always kind.
She was a little too kind, perhaps, as if to show him
that he wasn't an inferior, and now that his presence
was so taken for granted at the Pascalls' he found it
somewhat irksome to see Miss Brixworth. But the old
girl meant kindly, he told himself, and it was plain
that she did her best to entertain him. Once or twice
when he was having his evening meal with her, Mrs.
Fernandez came in.

It was only on the rarest occasions that Mrs.
Fernandez dared to go and talk to Alston in his own
room, but whenever she did so she said she was sorry
for neglecting him but she felt sure he understood the
reason why she inquired after his needs so seldom—
if he wanted anything, she said, he could always send
word to her by Carol. She had up to now been
rather reserved, but now that she found him occasionally with Miss Brixworth she allowed herself to

speak a little more freely before him, though she once
or twice turned to him with a pleading look and said,
"Of course you won't let this go any further, Mr.
Alston, will you?" Watching her, his slow brain
gradually came to understand the fascination which
Fernandez exercised over her: how much her heart
was at her husband's mercy becoming slowly made
plainer by a hint here, a glance there, a fragment of
gossip, a footstep on the stairs, or the distant shutting
of a door. . . .

Since Mrs. Fernandez addressed herself mainly
to Miss Brixworth, as woman to woman, Alston sat
apart, almost like somebody sitting in a theatre and
watching an actress on the stage. The comparison is
not a bad one, for Mrs. Fernandez, frank and honest
as she was by nature, and genuine as she was when
pouring out her talk to Miss Brixworth, feeling the
relief of confession and the pleasure of sympathy,
was a woman and seldom forgot her audience. She
was aware that Alston watched her intently, and
would glance now and then at his blue eyes, so young,
watching her with a steady and troubled expression,
and then she would speak a word or two to him or
invite his opinion about something. And whether on
account of Alston or not, a very slight suspicion of
a faint mutual disdain crept into the acquaintance-
ship of the two women. "Poor thing," Miss Brixworth would say to Miss Haymer, "I'm afraid she
has really very little future to look forward to," and
"Poor thing," Mrs. Fernandez would say to Mrs.

Gambitt, "you can see she lives a good deal in the past."

Late one afternoon Alston arrived outside Miss Brixworth's door exactly at the time he had been expected, knocked, mistakenly thought he heard a voice say, "Come in!" and opened the door. Mrs. Fernandez was sitting on the sofa. She was crying. He stood awkwardly on the threshold, feeling rather a fool, then, meaning to say "I'm sorry" and to withdraw, he somehow couldn't move. He looked at Miss Brixworth, who, with a sigh, motioned to him to come and sit down, and then at Mrs. Fernandez, who hadn't yet seen him, her face hidden in her plump white hands, while her fuzzy, wiry hair, so healthy and plentiful, stood out in a bush all round her head. And when she moved her hands, rubbed her eyes with a handkerchief, and then looked up and caught sight of him, she didn't seem at all surprised, while he was quite dazzled by her beauty in its sorrowful aspect, so that the apology he had meant to make for his intrusion he somehow couldn't utter.

"I think, if you wouldn't mind shutting the door—" said Miss Brixworth. "Come in and sit down."

He turned to close the door, saying as he did so:

"I'm sorry. I thought I heard you say 'Come in' when I knocked."

"It's all right," said Mrs. Fernandez. She was smiling, but the tears ran freely down her face. "I'm sure Miss Brixworth was expecting you."

"Of course I was," said Miss Brixworth, pointing

to a chair, and in a moment she and Mrs. Fernandez were chatting away about all sorts of trifles, as though a spate of small-talk would drown the reality of Mrs. Fernandez' tears.

Everybody in the house knew that Mrs. Fernandez and Alston occasionally met in Miss Brixworth's room, and it was asked when Fernandez would begin to get jealous of Alston. But Fernandez hadn't yet forgotten the milkman, and was keeping a close watch on his wife to discover whether she was still seeing him. The milkman, being a sensible fellow, gave the house a wide berth in these days.

Miss Brixworth, in her comparative innocence, didn't realise the strength of the forces that were stirring under the roof of 45 Cambodia Crescent, but then it was true, as Mrs. Fernandez had remarked, that she was rather taken up with the past. She had reached an age when people tend to indulge in the pleasures of memory and reminiscence, and when these pleasures become at times so intense that the past seems more real than the present. For instance, in Parthenon Street there was a shop that sold trunks and boxes and suitcases and such things. Miss Brixworth had paused one morning to admire a certain solid leather travelling-case with glass and silver fittings and a velvet lining. It was very moderately priced, and she had said to herself, "Now I must really think about getting that case, it'll be so useful when I travel"—when she had suddenly remembered that she had no money to buy it with, and that it was pretty certain that she would never travel again. And walking sadly home she passed the public-house called "The Case is Altered," and said to herself, "Yes, indeed it is, sadly altered," and with a resigned smile, passed quietly homewards.

In bad weather she didn't at all mind being in London, but fine weather (fine mornings in particular) always made her wish that she was back again in the country, in her own house, where many years of her life had been spent until a defaulting American railway had curtailed her income. How contented she had been! Often she seemed to smell in imagination the stocks, the freshly-mown grass, the apples, the hay and the mignonette. She wished that she could again put on a pair of old earth-stained gloves and dawdle about in the garden, snipping off the dead flowers. But now her only garden was a public park.

Her house, when she had first gone to live in it, had seemed to be quite in the country, although it was actually just on the edge of a country town not very far from London, but lately she had heard that all the land round there had been built over, and felt that she would never have the heart to go back and look at the change. She preferred the house and surroundings as they were, that is to say, as they still were in her imagination. In retrospect that old life all seemed so secure and comfortable and elegant, and of course the working people always touched their hats to you in those days. . . .

What was strange was the way in which she dreamed

nowadays of her old surroundings. Night after night she returned to the house and garden, and not only did she encounter there people she had known in the old days, but also people who couldn't possibly know that the house ever existed. Sometimes she was in the kitchen garden, discussing with the gardener what he should plant, then going into the greenhouse with him, and standing talking to him in the moist, scented tropical air with the wire baskets full of coleus and smilax overhead. Sometimes a woman who lived not far away came to call, and in one dream this woman said, "I'm sorry, but we've decided to turn the meadows into a big housing estate. London's getting so big now, you know, that it won't hold the people. I'm afraid you'll lose your view. . . ." Then she dreamt that Miss Haymer came to stay with her, limping along the lavender walk and admiring the roses, complaining of the stairs, and making a demonstration in the spare room because she objected to a picture that hung there. In another dream little Rosy Fernandez came up the drive, running along under the flowering lime-trees. She was crying, and when asked what was the matter said she was looking for her mother, but before there was time to answer Mrs. Gambitt came running along after her and picked her up and carried her away. And then finally, in a dream that occurred twice, the old servants, even the gardener, had gone, and Empringham had taken their place. He wiped his hands on a dish-cloth and went out into the garden with a basket, saying that he was going to cut some rhubarb, but instead of that he got into a taxi of which the body was made entirely of marquetry. In the dining-room she found Alston, just finishing a meal. He wiped his mouth with a table napkin, smiled, and said, "Now I must be going." She watched him with fear in her heart as he walked across the room to where a certain travelling-case, with a blue velvet lining and silver-topped glass bottles, was standing open on a side table. He fastened it up, locked it, took it in his hand, and, without even glancing at her, went off down the drive. "Come back, come back!" cried Miss Brixworth, but he was already out of sight—and she woke up with a pang of despair, her face wet with sweat. . . . The feelings these dreams gave her seemed unreasonably intense, and she began to wonder if they had any meaning.

Alston had not only found a place in Miss Brixworth's dreams; he had become, without knowing it, of interest to Mrs. Rudd, who was getting more and more discontented with her life. Her husband's limitations, a want of money and a scarcity of friends, combined to turn her appetite for life into peevish restlessness. The few pleasures they allowed themselves were only to be had at the price of careful economies. They waited on themselves in an atmosphere of joint slovenliness and mutual abuse, though they were held together by that marital bond which time, necessity and familiarity so often tend to strengthen in a couple not held together by love or even mutual respect. Although Mrs. Rudd didn't love

her husband, and would have been capable, had a
chance offered, of being unfaithful to him, she could
scarcely have been persuaded to leave him, for she
knew how much her husband was devoted to her.
Painfully aware of his own shortcomings and ever
anxious to please her, he gave more time than ever to
sweepstakes and prize competitions in the hope that
one day he would win a huge prize and with it his
wife's whole heart. At the same time he had a vague
idea that he would begin to collect stamps, for an
acquaintance of his had assured him that there was
money in it. Money, perhaps, was not his wife's most
pressing need.

Now the window of the Rudds' room faced the
street, so by standing at it and peeping through the
lace curtain she could see any coming and going
that there might be at the front door. In this way
she had caught frequent glimpses of Alston, and had
begun to endow him in fancy with all the qualities
in which she found her husband deficient. But Alston
was entirely ignorant of her growing interest in him
and indeed scarcely knew her by sight.

It is strange how great a part the windows of a
house play in the lives of its inhabitants. The large
and heavy Victorian windows of 45 Cambodia
Crescent might well have been openings into eternity,
to judge from the aspirations for which they served
as channels. It seems to be especially when they
think vaguely of the future in contrast to present
dissatisfaction that people stand at windows.

Fernandez, frowning, would stand at a window to prevent the arrival of imaginary lovers of his wife; Alston, we have already seen at his window embodying his dreams in a motor car; and Miss Brixworth, on fine mornings, standing at hers and thinking of the past and the country; while Mrs. Gambitt even would sometimes stand gazing out of the windows of the "office," her little dog in her thin arms and her liverish eyes directed to some small patch of sky showing through the leaves of the plane tree in the back garden. It was no wonder if the world looked unpromising to her, poisoned by years of feeding on the thought of her misfortunes, as well as on meat three times a day, soggy pastry, sweet-stuffs and the strongest of tea. In the whole house Mrs. Fernandez and Carol were the only ones too busy or preoccupied to spend much time in gazing out of the windows, at least in any dreamy mood.

"Why are you always standing at the window?" Rudd asked his wife.

"Can't I stand at the window if I want to? Must I ask your leave?"

"Are you expecting anybody in particular?" he said.

"Oh yes, I'm waiting for my dream-man," she said irritably.

And then one evening she had a surprise. She saw Alston, who always entered and left the house by himself, standing on the pavement outside and talking to a young woman. She couldn't hear what they were saying, but she could see the young woman's face, and was so little impressed by its beauty that she immediately saw herself as a successful rival in Alston's affections, and began to wonder how she could get to know him. The young woman was Amy, and she and Alston were having an argument. She was reproaching him for being rather silent.

"I never was much of a one for talking," he said.

"For talking!" she said.

"You could go out with some other fellow," he said, as a joke.

"There!" she said, taking him seriously, "I don't believe you care a button for me!"

How could he tell her that in order to be able to take her out this very evening he had practically done without cigarettes for a whole week?

"I never was one for fooling around much," he said.

"Was I asking you to fool around?" she said. "You know I wasn't!"

She turned away from him, her head a little cast down. The paste ornament in the shape of a swallow which she always wore in her hat glittered in the light of the street lamp near which they were standing. Alston looked down at her.

"Amy," he said.

She pretended to take no notice.

Seeing that there were not many people about, he caught hold of her, lifted her right off her feet, and gave her a kiss which seemed to last a long time, so that she could hardly breathe.

"Oh, *Eric!*" she cried, trying to push him away and looking hurriedly round, half delighted and half afraid of a scandal. "What would mother say?"

"That's a good one!" he said.

And Mrs. Rudd, standing at the window, felt a thrill of envious excitement run shuddering all through her veins. . . .

A few evenings later Alston and Amy were sitting in the Parthenon Cinema, waiting for the show to begin. Amy liked best the long films about rich and romantic lovers, but Alston's tastes were different. He liked "Western" pictures, with plenty of riding and shooting. And especially any picture that dealt with swimming, preferably when it was a matter of heroism rather than pleasure.

"My dad was a fine swimmer," he once confided to Amy when they were watching a film of a swimming race. "They've got all his prizes at home."

"That's what Willy likes better than anything," said Amy. "You should just see him in the water."

And this gave Alston's thoughts about Amy's brother a new turn. He began to imagine Willy Pascall as a kind of version of his father, and this made him all the more eager for the day when he should see him.

More than any films he liked news films showing the activities of Fascists or Nazis—enormous crowds of young men raising their right arms in salute, all vigorous, all believing in one thing, all enthusiastic, all living for the same purpose. When he saw these films he was deeply stirred by them; they gave him glimpses of the possibility of an active life led by many people with a common aim and altogether outside his own petty, personal existence. It would be grand, he thought, to be mixed up in a business like that—but what a pity all those people were only foreigners! Even films about airmen or gunmen, showing lives lived dangerously among death-dealing machines, pleased him better than the cocktails and seductions which enchanted Amy.

This particular evening was different from any previous one they had spent together, for the Parthenon Cinema was the scene of an unpleasant happening. In the middle of a comic film the image on the screen suddenly became blurred, and disappeared, leaving first a blank then a confused shadow. People at once began looking round to see what was the matter, and it was with horror that they saw a thin stream of smoke issuing from the projection room. There was no music, and for a brief instant there was a dead silence. Then somebody cried, "It's on fire!" and there was a rush for the exits. Everybody was so intent on the effort to escape that for some moments there were few screams or cries. Amy threw herself upon Alston for protection, and they were among the few people who were able or willing to keep their places, which were near the middle of a row of seats. The thick carpet and the thickly upholstered seats deadened the sound of the audience's sudden rush and struggle, but at the same time made it more awful. It was like that breathless silence which goes with some dangerous feat of strength.

Dense smoke was now pouring out and spreading overhead, and the crowd was beginning to get jammed round the doorways. Then the lights came on, and the band, with what the newspapers next day called "admirable presence of mind," struck up with a popular tune which they had been playing earlier in the evening. But they played it much too fast and loud, and it did little to calm the audience, now mostly in a state of panic. Round the doors people were beginning to fight to get out, voices called out excitedly, and a man could be seen trying to scramble over the heads of the crowd. It was an ugly moment.

"We're safer here," said Alston with his arm round Amy, "we shan't get trampled on. It's only smoke; they'll have it out in a minute."

He was very frightened himself, but appeared calm, and at the back of his mind was the thought, "Her brother'll hear of this sooner or later, and I mustn't show I've got the wind up." This was even more important to him than what Amy might think, for Amy loved him and would forgive him most things, but her brother's ideas would be those of a person of experience, and he mightn't be easy to please. Although Alston wasn't conscious of it, Willy Pascall now took in his mind a place that his father had once held—the place of a person who was wise, good and beautiful, and whom one's actions must please.

Amy clutched his arm, and cried:

"Oh, Eric, whatever shall we do?"

"It's all right, dear," he said, "listen to that."

A man in evening dress was running wherever there was space to run and calling out in a loud voice through a megaphone, "There's no danger! Please keep your places!" But nobody took any notice of him, nor of two commissionaires in uniform who were struggling to establish order. All this time the band was playing frenziedly. Suddenly a powerfully built man ran amok, rushed at one of the commissionaires, took a flying kick which caught him in the abdomen, at once doubling him up with pain, and rushed savagely at the crowd, trying to tear his way through.

"Oh!" cried Amy, clinging tightly to Alston, hiding her face against his arm, and then looking up at him.

There was a very strange expression on his face. He not only looked calm, he looked almost pleased. The alarm, the danger, the naked fear of the crowd, the insistent nervous jazzing of the band, too quick and out of tune, the smell and sight of smoke, the angry voices and dull sounds of struggle—all these things had combined to give him, as the letting loose of violence always had done, an extraordinary sense of excitement, which was nothing like fear, but rather the double joy of seeing destruction and standing firm in spite of it—it was almost the joy of the hunter. Amy was at the same time frightened and pleased at his behaviour, and loved him for it.

Policemen and firemen were already on the scene, and order was quickly restored, the fire, which had only been a small one, having been put out. In the reaction from the strain of the last few minutes Amy began to laugh a little hysterically.

"If it hadn't been for you," she said, "oh, I know I should just have died!"

He squeezed her arm, but made no reply. He felt that by keeping his head he had made a first small effort towards winning her brother's approval.

IX

Soon after the fire at the Parthenon there were two unusual occurrences at 45 Cambodia Crescent which might have been regarded as ominous. The first concerned Miss Brixworth, the second a maidservant called Lottie who came in two or three times a week to help Carol.

In view of Miss Brixworth's enthusiasm for cleanliness, which has already been mentioned, it may be imagined how much she enjoyed her daily bath. She never put less than twopence in the geyser, because she had very soon found out that if you put only a penny in you didn't get nearly enough water. And she took her time. "Only rich people," Miss Haymer was fond of saying, "can afford to be really clean." But to this Miss Brixworth would reply that she mightn't have many luxuries, but she was determined to be clean. And that, no doubt, was why she took her time in the bath. Most of the inhabitants of 45 Cambodia Crescent were rather indifferent about washing, and a weekly bath, taken at night, seemed to satisfy some, while Mrs. Petherham-Porter never had a bath at all. But it sometimes happened that while Miss Brixworth was in her bath somebody would come and try the door. This always seemed to happen just at the moment when Miss Brixworth, having thoroughly washed herself all over, had settled down to a quiet five minutes extended at full length with only her head and her toes sticking out of the water. When she heard the handle being turned, she began to splash vigorously, partly because she was afraid somebody might force a way in if they heard no sounds of washing going on, but mainly because she wanted to give an impression that she was actually using the bath to wash in and not to lie dreaming in.

After a time it became generally known that Miss Brixworth not only took a daily bath, but took a good twenty minutes over it. "I can't think what she does in there," said Mrs. Porter indignantly, and apparently no spirit-voices told her the truth. But Miss Brixworth was left undisturbed, and only rose, not at all like Venus from the sea, when the water began to get chilly. And then one morning this extraordinary thing happened. With a sense of guilt, she did something which she had never done before—she took a book with her to the bath. The young lady at Boots' library had most kindly obtained for her a novel which was only just out, and Miss Brixworth had found it so enthralling that she could scarcely put it down. She had sat up late reading it the night before, had picked it up first thing in the morning, and when it was time for her to go to the bath had simply taken it with her. But the danger that she might form the bad habit, or rather indulge in the secret vice, of reading in her bath was averted by the following accident.

Whether the bath water was warmer than usual, or whether reading so late the night before had tired her, Miss Brixworth had scarcely picked up the book when she began to feel drowsy, so she closed it, put it down, and actually fell asleep. . . . When she woke up, she felt queer, confused, a little giddy. "Oh, I must have fallen asleep," she said to herself, aware that the water was getting quite cold. And then suddenly she saw that the bath was full of blood! Her heart gave a jump. Thoroughly frightened and wide awake, she sat bolt upright and began to speculate on the source of the haemorrhage—had her nose been bleeding? had she cut herself? No, the novel she had been reading had fallen into the bath, and most of the colour had come out of the cover, which had been a dark red, but was now flabby and a pale pink.

When Miss Brixworth thought how astonished the young lady at Boots' would be when she heard why the novel couldn't be returned she began to smile, but when it occurred to her that she might have to forfeit her small deposit at the library her smile faded. One thing was certain, she would never read in her bath again, for she had spoilt a book, given herself a nasty fright, and continued to feel giddy for the rest of the day.

Shortly after this episode—which nobody heard about, for Miss Brixworth was careful to remove all traces of the red dye from the bath, ashamed to tell anybody in the house what had happened, and afraid to tell Miss Haymer, for fear of provoking ridicule—shortly after this, the bathroom was the scene of something much less pleasant. Lottie, the girl who came in to do the housework, was rinsing a tumbler, when it slipped out of her hand, caught the edge of the bath, and was of course smashed. A piece of broken glass flew upwards and into Lottie's bare arm, which was badly cut and at once began to bleed profusely. The poor girl, more frightened than hurt, rushed out on to the landing and called for Mrs. Fernandez. It was significant that in such a moment of stress she should have instinctively called for Mrs. Fernandez rather than Mrs. Gambitt, the last person she had seen just before coming into the bathroom a few minutes before. However, Mrs. Fernandez happened to be out of call, and it was Mrs. Gambitt who replied, in an ungracious voice, from downstairs.

"What is it, Lottie? What do you want?"

For a moment Lottie hesitated, most unwilling to let herself become in any way indebted to Mrs. Gambitt, who gave herself such airs. But when she saw how badly her arm was bleeding she called over the banisters:

"I've cut myself badly, Mrs. Gambitt. I'd be obliged if you'd come and help me."

And she rushed back to bleed into the bath. Mrs. Gambitt came sulkily upstairs. At the sight of blood her face took on a sicklier tinge than usual, and she hunted round for a towel. By this time Mrs. Porter had appeared on the scene, and between them they managed to stop the bleeding and tie up the arm. Poor Lottie was by then feeling so faint that they led her into the nearest room, which happened to be the bedroom occupied by the Fernandezes, and there they persuaded her to lie down for a while, and left her.

Lottie looked uneasily round the room, felt light-headed, and after a few minutes went off into a kind of doze. When she opened her eyes again, she wondered where she was and how long she had been there, and then had an uncomfortable feeling that somebody was watching her. And indeed somebody *was* watching her. "When I saw who it was," she told Carol afterwards, "it was all I could do to stop meself screaming—oh, I could have screamed the house down!" It was Fernandez. And if there was one person in the world of whom Lottie was mortally afraid, he was the one. If you had asked her why, she couldn't have given you any reason; she would simply have said, "Oh, I think he's awful." Awful he undoubtedly was, standing there quite silent by the side of the bed, smoking his usual stinking cigarette, and looking down at her. He had heard Mrs. Gambitt telling Mrs. Rudd what had happened, and when nobody was looking had come quietly upstairs and into the bedroom, so quietly that Lottie hadn't been disturbed by his entry, and there he had stood looking down at her. It wasn't her face that interested him, or her body, but the bandage on her bare arm, in the middle of which he had been able to watch a tiny red spot gradually increasing in size till it was as big as a florin, for the bleeding hadn't yet stopped. The sight fascinated him, and even when Lottie opened her eyes he could hardly take his from the bandage. First seeing him, and then noticing his interest in her injury, she was so frightened that she couldn't speak.

"How are you now, Lottie?" he asked, in that husky voice of his, his face infinitely sombre, like the dead face of a person of bad character.

"Better now, sir, thank you," said Lottie.

She didn't scream, but sat bolt upright, pulling her skirts down over her knees with one hand and giving her hair a pat with the other. And she immediately got up, brushed past him, and hurried downstairs.

Half an hour later Mrs. Gambitt went into the bathroom, meaning to tidy it up and to collect the pieces of broken glass. She was surprised to find Fernandez there, standing and smoking, and looking down at the blood which still remained in the bath.

"Come along now," she said, as if she were speaking to a child, "let me come and clean up the mess."

And she gave him a slight push to show that he was to leave the room, which he obediently did. Mrs. Gambitt was the only person in the house who would have dared to treat him like this, but he made no protest, for he felt gratitude to her for loving his wife. . . .

Miss Brixworth had made up her mind not to tell Fanny Haymer how she had fallen asleep in the bath, for she knew she had made a fool of herself and would be told so in plain terms, but now that such a strange accident had happened to Lottie in the same place so soon afterwards she decided that it wouldn't matter if she told both stories. Miss Haymer interrupted her with occasional snorts and satirical exclamations, and when her friend ended by asking her if she didn't think the first incident to be in some mysterious way connected with the second, she said:

"Nonsense, my dear. First you were careless and then the servant was careless. I hope it will be a lesson to you both. And don't let me hear of your becoming such a slave to twopenny novelettes."

"Seven-and-sixpenny, Fanny," Miss Brixworth protested meekly, "and you know I'm very fond of reading."

"When I say twopenny I mean twopenny," said Miss Haymer, prodding the air with a gouty forefinger. "You're much too fond of reading novels. And for heaven's sake don't be superstitious about a piece of carelessness."

If Miss Brixworth wondered about the mishap in the bathroom, Mrs. Porter could think of nothing else, and said that she had actually foreseen it—a crimson aura with jagged edges had surrounded the girl Lottie for some time.

"I'm very glad I never have her in to do my room," she said to Mrs. Gambitt. "I knew something like this would happen. Don't you remember my saying to you last week that the crystal showed indications of bloodshed?"

Mrs. Gambitt didn't actually remember, but she so much wanted to do so that she said she did, and as soon as she had said it she really thought she did remember after all.

"And you remember how my planchette tried three times to spell out a name beginning with L?"

This Mrs. Gambitt remembered having been told, and she was now genuinely impressed with Mrs. Porter's clairvoyance in the matter.

"Och, these women," Carol would exclaim to Alston, casting his eyes up to heaven as he did so, "aren't they too damned awful? Why, Mrs. Fernandez is the only one among them you could even touch. As for Mrs. Porter and Mrs. Gambitt, those two'll drive me silly one day. Oh, I hope somebody'll come along some day and give that Mrs. Gambitt all she deserves. What she wants is——"

Alston laughed.

"Mrs. Porter's husband left her years ago, so they say," Carol went on, "and small wonder. I expect it was all this spook business that did it."

The facts about Mrs. Porter were not known to anybody in the house until she herself told them to Mrs. Gambitt. People thought of her simply as an isolated old woman, rather odd in her behaviour, and had just conveniently decided that her husband had left her. Nobody bothered to look below the surface. Indeed, nobody had much of a chance. Only Mrs. Gambitt ever caught much more than a glimpse of that face which, though it had something cloudy and fanatical in its expression, was not without gentleness. The greyish London light, glimmering through lace curtains, sometimes caught Mrs. Porter's face at an angle, held still for a moment, perhaps, against a dark background, with the eyes lowered and the mouth in repose, and struck from it, as though with a spotlight instead of some straggling and smoky ray, an inner beauty. There was certainly no beauty of feature, for Mrs. Porter's hair was frowsy, her eyebrows were scanty and her eyes pouchy, the nose and mouth were commonplace, the chin more than double. She had none of the beauty that comes from present happiness in love, a lively intelligence, composure, or holy living; but she had the dignity that can be found in the faces of those who have given themselves up as wholly, heart and soul, for a fellow-creature as Mrs. Porter had given herself up for her husband.

One day she told the story to Mrs. Gambitt, not knowing of Mrs. Gambitt's misfortune in marriage, and thinking of her as one who had lived as an ordinary married woman. It wasn't a long story, and it was simply told. But the impression it made on Mrs. Gambitt, who was not a particularly impressionable person, was a deep one. It was clear from Mrs. Porter's face while she spoke that she was touching on the central ecstasy of her life.

"When I married him," she said, "my husband was somewhat older than myself. I looked up to him, and I still look up to him, as something far above me.

I'm not saying too much when I say there was something noble in him. . . . I was his second wife. There was a child by the first marriage—you've heard me speak of Claud, dear; that's his photo on the mantelpiece—and my stepson grew up, I'm glad to say, to be as good as a son to me. He's happily married and lives abroad, being employed by a cable company at one of their foreign branches, but he never forgets to write to me, and he and his wife are anxious that I should go and live with them when they return to England. . . . My husband was in business, the best and kindest man in the world, and always enjoyed the best of health until just before the War. In 1913 he had a kind of stroke which affected his brain, and had to give up his business. It happened like this. His new warehouse caught on fire the day before he was going to insure it. When he heard the news the shock was too much for him. He asked the typist for a glass of water, and when she came back he was on the floor in a fit. (A plain little thing she was, and thought a bit too highly of herself.) Fortunately there was some money to keep us going. 'You must take him about,' the doctor said to me, 'from place to place. A constant change of scene will keep him amused, and may do him as much good as anything.' But of course he knew even then, I'm sure the doctor knew, that nothing would do my Maurice any good."

"Yes, of course he knew," said Mrs. Gambitt. "Doctors never tell you the truth till it's too late."

"He said to me," Mrs. Porter continued, " 'Of course you know, Mrs. Porter, that what you're doing is illegal? Your husband ought to be certified and confined.' 'Doctor,' I said, 'I know.' Then he tried persuasion. 'Ah, Mrs. Porter,' he said, 'why ruin two lives instead of one?' But I wouldn't be persuaded. Maurice was my husband, I said, and I loved him dearly, and as long as I had the money and the strength I would do all I could for him. Well, I had him with me all through the War, and those weren't the brightest days you can imagine, as some of us remember. Mind you, his health remained perfect. It was only his brain that was touched."

"Only his brain, fancy," said Mrs. Gambitt sympathetically.

"I had to do everything for him all those years. He lived six years after the War, and was with me all the time, and every day I washed him, and shaved him, and bathed him, and dressed him, and fed him, and took him out with me. Wasn't it lucky that I had enough money to keep us going? He never turned on me but once, and that was one morning when I dressed myself before I dressed him. Usually I dressed him first, and then he sat on a chair (he was so good!) while I dressed myself. But this one morning I dressed myself first—in a hurry, without thinking—and I suppose he thought I should go away and leave him. . . ."

She was silent a moment (it was then that her plain, ageing face became almost grand) and then said:

"Natalie, don't tell anybody all this, will you?"

"Of course not," said Mrs. Gambitt. She wondered if Mrs. Porter's husband were still living. The other woman's next remark made this point clear.

"The memory of him grows stronger and stronger," she said, "and I look forward to the day when I shall join him for ever."

Mrs. Gambitt was silent.

"And when you complain to me about Mr. Fernandez, Natalie," Mrs. Porter went on, "I only know this, that if she loves him a quarter, yes, even a quarter as much as I love Maurice (even though he is no longer with me), then it would be cruel, yes, cruel and wicked to try and separate them."

"It isn't quite the same thing," said Mrs. Gambitt. "Fernandez isn't fit to be about."

"Just what the doctor told me about my Maurice, Natalie!"

Mrs. Gambitt was just going to reply, when she thought she heard voices, so she went and opened the door very cautiously and peeped out.

"Just as I thought," she said, closing the door again, "it's that Miss Brixworth gossiping on the stairs with Carol again. If only the old brute would leave the servants alone!"

The truth was that Miss Brixworth had a kind of assurance, a kind often to be found in people of similar breeding to hers, which made some people instinctively turn to her for advice and support and sympathy, just as certain servants instinctively turn to the right sort of master or mistress when they are in need of these things. And now Carol, like Empringham before him, came to her with his confidence. He was talking about his future.

"But, Carol," she was murmuring, "you're not always going on with *this* kind of work, are you?"

"Don't know, I'm sure, Miss Brixworth."

"But what would you *like* to do?"

"Well, I thought I should like to get into the police, but they wouldn't have me, because I'm not tall enough. You see, you have to be tall, and I'm not quite five foot seven. They said everything else was all right about me, but I just wasn't tall enough."

"Oh dear," said Miss Brixworth, her imagination at once fired by the thought of Carol in a policeman's uniform, with white gloves, directing the traffic with a lordly air, or perhaps capturing some dangerous criminal. "What is to be done?"

"Don't know, I'm sure," said Carol.

"Oh, but I've got an idea!" she said. "Isn't it possible to increase one's height? Don't you remember those advertisements you sometimes see in magazines—*Increase your height by our easy method, no drugs or difficult exercises—Why not be tall and distinguished looking?*"

"Oh, but I've tried them," said Carol, "and they haven't made any difference."

There were actually tears in his eyes as he spoke. One of them fell into a jug of hot water which he had in his hand. He licked his lips, and his hair fell across his forehead.

"Poor boy," said Miss Brixworth, thinking how pathetic he looked.

"And all for the sake of a couple of inches!" said Carol, indignation getting the better of self-pity.

X

Miss Brixworth was lunching with Miss Haymer.
They sat at opposite ends of the small dining-table
and were waited on by Empringham. It was extraordinary how Empringham and Miss Haymer had
taken to each other. Miss Brixworth told herself that
it was wrong of Fanny to treat Empringham with
quite so much familiarity, but the truth was she was
a trifle jealous of the attachment. She wasn't the only
one who disapproved. People living in the same
block of flats as Miss Haymer were saying how odd
it was that she should employ a man instead of a
maid, and some even went so far as to suggest that
she and Empringham were living together as man
and wife.

Miss Brixworth sighed. Empringham was still
always very polite to her, yes, very nice and polite,
but between him and Fanny there seemed to be a
real *understanding*. Miss Brixworth gazed sadly at a
Javanese mask which hung on the wall behind Miss
Haymer, and was on the point of regretting that she
had ever found Empringham this place.

"You're very silent, Connie," said Miss Haymer.
"I'm waiting for you to tell me some more about
this young man Alston. Empringham, it seems, just
vaguely disapproved of him. Servants are so odd. . . .

But does Alston ever come and have tea with you nowadays?"

"Now and then he does."

"You don't tell me about him. What are you hiding?"

"It's not so much what *I*'m hiding, Fanny, as what *he*'s hiding."

"Is he so mysterious?"

"I must confess I don't understand him. He seems quite sensitive in some ways. I'm afraid he only comes to see me because he's afraid I shall be hurt if he doesn't—I mean, I sort of encouraged him to come and see me. I think he likes it better when Mrs. Fernandez is there; I see him watching her with an admiring gaze——"

"Does she encourage him at all?"

"Oh no, I don't think it's *that* sort of gaze. He has a young woman he walks out with, takes to the talkies and so on. And that reminds me, I meant to tell you——"

"And what are his feelings about this young woman of his? Does he discuss the matter with you at all?"

"Well, you know he's naturally rather dumb, and when he's with me I'm afraid he's always rather worried by the feeling that he doesn't belong to our class."

"But have we got a class?" Miss Haymer demanded with a dramatic gesture. "I ask you, have we got a class? Really, Connie, we're not still living under the Widow of Windsor."

"Well, you know what I mean."

"Yes, you mean that he's always on his best behaviour with you?"

"I'm afraid so."

"Yes, you're too old-fashioned, too stuck-up and class-conscious. You ought to be a bit of a bolshy, like me."

Miss Haymer was secretly congratulating herself on her own ability to get on with men of all kinds—and especially Empringham—better than Miss Brixworth could.

"He seems to me about the most interesting person in that house of yours," she said.

"Oh, I meant to tell you what happened, "said Miss Brixworth. "You've seen in the papers all about this fire alarm and panic in a cinema near where I live, the Parthenon?"

"Yes, indeed."

"It was a dreadful affair, and several people were injured. Well, Alston and his young woman were in the place when it happened."

"Really! And didn't they get squashed? Did he tell you about it himself?"

"Yes, he gave me quite a vivid description of it. And he did what he has never done before, at least to me—he described his own feelings."

"And what were they?"

"Apparently he found it so exciting that he forgot to be afraid."

"H'm," said Miss Haymer, and was silent for a

L

moment. "Extraordinary, isn't it, all this film business?" she said then, and Miss Brixworth at once anticipated a lecturette.

"Yes, it is," she said meekly.

"Connie, has it ever struck you," Miss Haymer went on, warming up to her subject, "that the cinema has really become a sort of church? Just as they were putting up churches everywhere in the Middle Ages so now you see cinemas going up everywhere. You see these huge, clean, costly buildings rising up even in the slums. The entrance is often almost as imposing as the west door of a cathedral, and you pause to read the posters outside just as you might pause to read the times of services and diocesan notices. As soon as you get inside, a sort of verger in vestments directs you to a small shrine, where a vestal virgin (or not, as the case may be) receives the offertory, without which you couldn't possibly go in. Heavy curtains, as in a church, screen the main body of the building from its porch or vestibule, and once inside, you're ushered up the aisle by a sideswoman, equipped with a flashlight, to a dark pew, where you take your seat as quietly as possible. All round you rises a rather doubtful incense from the cigarettes of the worshippers. The light is dim and religious, and the whole atmosphere is made as dreamy as possible, so that you're quite ready for miracles to happen. Near the chancel a vast electric organ pours out its music and plays on the feelings of the congregation, whose attention is fixed on the screen, which stands exactly where the altar stands in a cathedral. And what a labour-saving religion! You just sit in an arm-chair to be preached at, you never have to kneel down, and you only have to stand up at the very end when *God save the King* comes instead of the benediction."

"Well, I must say, Fanny, you do have some extraordinary ideas," said Miss Brixworth. "Nobody but you would ever have thought of making such a comparison," she said, feeling a little shocked, and wondering if the comparison wasn't perhaps in a way rather blasphemous.

"Ah, but the real point is," said Miss Haymer, "that only the Russians have been clever enough so far to make the cinema a living thing."

"Have they?"

"Yes, they've turned politics into a real religion."

"And tried to destroy true religion!" Miss Brixworth exclaimed.

"They're far more alive than we are, I assure you. We shall have to come to something very like communism before long. Connie, why don't you join the Film Society this winter and see some Russian films?"

"I can't afford it," said Miss Brixworth, and with a quickness and bitterness unusual in her she added, "You see, I belong to the proletariat and we can't afford these luxuries."

Miss Haymer laughed. Perhaps there was just a touch of superiority in her laughter, as there was in her income, her experience and her brains. She had an idea that her friend had few secrets from her, but in this she was somewhat mistaken. She didn't even know that Miss Brixworth was a keen Anglo-Catholic. It was true that by browbeating her she sometimes hustled her into speaking of things about which she would otherwise have remained silent, but just as often she managed to frighten her out of confidences she was ready to make. For instance, there was a little matter just now occupying Miss Brixworth's mind, and Miss Brixworth had no intention of telling her friend a word about it.

She had known for a long time that Rosy Fernandez wanted a rocking-horse, and it always gave her so much pleasure to see Rosy pleased, that she had secretly made up her mind that the child should sooner or later have the rocking-horse at all costs. How very soon, she reflected, Rosy would reach an age when rocking-horses can give no pleasure! It was one thing to decide to buy her a rocking-horse, and quite another to find the money to buy it with. Miss Brixworth wasn't the sort of person to buy anybody a cheap present. She believed in giving something good or nothing at all. And of course it so happened that just at this time her wretched finances were in a more wretched state than they had ever been before. As a poor member of the "rentier" class she began to suffer earlier from the revolution than Miss Haymer, who was able to predict it in comfort. Dividends that Miss Brixworth had thought certain were now either smaller, delayed, or not paid at all, she was overdrawn at the bank, and had for some time past been practising strict economies. The sort of rocking-horse she meant to buy for Rosy couldn't cost less than thirty shillings—and thirty shillings seemed a lot of money. Of course she could always raise a little money by selling one of her few remaining possessions, but she didn't want to do that if she could help it; and of course she could always borrow a little money from Fanny Haymer—in theory, but she knew that she would somehow hate to do it in practice. She knew that if she were to tell Fanny that she wanted to give the child a rocking-horse there was a *chance* that Fanny would give her something towards it, for she could be very generous, but on the other hand it was more than likely that the proposal would provoke an outburst. "Preposterous, Connie!" she could imagine Miss Haymer saying. "I've never heard of such nonsense! Wanting to throw away money you haven't got on your landlady's child!"

So Miss Brixworth remained silent, and wondered how on earth she was going to find the money. She was already in need of several essential things which she had put off getting, but she had hinted broadly to the child that some day the horse might be forthcoming, and she was in dread of disappointing her. Actually, she was attributing to the child a sensitiveness which it didn't possess. People tend far too much to judge others by themselves, and Miss Brixworth was thinking of her own grief as a child when she was disappointed of some trifle. It didn't occur to her that Rosy was much tougher than she had been at the same age, and quite capable of turning set-backs into opportunities. Already Rosy had turned Miss Brixworth's hints into certainties. The child was nothing if not go-getting.

"Miss Brixworth's going to give me a rocking-horse," she announced pompously in the kitchen.

"Nonsense," said Lottie. "Miss Brixworth's got no money to buy rocking-horses for little girls with."

"I'm not a little girl," said Rosy. "My daddy says I'm a big girl."

"Or big girls either, Miss Dignity," said Lottie. "And what would you do with a rocking-horse, anyway?"

"I'd *ride* on it!"

"It wouldn't take you anywhere."

"I don't want to go anywhere. I just want to *ride*!"

"Go and ride a broomstick, then. And then you'll be a witch."

"Like Mrs. Porter," said Carol, looking up from his work.

"Oh, Carol!" said Lottie. "Don't go giving the child ideas!"

"What's a witch?" said Rosy.

"Which is a what?" said Carol. "Now you run along, Rosy."

Rosy looked extremely coy, put her head on one side, and edged her way out of the room.

"What a little flirt she is!" said Carol, watching

the child's coquettish ways. His judgment wasn't slow where women are concerned, and it was true that Rosy seemed to behave as if she knew in what lies the main business of a woman's life, and was unconsciously beginning to fit herself for it.

"I'll tell you what," said Carol, "have you noticed how that child likes Alston?"

"Oo, I know. I've seen her clap her little hands to see him come in of an evening."

"That must be why Fernandez hasn't picked on him yet. He thinks the world of that child."

"What'd Alston do if he *did* pick on him?" said Lottie. "I suppose he'd just have to clear out."

"Alston's not one to put up with a lot of nonsense, though he's a funny chap, I can't quite make him out."

"Well, Carol, if you ask me," said Lottie, "most of them are funny in this house. That child's funny, now, and funny things she gets into her head sometimes. The other day Mrs. Fernandez wanted to amuse her, so she put two white pansies in a bottle of red ink on the window-sill. You know when you do that all the veins in the flowers turn red. Well, there the child stood, just staring and staring. Couldn't take her eyes off them flowers. 'Now, Rosy,' I said, 'you leave them flowers for a bit and come downstairs.' I thought she'd go balmy looking at them like that. 'Oh no, Lottie,' she said, 'I like them. They're like blood.' What a thing for a child to say!"

"That's nothing," said Carol. "You should see what she did to the cat the other day."

"What did she do?"

"Well, I don't think I'll tell you."

"Why not?"

"Well, Lottie, I've got something better to talk about."

"And what's that, may I ask?"

"Well, if you want to know, it's another little girl."

"Oh, and who's that?"

"Don't be so inquisitive," he said. "But if you really want to know, shut your eyes and I'll be telling you."

Knowing perfectly well what was going to happen, Lottie shut her eyes, and of course Carol kissed her. She shivered with pleasure, but opened her eyes, put on an indignant expression, said, "Oh, you—you——" and was just going to slap his face, when he caught hold of her hands, held them down and kissed her again. She screamed, and at the same moment Mrs. Gambitt, looking thinner and more whey-faced than ever, and carrying her little dog in her arms, walked into the room.

"A nice way to behave in the kitchen," she said bitterly. "No wonder nothing ever gets done but the smashing of plates."

She wasn't born a kill-joy. She had got like that. And after all, a woman who has lost both love and youth, and has enjoyed little of either, must be expected to take offence at anything—she is trying to assert herself in one of the few ways left open to her.

"Pardon me, Mrs. Gambitt," said Carol, "but I'm not aware that I've smashed any plates to-day."

"Don't answer back, Carol, and please do your *courting* on your evening out." She put a special sneer into the word "courting".

"Who said I was courting?"

"I'm not going to bandy words with you, Carol." Mrs. Gambitt sniffed, drew herself up, and made as if to go out of the room. Then she looked over her shoulder and said sourly:

"I may tell you I'm used to being obeyed."

"She-who-must-be-obeyed and her dirty little dog," muttered Carol, making a long nose and putting out his very red tongue at her almost before she was out of the room. And he turned, with his eyes twinkling merrily through a lank fringe of black hair, to Lottie again.

Mrs. Gambitt made her way upstairs to Mrs. Petherham-Porter, for it was close on tea-time, and for once they were expecting a guest. The guest, a Mr. Swanage, with whom Mrs. Gambitt had formerly been slightly acquainted, was coming at her invitation. She had at one time been interested in those occult matters which were now occupying Mrs. Porter's attention more and more, and as Mr. Swanage had been her guide, she saw no reason why he shouldn't be Mrs. Porter's as well. The arrival of this personage was a source of annoyance to Carol,

who, on hearing the front door bell, had to break off
in the middle of his attentions to Lottie, slip into a
coat, admit the visitor, and show him upstairs to
Mrs. Porter's room.

Ernest Swanage had never been to this house before, and took stock of it, as he went upstairs, out of
the corners of an exceedingly sly pair of eyes. For he
had to consider 45 Cambodia Crescent as a possible
source of income. Mrs. Gambitt came forward to
receive him, and immediately introduced him to Mrs.
Porter. Feeling at once that he would be able to get
his own way with her, and being on the look-out for
a widow with money, he made her rather an ex-
aggerated bow. And Mrs. Porter, feeling very nervous
and embarrassed, asked him if he wouldn't take a
chair. She had felt that the proper thing to do when
Mr. Swanage arrived would be to offer him tea at
once, but Mrs. Gambitt said she mustn't do this on
any account, as he might want to go into a trance,
and nobody (she said) ever ate anything for at least
three hours before doing that. The proper thing to
do, she said, would be to have the tea all ready on
a side table, so that when Mr. Swanage had finished
his spiritual proceedings he could satisfy his physical
appetite. This Mrs. Porter had accordingly arranged,
and the spread was even more complicated than the
ones she usually provided for Mrs. Gambitt. There
was a marked contrast between Mrs. Porter's teas and
Miss Brixworth's. Miss Brixworth laid a plain cloth
with plain food on plain china; her food was good

and fresh and nourishing, and she liked preparing things herself, refusing to eat anything out of a tin except sardines. But Mrs. Porter liked to lay a fancy cloth with bad but elaborate-looking food, and though she herself ate little was especially lavish with sauces, pickles, tinned foods, and, since Mrs. Gambitt had become her daily guest, with stodgy pastries, sweets, dates and cheap chocolates. To-day she had excelled herself, and her preparations didn't escape the small, sharp eye of Mr. Swanage, who carefully sat down with his back to the tea-table, as though he hadn't noticed it at all.

He appeared to be between forty and fifty, was of medium height, rather stout, with a puffy face, scanty hair, very thin lips, and one or two of his front teeth discoloured or missing. When he sat down, he spread out his hands on his rather fat thighs. There were scarcely any nails on his fingers, as he had had the habit of biting them away as a young man, and he wore a large turquoise ring in the shape of a scarab, which immediately fascinated Mrs. Porter, who felt sure that it must have some mysterious psychic importance—the word "Isis" at once passed through her mind. While she was looking at it, Mr. Swanage slid his hands forward as far as his knees, and then, leaning towards her, said in a solemn tone of voice:

"You are one of those who desire to lift the veil—to get in touch, perhaps" (and here he lowered his voice), "with someone who has passed on?"

"I do," said Mrs. Porter firmly, though she still felt very nervous.

"Then I must give you a warning. The Beyond can only be approached in a spirit of reverence, by earnest seekers after truth. No mere curiosity-seeker will ever pierce the veil. . . . But I'm sure we need have no doubts about you, Mrs. Porter, or the reverent feeling with which you approach these matters."

"I do," said Mrs. Porter again, just as if she were in a church replying to a priest.

"Then we must try and establish a home circle," said Mr. Swanage, "for should you be so fortunate as to get in touch with some loved one of yours, I'm sure you'll be glad of the privacy of your own apartments?"

Mrs. Porter, who was flattered to hear her room spoken of as "her own apartments," said she was sure she would.

"You've heard of automatic writing, I suppose? A couple of years ago I was so fortunate as to have a message written through my hand by the late Cecil Rhodes. 'Spiritualism,' he said, 'is the only thing that matters. It is the only thing that counts,' he said. 'Knowledge of this other world of ours is beyond aught else. . . .' Isn't it wonderful to think that a man whose earth-deeds were so grand should be still building empires in heaven?"

"Wonderful!" said Mrs. Porter and Mrs. Gambitt together.

"Of course, we may not get an immediate phenomena. Much depends on your state of mind. Unless there is harmony among the sitters, and an earnest, reverent attitude of inquiry, I may not be able to go under control, and then you won't get a phenomena. You see, there are deep trance subjects and light trance subjects. I'm a light trance subject myself. A delicate balance, you know."

At this moment he gave a tremendous sneeze, and Mrs. Porter nearly jumped out of her skin, thinking that he might be going off into a trance. But after blowing his nose, Mr. Swanage continued:

"We will not hold a *séance* to-day," (He pronounced the word *sea-ants*). "But to-morrow, D.V., my psychic force will be at your service."

With this he looked very hard at Mrs. Porter, and a thrill ran up and down her spine.

"As St. Paul says," he added severely, " 'The manifestation of the spirit is given to every man to profit withal.' "

Mrs. Porter was wondering whether this meant that he wanted her to write him a cheque there and then, when he addressed her and Mrs. Gambitt together:

"My dear sisters," he said, "we seek the truth together. To-morrow I will be with you, a little earlier than this."

"And now I think we might offer Mr. Swanage some tea," said Mrs. Gambitt, who was feeling in need of some herself.

When they sat down to tea Swanage's manner completely changed. He was anxious to show that he could be as hearty and human on the earth-plane as anyone.

"I'm not particular," he cried in a falsely jovial tone of voice, when Mrs. Porter asked him how he liked his tea; "I'll take it just as it comes! And what a gorgeous spread," he added, almost boyishly. "I shall do full justice to it, I assure you."

He did. It was only when he was leaving that he grew momentarily serious again, producing several pamphlets for Mrs. Porter to read, and carefully treating Mrs. Gambitt as an initiate, which made her feel flattered, and so gave her a feeling of superiority over her friend.

"He's a most remarkable man," Mrs. Porter declared as soon as he had gone, "fascinating! I can't thank you enough, Natalie, for getting him to come here."

"You must have made a good impression on him," said Mrs. Gambitt, "if he's coming again to-morrow."

"Oh, I'm so pleased if I have," said Mrs. Porter, and she gazed out of the window. It had begun to rain, and a miserable sky was darkening over the roofs and chimneys, but she felt strangely excited, more stirred than she had been for a long time past, rejuvenated almost, as if a new chapter were opening in her life.

On the following afternoon she was convinced of it. The rain was falling more heavily than ever, but she was as excited by the arrival of Swanage as a young girl at the arrival of her lover. He didn't fail to notice the effect he was producing, and on the spirit-plane, as it were, rubbed his hands gleefully together. But his manner was the solemn one he usually assumed when in tune with the infinite.

"It isn't necessary to *darken* the room," he said, "but a *dim* light is usually helpful. A dim, religious light, as I call it."

"I shall draw down the blinds," said Mrs. Gambitt, and proceeded to do so, while Swanage arranged three chairs in a circle in the middle of the room. He seemed as calm as Mrs. Porter was agitated, while they seated themselves in the semi-darkness.

"Remember," said Swanage, in a voice grown almost sepulchral, "we are about to use one of God's most precious gifts so often spoken of in the Bible. I would be glad, Mrs. Porter, if you would sing us a hymn."

At this Mrs. Porter felt more agitated than ever, for her voice wasn't fit for singing, and she didn't know if she could think of a suitable hymn.

"Any hymn, Natalie?" she whispered, with an appealing look.

"Yes, any one," said Mrs. Gambitt. Mrs. Porter began to sing *Abide with me*. Her voice was at first thin and dry and shrill and quavering, but with the second verse she gained confidence. However, it was a hymn which had melancholy associations for her—it had been one of her husband's favourites—and in the third verse she broke off with a little sob.

"I can't—go on," she said, almost in a whisper, and sniffed.

After that there was a complete silence. A silence which lasted a long time. Neither of the two women dared to make the slightest movement. They waited expectantly, and nothing happened, but they were both convinced that something was going to happen. It was impossible to tell how long they sat like that, but the silence began to tell on their nerves. It became tense. It seemed to work itself up to a climax. Mrs. Porter felt almost hysterical. She was staring at the vague form of Swanage, sitting in rather a huddled position. She could hear the blood singing in her ears.

Suddenly Swanage sat bolt upright, gripping the arms of his chair. His chin was thrust slightly forward, and he began to mutter in a voice quite unlike his own. As his voice got clearer, the two women paid very close attention.

"Keep smiling," he said, somewhat inappropriately perhaps, "ke-ee-eep smiling. It helps us, you know. When you've passed over too, you'll know it's a help to us. . . . Don't you know me? I'm watching over you. . . . Do you remember Tiny? She's here too——"

Mrs. Porter started violently. Was it, could it be, her husband's voice?

"Maurice!" she cried, in a breathless, incredulous whisper.

"It isn't easy," said the voice vaguely, "it isn't so easy . . . kee-eep smiling . . . you remember . . . take care . . . ah!"

Then a few moments later:

"There's music over here . . . playing softly . . . old favourites. . . . Sir Arthur Sullivan——"

There was a long pause, during which the medium muttered and groaned. Then all at once his figure shuddered in the chair, uttered a loud, long-drawn sigh, sat up, and opened its eyes.

"Please pull up the blinds," said Mr. Swanage, in his ordinary voice.

Mrs. Gambitt went and pulled up the blinds.

"Oh, I don't know how to thank you enough," said Mrs. Porter, dabbing at her nose with a handkerchief.

"Don't thank me, I'm only a channel," said Mr. Swanage, wiping his sweating forehead. "Did you hear any familiar voices?"

"My husband's!"

"And who is Tiny?" Mrs. Gambitt asked.

"Our darling little fox-terrier! It's too wonderful —oh, I can hardly bear it!"

"Well," said Mr. Swanage, "it looks as though we may be able to develop a home circle here. Many people, you know, have psychic powers within them, but it's only by sitting regularly for development that those powers can be brought to light."

His small eyes twinkled, for he knew that Mrs. Gambitt knew that he expected some solid reward for his services, and he knew that she would make Mrs. Porter see that he got it. Before leaving, he was careful to make an appointment for a further "sea-ants."

M

XI

MRS. FERNANDEZ was delighted, for a room which had stood empty ever since she had taken over the house was now to be occupied. It was true that the new lodger was a man, and a coloured man at that, an Indian gentleman called Ramsamy in fact, and she was by no means sure how her husband would take the news. When she told him, he was silent.

"Now please, Paul, don't get ideas into your head about him," she said. "Remember a tenant's a tenant," she said, for she never could bring herself to use the word 'lodger.'

Still Fernandez was silent, and it was with no little misgiving that she made things ready for the arrival of Mr. Ramsamy, for she was by now more definitely afraid of her husband. But this very fear was what kept her passionate love for him alive. If she could have ceased to fear him, she might very quickly have grown tired of him and cast him off, but there had always been little doubts to calm, little doubts which had gradually turned into a haunting fear as to where his mania would lead him and as to how it would affect the child—as though it were not enough for Rosy to be her father's daughter! Mrs. Fernandez wasn't a fool. She was in love. Quite shrewd enough to understand certain facts about her husband and the possible results of his behaviour, she felt so strongly about him that her judgment was swamped. She had concentrated on his one praiseworthy trait, and that was his overwhelming devotion to herself and the child. That she was the subject of a monomania on the part of a person with strong feelings, this alone was enough to make her heart master of her head, and Fernandez master of both.

In Miss Brixworth's room, one evening when Alston was present, she spoke openly of her fears and sufferings.

"You'd never guess what happened just after this Indian gentleman came," she said. "Do you know, my husband threatened to throw me out of the window unless I promised to get rid of him at once. But what am I to do? We must live. Yes, he actually held me out of the window for about ten minutes on that very cold night we had last week, and kept threatening to let go."

"But, my dear," exclaimed Miss Brixworth, "that sort of thing can't go on. Why do you put up with it? Oughtn't you to separate from him?"

"That's what Mrs. Gambitt told me long ago. 'Put him out into the street,' she says, 'and you and I will carry on.' But I haven't the heart to do it, Miss Brixworth, I haven't really."

"But if, as you've hinted to me before this, he's sometimes, to put it plainly, not altogether in his right mind, do you think you have the right, either for your own sake or the child's or that of the other people in the house, to go on as you are doing? Remember you haven't only yourself to consider."

"But what can I do?" she said.

"You could——"

"Ah, I know what you're going to say. But, you see, it isn't as if he ever lays violent hands on me."

Being held out of a window at midnight she didn't regard as violence.

"Or there's another way," said Miss Brixworth, with some hesitation.

"I know what you mean. I *have* spoken to the doctor about that. But he says he couldn't certify him. 'Lots of men are jealous,' he said. But the truth is, he's afraid. You see, there have been these cases lately of people being certified in error, and the doctors have had to pay heavy damages. Besides," she added, "I'm not at all sure that I'd allow it in any case."

"But you can't go on indefinitely like this," said Miss Brixworth.

Mrs. Fernandez didn't answer. She began to weep.

"It's terrible," she said, in a whisper. "I don't know what he'd say if he knew I was in here talking about him to you and Mr. Alston. You know, he lies awake all night watching me. If he does drop off to sleep at all, and I stir, he's awake at once."

She said this almost with pride.

Alston had listened so far without saying a word. His heart was beating rapidly, and his mouth felt dry, as if he couldn't speak even if he wanted to.

What a pity, thought Miss Brixworth, that Alston was so young. If only he were older, stronger, more experienced, more a man of the world, he could act with decision, fly into a rage, storm and threaten, and grimly *command* Mrs. Fernandez that she must at once make arrangements to have her husband confined, or at least to separate from him, that she had a duty to the public and must run the house properly or he would leave it and would advise everybody else to do the same. . . . And looking at him, sitting there, young and silent, unable to take his eyes off Mrs. Fernandez, she thought he was as helpless as she was herself, and suddenly (and for the first time) she felt displeased with him, resenting what she considered his lack of initiative. But after all, she told herself, what right had she to blame him? And what right (as Miss Haymer said) had any outside person to interfere (though Miss Haymer was by no means above interference herself, when she got the chance) with this woman's private life, and indeed her happiness?

Alston sat staring at Mrs. Fernandez. Her weeping eyes had the dewiness of a lover's eyes; her lips quivered like a lover's even while they prayed for deliverance from love; even to Alston the erotic nature of her love for Fernandez was plain. "Like the dove and the snake, aren't they?" Carol had said. "You can see he just fascinates her."

But was the matter to be so easily explained, after all? Mrs. Fernandez wasn't just any weak woman:

she had character, independence and spirit. Nor was she alone in the world, without advisers. She had relations to turn to, as well as Mrs. Gambitt. What a mystery it all was! Here was this woman, with strong instincts towards order, comfort and security, towards health and goodness and youth and strength, and yet when you looked at her, you saw she had a bit of a devil in her, and that was just what made her so attractive, and just what drove her at the same time to unite herself so unreasonably to disorder and disease and anxiety and evil. For there was no doubt that Fernandez himself was beginning to seem to others than herself almost as evil as a human being can be, a light had gone out in him, he had a "closed" face in which evil seemed to prevail entirely—and yet he was fond of the child, "worshipped it", as Carol said, and as for his wife, if he loved her madly, wasn't that love?

The next morning, when Carol brought Miss Brixworth her breakfast, he was grinning broadly and carrying a leaflet in his hand.

"I was asked to bring you this," he said, "by that old woman down there, Mrs. Porter, and to make sure that you got it."

Miss Brixworth took the paper from him and read as follows:

Life's Riddles answered by the Seer

"Are you one of those who would pierce the Veil? Here is a naked revelation for you. The Urim and

Thummim of the Kosmos can be an Open Book to YOU. One who has walked this earth since the Beginning and from whom nothing is hidden, is now at your service to answer the Great Questions you have always been asking yourself and could never answer. Write now to the SEER himself, MR. P. ERNEST SWANAGE, who will advise and guide you. Arrange an Interview NOW—you will be surprised, delighted, and uplifted!"

"What dreadful nonsense and blasphemy," said Miss Brixworth mildly. "And who on earth is this Swanage?"

"He's the Seer!" cried Carol triumphantly. "That's him! And they both believe in him as if he was a god. He comes into the house here sometimes, and I bet he doesn't go away again empty-handed, either." He winked.

"But who is he, Carol? He must be mad."

"Not he, Miss Brixworth. He knows how to make a good living, sure and he does."

"Have you seen him, Carol?"

"Oh yes, indeed I have. He sometimes comes to tea with Mrs. Gambitt and Mrs. Porter and they all shut themselves up in Mrs. Porter's room and call up spirits and all that."

"Never!" cried Miss Brixworth. "How very shocking! I hope Mrs. Fernandez doesn't have anything to do with all that."

"No, she doesn't," said Carol, "but Mrs. Gambitt's always nagging her about it."

"As if she hadn't enough troubles already! As if we

all hadn't enough troubles in this world without trying to monkey with the next!"

"Then you don't like spiritualism, Miss Brixworth?"

"Indeed I don't, Carol. I won't have anything to do with it and I hope you won't either. Please return this silly leaflet to Mrs. Porter with my compliments and regrets."

When Carol did so, Mrs. Porter burst out indignantly with the one word, "Unbeliever!"

Miss Brixworth of course reported what Carol had told her to Miss Haymer, who said dryly:

"We shall have so much time to talk to the dead when we join them."

"Just what I told Carol!"

"Did you, Connie? You know they say there's a hollow spot in the brain, just as there's a little spot in the eye which doesn't see anything. Well, of course, if one pays too much attention to this hollow spot it soon leads to trouble. It's the swarming-place of bees in the bonnet. Your Mrs. Gambitt and your Mrs. Porter, being women without men, naturally feel themselves a bit cheated of reality. So they make their minds a blank (it can't be very hard for them to do that, I should say) and in fly all the enemies of sweet reasonableness."

"Evil spirits, I should call them," said Miss Brixworth.

"Very well, my dear, do, if you want to be mediaeval. . . . But one realises now why nature abhors a vacuum. It's because of all the poisonous rubbish that flies to fill it. And after all, if people's lives are dull and idle enough, they can scarcely be blamed for feeling the need of some more or less unlawful thrill."

"Still, it's disgusting, Fanny."

"What, spiritualism you mean? Yes, or just ridiculous."

It so happened that when Miss Brixworth returned home that afternoon she made an absurd mistake. She was astonished to encounter a black stranger in the hall. Her head was still full of spiritualism, and she had confused Carol's account of the Seer with what she had heard about the Indian lodger, Mr. Ramsamy. So as soon as she saw him she was both surprised and alarmed, partly because she was unfamiliar with coloured people, and partly because she imagined that this was the Seer. She accordingly drew herself up to her full height, gave him a very cold look, and sailed majestically upstairs. The unfortunate Mr. Ramsamy, a most harmless individual, was even more frightened by Miss Brixworth than she had been by him, and quailed beneath the look she gave him, immediately supposing that it was a display of colour prejudice, or else that she must be a trifle unbalanced. Mrs. Fernandez and Carol had been so nice to him that he was more than a little distressed to find a fellow-lodger so hostile, and let himself out at the front door in a very miserable frame of mind indeed.

"You should have told me, Carol," said Miss Brixworth reproachfully, "that the Seer was a black man."

"A black man, Miss Brixworth! But he isn't! He's Scotch!"

"Scotch? Then who is the black man that I met in the hall?"

"Oh, that must be Mr. Ramsamy, the new Indian gentleman upstairs. Nice and quiet he seems."

"Oh dear, what *have* I done?" said Miss Brixworth.

"Well, what *have* you done?"

"I treated him *so* badly." Miss Brixworth explained what had happened.

"Oh, well, I expect he'll get over it," said Carol philosophically. "They're used to that sort of thing. After all, they're only foreigners, aren't they. . . . Of course Mrs. Fernandez is as pleased as Punch at getting somebody to take that room. She says her husband disapproves of coloured men (though, if you ask me, you might almost take him for one himself), but as she said to him—I heard her say it—'You can't very well take exception,' she said, 'to a bachelor of science.' Yes, that's what he is and all, a bachelor of science. But he won't be a bachelor long, I should say. Women like them, you know. It's funny how they'll take up with a darkie."

The new addition to the household pleased Mrs. Fernandez so much that she took a plunge and fulfilled one of her long-cherished ambitions—the provision of a new stair-carpet. It was bought as a bargain, on the hire-purchase system, and at once laid. She paid a special visit to Miss Brixworth in order to ask her opinion of it.

"It's very handsome, I think, very handsome indeed," said Miss Brixworth, watching the pleased expression on the face of Mrs. Fernandez, who was feeling the carpet with her feet, and taking a delight in its muffled softness and springiness instead of having to walk on bare boards.

But when Miss Brixworth happened to come face to face with Mrs. Gambitt, or heard Fernandez coughing his graveyard cough behind closed doors, or saw him, always as silent as a cat in his movements, going up or down stairs, she began to resent the existence of the stair-carpet. It seemed to add an air of secrecy, of mystery even, to the house. By silencing the footsteps of all the inhabitants it made Mrs. Gambitt's peevishness seem almost menacing; it made the unpleasant Fernandez seem sinister, and even seemed to turn the parlour witchcraft and spookish hanky-panky of Mrs. Petherham-Porter into something uncanny. All that was strange and reserved and remote in the house—the puzzling character of Alston, the "old-fashionedness" of Rosy—became intensified, and the carpet, by making their movements more private, seemed to lay stress on the separateness of each individual in the house, whereas formerly the sharing of one roof had seemed to unite them all into some sort of community. Their outward differences were accentuated, their inner lives made more secret, by this cheap but downy stair-carpet, bought at a few shillings a yard.

"Fernandez doesn't like the Indian at all," Carol reported, and he was right, for a triangular discussion had taken place in the office and had made the fact plain.

"I know why you're sulking," Mrs. Fernandez had said boldly to her husband. "You're still sulking because of the new tenant."

"You're right," he said, without taking his gaze away from the fire by which he was sitting.

"Well, what's wrong with him?" said Mrs. Gambitt in her harsh voice.

"There may be nothing wrong with him," said Fernandez.

"Is it because he's an Indian?"

"No."

"You ought to be used to coloured people, considering that you've lived abroad. Do you realise that he's a decent, educated man, and that if you annoy him he'll just go? A nice name this house'll get if you go on chasing every man away from it. They'll be calling you Bluebeard or something."

He didn't reply, but looked at her angrily.

"Don't think I'm afraid of you," she said, leaning towards him over the cup of very strong tea which she had in her hand. "Remember, I've got my money in this house, and as long as my money's in it the house has got to be looked after. I won't have the tenants insulted, do you hear? Do you want us all turned into the gutter?"

"Oh, leave him, Natalie," said Mrs. Fernandez; "he won't annoy Mr. Ramsamy, I'm sure, now you've asked him not to."

Fernandez darted a malicious glance at his wife, but neither of the women noticed it. Why, he wondered, should she fly to the defence of the Indian? How very significant! This was something to be watched. . . .

XII

From day to day life at 45 Cambodia Crescent was as
full of richness and variety as a sky full of clouds, all
moving on different planes but in the same atmosphere, driven by varying currents of air, caught by
changing rays of light, now hiding and now revealing
heaven, all light and shade and movement. And
nothing could be more touching than the way in
which the pleasures of hope could warm the hearts of
the inhabitants. There were times when it really
seemed that Fernandez was returning to a more
normal frame of mind, and then the joyousness that
radiated from his wife infected others, making Rosy
seem a more innocent child than she was, and exciting
Mrs. Gambitt, who tried to express her feelings by
cuddling her little dog. A temporary reconciliation
sometimes sweetened the life of the Rudds; on one
occasion Rudd himself actually won a small prize in
a newspaper competition, and the poor man at once
found life infinitely more attractive. Carol, in his little
basement bedroom, had devised an exercise, or rather
a torture, which he imagined would increase his
height, and in his spare time he suspended himself
from a hook and struggled to touch the floor with his
toes, in the hope of eventually being accepted as a
policeman. Even Mrs. Porter had a new excitement

to add to her enthusiasm for Mr. Swanage. She was thrilled by the idea of Mr. Ramsamy. They had never set eyes on each other, and while he didn't even know of her existence, she couldn't think of him or hear his name mentioned without a tremor of curiosity—he was Indian, therefore he was a Hindu, probably a *yogi*, must certainly be very "psychic", was bound to be full of knowledge of ancient mysteries and of the occult, and might even be a sort of Krishnamurti. And when Mrs. Gambitt, who was almost ready to share these imaginings, declared that Mr. Ramsamy was a bachelor of science, Mrs. Porter felt sure she was on the right track, and said she shouldn't be surprised if in a very short time they had Mr. Ramsamy lecturing to them about Vishnu and Siva and lotuses and nirvana and *pranayama* and so on.

Miss Brixworth, returning from church one Sunday, was pleasantly surprised to meet Empringham in Parthenon Street. For the first time since he had gone to work for Miss Haymer she had the chance of some private words with him, and hurried to take it.

"Well, Empringham, and where are you off to, I wonder? You weren't going to notice me, were you? It's a long time since I've seen you except to say 'good morning' to, isn't it?"

"Yes, madam. And I should like to take this opportunity of thanking you for getting me a place like I've got with Miss Haymer. I couldn't wish for a better."

Empringham was as polite and deliberate as ever.

"I'm very glad," said Miss Brixworth. "I hoped it

would be so. Miss Haymer is such a very old friend
of mine, and I know how good and kind she is. If
you ever don't quite understand her, Empringham,
or find her a little trying, you must try and bear with
her. As you know, she's troubled with the gout, and
I'm afraid she's sometimes a little bit, well, *eccentric*
in her opinions."

"Yes, madam. Of course she must have seen a bit
of the world in her time."

"Oh, she has, indeed."

"She loves to talk a bit, doesn't she, and no matter
what you talk about, she always knows something
and has got something to say about it."

"She's a very clever person, Empringham, and of
course she's read a great deal."

"Mind you, I don't know I always see eye to eye
with her. Especially in politics, now. But that's
always a tricky thing to talk to anyone about."

"I'm afraid Miss Haymer's a bit of a bolshevik,"
said Miss Brixworth. "Not, of course," she added
hastily, "that she wishes to do anybody any *harm*."

"Oh no, madam, of course not."

"But, you see, she's got an idea that the world's
got to be run quite a different way to the way it
always *has* been run. And who knows? Perhaps she's
right."

"Yes, madam."

"But, Empringham, although I'm glad to see you
in a fairly snug position, I can't help thinking sometimes about that little restaurant of yours and all

those beautiful fittings just lying idle year after year."

"Ah, well," said Empringham, "some day, perhaps. . . . But I don't know whether I'll ever do it now, I'm sure. I suppose everybody has a little dream they hope'll come true, and what I say is this, when your dream comes true it isn't a dream any longer, so if you've gained something you've lost something too. And you know, you want something to look *forward* to, that's what it is."

"Empringham," said Miss Brixworth, "you're a very wise man."

"If you'll excuse me asking you, madam," he said, "I hope things are all right at Cambodia Crescent?"

"Not so good as when you were there, Empringham. But still, we scrape along somehow."

"That Mrs. Gambitt——"

"I know," said Miss Brixworth.

When she left him she felt a little sad. He was so nice to talk to, so steady and reliable, like servants in the old days, a treasure really. How lucky Fanny was to have somebody so dependable to look after her. . . . With these thoughts running in her head, she returned to Cambodia Crescent, and was going up the steps with a sigh when she noticed a curtain abruptly drawn back, and a face appeared for a moment. Why is Mrs. Rudd suddenly so interested in my movements? thought Miss Brixworth.

But Mrs. Rudd wasn't in the least interested in her movements. She had looked out, thinking it might be Alston who was coming in. For to tell the truth, except during those rare and brief periods when her husband brightened up, she now measured time by the moments when she caught a glimpse of Alston. The clock and calendar of her heart was at present made up of sidelong peeps at him through the lace curtains at her window. It had become a fixed idea with her that she must get to know him, and she knew it was no good waiting for him to use some stray excuse to seek her out.

He was still entirely unaware of her feelings when they came to such a head that she felt she must let him know them or burst. She thought at first that she would write him a letter and put it in the post, then she thought she would just write him a note and pay Carol to slip it under his door, and then she prudently decided to commit nothing to writing, for she had a fear of scandal and a love of secrecy. Obviously, she thought, the best plan would be either to meet him out of doors as if by chance, or to waylay him when he was just entering or leaving the house. She decided on the latter course.

So one morning, when Alston was just going out to work, and was crossing the hall, he was astonished to see a female head emerge from a doorway, and to hear it say, in rather a choked voice, "Mr. Alston, could I speak to you a minute, please?" He was very surprised, for he had never addressed a word to Mrs. Rudd in his life beyond an occasional "good morning."

"Certainly," he said, for he rather prided himself on knowing exactly how to behave at any given moment in a suitable way.

"Won't you come in?" she asked, rather coyly, and showed the way into the room. Alston refused a chair and raised his eyebrows. Fiddling uneasily with his cap, he wondered what was coming next. It was the first time in his life that he had been in any woman's bedroom but his mother's.

"You'll excuse me asking you in like this," said Mrs. Rudd, fluttering her eyelids, "but it's about something rather important—to me at least."

She laughed nervously. He could see the division of her breasts, and her bosom rapidly rising and falling above it. A common little thing with her fluffy hair and cheap pink kimono, she went well with the surrounding furniture of fumed oak decorated with rather soiled bows of ribbon. An aspidistra, the *Daily Express*, and the remains of a breakfast could be seen on the table.

"All right," said Alston.

She didn't quite know what to think of him. Perhaps his apparent coolness hid reserves of passion. She asked him for a cigarette.

"Sorry," he said, offered her one, lighted it for her (she took care that their hands should touch at this moment, and derived a thrill from the contact), and then, without taking one for himself, put the packet back in his pocket.

"Oh, aren't you going to have one, too?" she said.

"No, thanks, I had one just five minutes ago," he said.

This wasn't true. He was rationing himself strictly in cigarettes in order to have enough money when he went out with Amy. Giving a cigarette to Mrs. Rudd meant that he had to do without one himself. He now began to feel uneasy.

"Do you like dancing?" said Mrs. Rudd abruptly, looking at him with a sweetly vampish expression on her face.

"Well, yes," he said. "But I haven't done much lately."

"Oh, nor have I. But I wish I could. I just love it!"

Does she mean me to ask her out dancing? he thought: if so, she's going a straight way about it. He said nothing, and there was an awkward silence.

"Oh, I wanted to say——" she said, "oh, I hardly know how to begin."

"Well, try," he said. "I can't stay very long. I must get to work."

"Well, you see," she said, "it's really about my husband."

"Yes."

"Well, we've been married six years."

"Yes."

"And, well, you see—we have no children——"

"And whose fault is that?" he asked, with the directness of a countryman.

"Well, that's just it," she said. "I don't know, of course, but I think it must be my husband's."

And at that moment even Alston vaguely realised that Rudd looked the sort of man who would only be tender and caressing when cleaning his spectacles, and only eager when opening an umbrella or news-paper.

"And do you want a child?" he said, surprised at his own boldness. "What are you going to do about it? Get a new husband, or what?"

"Well, you see, I don't know for certain whether it's his fault or not, but I'd like to *try*—what I mean is, I've sometimes seen you—I mean I've often noticed you going in and out of the front door—and I thought perhaps—I thought I'd ask you—if you'd like——" Here she simpered, cast her eyes down, and turning away cried out, "Oh, I hope you'll forgive me for asking!"

Alston could hardly believe his ears. But where many a man would have been touched or amused or excited by such an appeal, he felt a little repelled by it.

"Well," he said, "I'm sorry, but I'm afraid you haven't picked on quite the right man." He smiled, and buttoned up the topmost button of his coat, which was undone. The gesture was characteristic, and as significant as a snail's retreat into its shell. And leaving her standing in the middle of the room, he went out.

She had allowed her kimono to slip down over one shoulder, and she stood there motionless for an instant. But directly she heard the front door close behind him she hitched up the garment, and instead of going to the window, as she had so often done before, she hammered on the table with her fists till the dirty cups danced in the saucers and the cigarette ashes danced out of them.

"Oh God!" she cried aloud in her humiliation. "I'll make him pay for this!" And she went to a drawer and took out one of her own cigarettes, at which she began to puff furiously, while she strode up and down the room, stamping her foot from time to time. In which condition she may for the moment be left.

Alston, leaving the house, took a deep breath of the outside air, partly to rid his senses of the mingled odour of cheap powder, scent and tobacco, stale cooking and unaired bedclothes, and partly with a feeling of relief at having escaped from an uncomfortable situation. Was it possible, he wondered, that she really meant what she said? Perhaps the whole thing was a trick. Mrs. Rudd no doubt wanted to be divorced from her husband (hadn't Carol often spoken of their rows?) and he, Alston, was to be used as an excuse. She was trying to arrange that her husband should catch them together red-handed in the bedroom. Ah no, thought Alston, she won't catch me as easily as that. . . . First surprised, then embarrassed, then suspicious, he felt finally a little disgusted, where a little more experience of the world would probably have only amused him.

A decent young fellow, people said of him, without much to say for himself. And knowing him a little better, they said, "He seems a bit lost, somehow." Of course he was leading a double life. In him, as in many men, there wasn't a proper adjustment between the inner and the outer self. The trouble with many a man is that he dare not or cannot obey his heart for fear of offending society; and that, in trying not to offend society, he is in danger of altogether disobeying his heart; and with that of spoiling his chance of becoming a good citizen. We have a double conscience, and one part acts as a brake on the impulses of the other.

The top-layer conscience, closely concerned with the crowd, the herd, society in general, is the one we are educated to obey. But it is a doubtful guide, largely formed out of tribal taboos—we needn't look far to see how many acts of folly and violence throughout history have been done (and are still being done every day) in the name of "conscience" or "duty." It is the deeper conscience, the Quixote or Columbus, the Blake or Copernicus, in us which deserves the deeper respect. It is the individual mystery, not the common citizenship, that works the greatest changes, since men have at heart their insurgence as individuals, rather than their obedience as citizens, in common. But an individual is nothing unless he is related to a society or to some vital movement within a society. The power and the machinery are useless unless they work together; they are, in a sense, of equal importance; but it is the power that drives. And the power can only drive through its proper channel. Alston had found no means yet, no proper channel, through which to express himself. Deep down in him there was a desperate fear and a desperate courage, and one was bound to conquer the other in the end. It wasn't fame he wanted. He needed what every man needs, to play a part in the world and to feel that he is playing it to some good purpose. A vigorous youth movement of the German kind might have helped him, but unfortunately he lived in a country which could offer him little but to join the Boy Scouts or the Y.M.C.A.

His nature was like a ship sailing blindly away on a voyage of discovery. And in that ship there were two forces—the crew, who enabled it to travel, and Columbus, the captain, who directed their activities. Columbus was the master, and because of that the crew would in the end be obliged to obey him and follow where he led. Columbus sometimes overheard his crew calling him a selfish madman, but he didn't worry, for he knew that a certain degree of madness is necessary in order to get things done, or said, for the first time—pioneers are always thought to be selfish madmen at first, until it is seen that they have enriched humanity a million times more than themselves. The quixotic Columbus, brooding unseen in his cabin, is the mysterious guiding force that drives every one of us to fulfil our destiny; while the crew are all that necessary, lazy, worldly, conventional, grumbling, unenterprising part of us that is so full of common sense, wants to know that it will get its supper and wages at the proper times, and plays above all for safety, finding it better to squat warmly on a nest-egg than soar like an eagle in a thundercloud. The trouble is that there are so many Columbuses who never discover an America.

The Columbus in Alston, had he failed to sight land, might have grown too proud to turn back, and might have determined to run recklessly before the wind into all the anger of the elements, ice and fog, the hidden reef and the waterspout. Setting out to create, he might, in failing, have turned to destruction, for there was a leaning towards destructiveness in him. Just as no one can turn sourer than a frustrated sentimentalist, so no one can turn more violent and headstrong than a young man with the makings of will and energy who misses his proper vocation. The energy in Alston was ready to make a fine flower, but he was a plant no gardener had tended, and he seemed likely to grow wildly—a weed and yet not a weed, one could imagine him hungering for a light and warmth that might never reach him except in snatches. He wanted to act, but didn't know how.

And the cause of all this? That the love between him and Amy, though enough in itself to satisfy her, wasn't enough to satisfy him. His love for her was a steady thing, and grew more tender as time went on, increasing at times into a strong need of her. But where Alston answered almost the whole need of Amy, she only fulfilled the need of one side of his nature; it was the old story of a woman being content with a man's love while the man isn't content with loving her and receiving her love in return, but needs a kind of work that he believes in and comradeship of some kind as well. . . . And then, on the very day of Mrs. Rudd's attempt to seduce him, a great change in Alston's life began—a change which was to convince the crew, as it were, that Columbus had been right after all, and which would eventually lead Alston towards happiness and so make a good citizen of him.

The day passed like many another before it, except that Alston seemed a little absent-minded, felt a little out of sorts, and, moving about in his white coat among the oranges and apples, was a little less the good salesman than usual—he was even blamed for a stupid piece of carelessness in making up an order. When he came back to Cambodia Crescent in the evening he exchanged a few words with Carol, and told him about Mrs. Rudd's behaviour in the morning. Carol was much amused.

"Well!" he exclaimed. "That was cool, wasn't it! And you mean to say that you didn't——?"

"No," said Alston. "Catch me!"

"Well! Fancy throwing a chance like that away! I know what I'd have done if I'd been in your place!"

Alston answered him with a smile, and went upstairs to wash, before going out to see his uncle and aunt. On his way downstairs again he saw Mrs.

Fernandez in the hall. She was standing in the hall with the electric light shining full upon her, and she seemed to him quite dazzlingly beautiful as she smiled and said "Good evening" to him. Even when he had left the house he went on thinking about her, and he couldn't help contrasting her with his beloved little Amy, so unripe, childish almost, with something delicate and helpless about her in comparison to the buoyant and easy grace of Mrs. Fernandez; but though Mrs. Fernandez might appeal to his imagination, it was Amy, waiting to be woken up to the fullness of life, and not perhaps waiting very gracefully, who had his heart.

There was no doubt that as Fernandez' health gradually declined, as his passions became more violent and his understanding more governed by them than ever, so, in a precisely inverse proportion, did his wife's vitality increase. While her husband crept silently about, or sat moodily for hours, staring into a dying fire with bloodshot eyes, while he mumbled incoherently or coughed—with a long, resigned, shattering cough—through a cloud of tobacco smoke, his face grey and his hands clutching nervously at the arms of his chair, Mrs. Fernandez looked younger than ever. While she realised that her husband's condition was bad, she was too obsessed with her love for him to be able to understand how bad it was, and although she went about with vague fears in her heart, her eyes sparkled, her cheeks were pink, her step was light, and her image, photographed in

Alston's memory, was the image of a woman at the very climax of her existence.

His aunt gave Alston supper, and afterwards he sat listening to the wireless. But after a time his uncle, who had been sitting by the fire in his shirt sleeves and smoking a pipe, got up and went and switched it off.

"Eric," he said in a casual tone of voice and without taking his pipe out of his mouth, "do you want to buy any furniture?"

"Not that I know of," said Alston.

"Well, I'm only telling you, because if you do, you can get an extra big double brass bedstead with mattress complete, all as good as new, for fifteen bob."

"A double bed! What on earth should I do with that?" Even to Alston it seemed rather an irony that such a subject should crop up on the very day that Mrs. Rudd had called him into her room.

"Now, look here," said his uncle, "I'd have snapped it up myself if there'd been anywhere to put it. It's a wonderful bargain, and a young fellow like you—well, you'll be getting married one day——"

"I don't think," said Alston.

"Well, I *do* think. Like to have a look at it?"

"I don't mind, uncle. Where is it? And whose is it?"

"It's in the shed, and it's the baker's. He doesn't want the thing. Nowhere to put it. I said I'd keep it here a week to oblige him but not a day longer. There's two days left, and he'll take fifteen bob for it as it stands."

"What's your commission?" said Alston.

"Go on! You trust your uncle!" said the old man, who was promised half a crown if he could get fifteen shillings for the bed. "What do you take me for? Think I want to make money out of you?"

"All right, let's see it, then."

They took an electric torch and went out to the shed, which his uncle unlocked with a large key.

"Full of mice," he said, as he opened the door. "I must put the cat in again. There you are!"

There was the bed. The brass knobs on it were many and gleaming. The bright globes reflected the faces of the two men, distorting them slightly.

"Isn't it a beauty?"

"Oh, a beauty," said Alston. "And you didn't have to be such a red-hot salesman to get anybody to want to buy it. If I had the money I'd take it. It's not much of a bed that I've got now."

"If you had the money! You'll never get a chance like this again. You could get some sleep in that. And a bit of fun too." The old man (a dirty old man, like most of the old men our civilisation produces) chuckled and gave his nephew a dig in the ribs. "When I was your age I could have made the springs creak, I can tell you."

"I'll oil them," said Alston.

"Then you'll take it?"

"Yes, I could do with it. But I can't pay for it in a hurry."

"Oh, that's all right," said his uncle, pleased at having settled the matter.

Alston didn't return home in a very cheerful mood. The lighted windows of the houses he passed suggested a warmth and contentment and intimacy that his life didn't yet possess. It wasn't that he hankered for a life of mild domestic bliss with Amy and hadn't the means to support it—far from it. What worried him was an unsettled feeling, a feeling that he was drifting, that he didn't really belong to London, and the knowledge that Amy, fond as he was of her, didn't and couldn't by herself round off his life and give it a proper centre and direction. Why, he wondered, had he bought this bedstead which he didn't really want, and couldn't easily find the money to pay for? And what was the use of his job? Was he to go on living like this for years and years? . . . As he got nearer home he felt still more depressed, and taking out of his pocket a few coins he decided to go and have a drink somewhere before going back to bed. He was then in Parthenon Street, and a few more steps brought him to " The Case is Altered."

It was near closing time, and the atmosphere was rather stale in the bar. The gloom with which the English take their pleasures had covered the walls with a murky brownish colour, and a half-hearted game of darts was going on in a corner. Alston ordered himself a drink and was just going to put his lips to the glass when a man near him dropped some money, and he stooped down obligingly to pick it up.

"Thanks," said the man. "I never seem to have any money but I chuck it about."

The speaker, a solidly-built young man something under thirty, with curly hair and a very frank and cheerful expression on a rather weather-browned face, looked at Alston very shrewdly, and then said, pointing to his glass:

"Drink that up, and have another one with me."

"Oh, thanks," said Alston, glancing at the clock. "There may be just time for a quick one."

"We'll make time," said the stranger. "Live round here?"

"Yes," said Alston, and as he spoke he thought there was something vaguely familiar in the stranger's face. "Do you know," he said, "I've an idea I've seen you before somewhere."

"Maybe," said the stranger. "but I don't remember you. . . . What do you do round here?"

"I work in a shop just down the road here. Fruiterer's, it is."

"Oh. Like that all right?"

"It's all right."

"Live with your family, I suppose?"

"No," said Alston.

He explained about 45 Cambodia Crescent.

"But there's too many old women in the house," he said.

"Leave you alone, don't they?"

"Yes and no," said Alston, thinking of Mrs. Rudd and then of Miss Brixworth.

"Time, gentlemen, please!" cried the barman.

"I'm not in a hurry," said the stranger. "I saw a coffee stall down the road; we could go and chat there for a bit. . . . What you want in London is a little place of your own."

"Is that what you've got?" said Alston.

"Me? My God, no!"

By this time Alston's curiosity was aroused. He couldn't understand the stranger's friendliness and wanted to know more about him. All the time they were talking he watched the stranger's face, wondering where he had seen it before.

"I've done a mad thing to-night," said Alston, as they left "The Case."

"What's that?"

"I've gone and bought a bed, a double bed!"

"What, are you going to get married or something?"

"Oh, not yet."

"But there is somebody——?"

"There is."

Alston didn't feel inclined just then to talk about Amy, but the stranger made him want to talk, and he found himself telling about Crotchester and his childhood, and about how he had come to London, which he mightn't have done if his father hadn't died and if his mother hadn't married again. . . .

"My dad was a wonderful swimmer," he said.

"Was he?" said the stranger. "That's just what I like myself. . . . But I never got on with my dad. We couldn't abide each other. He's been dead these ten years or more. Oh, I just cleared out from home, I couldn't stick it. . . . My young sister, now, she was different. You often get it that way, don't you? Fathers and daughters, mothers and sons, seem to get on best."

Alston's heart began beating very quickly, and he hardly dared to look at the stranger. He could hardly speak, but he managed to say:

"You live in London, don't you?"

"I can't say I live anywhere. I'm what they call a bird of paradise, I am, here to-day and gone to-morrow."

"But you've got a home in London?"

"How do you know that?"

"I'm just asking."

"Well, I have got a home in London, as it happens, and I mean to go there to-night for the first time in months. A surprise visit, like. They don't even know I'm in the country."

Alston looked admiringly at him, and said, with great joy in his heart:

"You know, I believe I could tell you something about that home of yours. . . . I shouldn't be surprised if there's a big photo of you over the mantelpiece and if your name's Willy Pascall."

It was indeed Willy Pascall back from Egypt, via Cardiff, and when he heard what terms Alston (whose aunt and uncle he knew) was on with his own mother and sister he was very surprised and pleased.

As soon as he had a little got over his surprise at the coincidence he said:

"Well, I mean to stay at home a bit now, and I want to see a lot of you. Come round to-morrow evening, will you? I dare say you know the way."

After a few minutes he said he thought he ought to go home before his mother was asleep, and clasping Alston's hand warmly, and smiling, he said:

"Good night, boy. See you to-morrow."

Alston, watching Pascall's retreating figure, felt quite overjoyed, and turned to go home. The night wind blew freshly in his face as he turned the corner near Pélagie's, and taking a deep breath of the fresh air he expanded his chest and began whistling quietly to himself, a thing he very rarely did. The odd chance of the way he had met Pascall seemed to him delightful, but Pascall himself seemed to him much more delightful. He had always felt a secret dread that Amy's brother would be rather a terrifying person who would despise him—and instead of that he seemed the most kind and easy and cheerful and frank and generous person imaginable. . . . As he turned down Cambodia Crescent he noticed the sports car standing opposite the house, where it so often stood. But somehow to-night he felt less interested in it than usual. It was as if speed and power were in his heart.

When he let himself into the house and went upstairs, the stair carpet made his ascent as silent as a ghost's. It wasn't even possible to kick the stair-rods inadvertently, for there were none, the carpet having been simply tacked down. Having arrived in his own room, he was about to undress, when he was startled to hear a knock on the door. Thinking he was mistaken he made no reply, but it was repeated, so he said "Come in!" hastily buttoning up his waistcoat again as he did so. It was Mr. Ramsamy.

"I beg your pardon," said the Indian in a low and rather nervous voice, as he advanced into the room, "for disturbing you at such a time, but I heard you come in and would like to ask your advice about something."

"Well, it's rather a funny time for a visit, isn't it?" said Alston. "But suppose you sit down. Smoke?"

"No, thanks," said Mr. Ramsamy, refusing the proffered cigarette. "It is about Mr. Fernandez, our landlord."

"Oh, yes."

"I understand from the servant that Mr. Fernandez thinks I came to live in this house because I am interested in his wife. Of course it is absurd, as I had never seen her before I came here. Now, almost every time I come in or go out I catch sight of him watching me, and this makes me feel uneasy, especially as I hear he is threatening to get his revenge on me. It is beginning to get on my nerves. Once when I opened my door he was standing just outside, and he didn't move away when I came out. And now I think he is there when he is not there. He moves very lightly, like a cat."

Alston tapped his forehead with his finger.

"Yes, I fear he is mad," said Mr. Ramsamy with a sigh. "The servant says he is suspicious of all men where his wife is concerned. Has he never threatened you?"

"Not yet," said Alston, "but I dare say my turn's coming."

"Now I wish to ask your advice," said the Indian. "Would you advise me to stay in the house or not?"

"Well," said Alston, "it's hard for me to say."

"What would you do, Mr. Alston, if you were in my place?"

"I think I should go."

"So you advise me to leave? It is a great nuisance, as I have only so lately moved in, but I cannot settle down to work with the thought that that man may be just outside my door, plotting some mischief."

"Well," said Alston, "I dare say nothing will happen if you stay. But you'd certainly be safer out of the way."

"Thank you. That was all I wanted to know. Then I think I shall leave."

And again apologising for his intrusion he said good-night and retired.

All the time the Indian had been in the room Alston had felt impatient. He was so excited and had so much to think about that he was afraid he would never get to sleep. He wondered why so many things had happened to him in one day, and looked eagerly forward to going to the Pascalls' the next evening. He also tried to imagine what Amy and her mother would tell Willy about him. More than anything in the world just then he wanted Willy Pascall to have a good opinion of him. . . .

When at last he fell asleep his sleep was full of wild dreams. He dreamed about the girls at Pélagie's, not at first about Amy, but about the girls he sometimes encountered as they were coming out of a side entrance when he was on his way back from work. Some of them were dressmaking hands, and others, prettier, were mannequins. With fluffy hair and painted lips, with chatter and silk stockings, they hurried past him, but one of them stopped and pointed to a motor car waiting at the kerb, a sports car, painted dark brown and light brown, with shining fittings. Amy was leaning out of the window of the car and beckoning to him to come and join her, which he did. Then they drove off. He could see the chauffeur's back, in a dark blue livery. He could also see the chauffeur's smiling face reflected in miniature in the little mirror attached to the side of the windscreen. Leaning forward, he recognised the face of Willy Pascall.

Then the dream took another form. He found himself in a large room which was evidently one of the dressmaking rooms at Pélagie's. The windows were heavily curtained, dressmakers' dummies stood here and there, and on a large table there were pieces of stuff, scissors, packets of pins, and sprays of artificial flowers. There was nobody in the room but Mrs.

Fernandez, who was sitting at a sewing-machine.
When she saw him she got up with a smile of welcome
and went out of the room. Then a door opened showing a room containing a large brass double bed. Amy
appeared in the doorway with some sewing in her
hand, but directly she saw him she took the pins out
of her mouth and the thimble off her finger and
beckoned to him to come into the other room. "Have
you seen Miss Brixworth?" he said. "Yes," said Amy.
"And what did she say about me?" he asked anxiously.
"She says she is very offended because you don't
come to see her more often." This worried Alston for
some time (or so it seemed), until Amy had disappeared, when he found himself face to face with his
father in a wet black swimming suit. His father said,
"Come on. Willy Pascall and I have been waiting for
you at the baths." Then Alston felt terribly ashamed
because he wasn't a very good swimmer and couldn't
dive very well either. He was so ashamed that he
woke up. . . .

Carol said to him next day:

"The Indian bloke's leaving."

"I know," said Alston, "I told him to go."

"You told him!"

"He came and asked me what he'd better do, and
I told him he'd be safer out of this house than in it."

"But you realise what you've done, don't you?
He's sure to pick on you, now."

"Who is?"

"Fernandez, of course."

"Why on me? Why not on you? Or on Mr. Rudd?"

"Because," said Carol mischievously, "you're younger and you've got more 'it' than either of us."

Alston laughed. He was only just beginning to be aware that he might be physically attractive to other people.

XIII

IT was very early in the morning, one of those autumn mornings which seem to belong more properly to summer, when there isn't a cloud in the sky, and the light, before the sun rises, is so clear and still and tinted that anybody who is awake, and who notices how this light lends to familiar scenes an air of enchantment, may well imagine themselves to be in a foreign country. The child Rosy Fernandez, lying awake in her little bed, was looking out of the window. Between the branches of the great plane tree which grew in the back garden could be seen a long row of tall houses, mostly greyish or dun-coloured (though one was a dull red) standing very silent and clear-cut against the sky, with all their chimney-pots crowded together and intersected with the thin lines of wireless aerials, like strands of cobweb. Beyond them stood that pearl-grey steeple, from which on Sundays and on one or two evenings during the week came a sound of bells which Rosy particularly disliked. No dog could have been more distressed by them. Perhaps some atavistic nerve, telling of panic or pogrom, was touched by those loud chimes—they seemed to madden the child, filling her with a mixture of fear and melancholy, so that she would thrust her fingers into her ears and hide in a cupboard or under the table. "I can do nothing with her," Mrs. Gambitt would say, having tried to banish these fears by reason. But this morning the steeple was silent, was just turning golden at the tip, the room was peaceful and filled with a faint greenish radiance that came through the fading curtain of plane-leaves outside the window, and Rosy, still barely awake, lay curled up deliciously in bed. Whatever she might have inherited from her father, she had from her mother the power of enjoying herself in little things, and loved her food, her games, the kindness of Alston or Miss Brixworth, her warm bed, the view from the window —it was a view she was to remember to her dying day, just as it was now, clear, peaceful, without bells, and seen through the thinning foliage of the plane tree.

As she became more wide awake, she would have liked to get into her parents' bed, which was her usual early morning privilege, but it was a pleasure she wasn't allowed to enjoy until they were both awake, and she knew now, without turning over, that her mother was still asleep, because she could hear her deep and easy breathing. She wondered if her father was yet awake. She could hear his breath rising and falling huskily in the intervals of her mother's, but she couldn't be sure if he was awake or not, and felt too comfortable to turn over and make sure. Probably he was still asleep, for at this time he was usually asleep—she had heard him tell Mrs. Gambitt that he never slept more than three hours a night, and that was usually in the morning.

This remark had made a deep impression on her, and when she asked her mother what it meant, Mrs. Fernandez said, "Because daddy isn't very well." That explained away all her father's eccentricities, and, unlike so many of the explanations that are given to children, it happened to be a truthful one.

Fernandez was awake. He had hardly slept a wink. He was sitting up against the pillows, which was his usual position, and smoking a cigarette, which was his usual custom when in bed. But he wasn't looking at the view. Nor was he actually thinking. He was brooding, with an uneasy sense of foreboding. He felt that something was going to happen. And he was right, for that very day something *did* happen, and proved to be almost more than he could bear.

The afternoon was one of those which Mrs. Porter and Mrs. Gambitt were in the habit of devoting to spiritual matters, not unaided by Mr. Swanage. In expectation of his coming Mrs. Porter had prepared an elaborately indigestible tea, and by four o'clock the two women and their visitor were all shut up together in Mrs. Porter's room. Of late Mrs. Fernandez had been rather impatient with Natalie Gambitt for talking so much about spiritualism and for trying to convert her to it. Mrs. Porter, too, seldom spoke of anything else. And both of them seemed to be quite obsessed with Mr. Swanage. Mrs. Fernandez, this particular afternoon, felt badly in need of someone to whom she could confide her troubles, and she went upstairs to find Miss Brixworth. But unfortunately Miss Brixworth was out, so she came slowly downstairs again to the office. It had become unusual for her to talk much to her husband about anything outside their own private, domestic affairs, but to-day she couldn't help herself.

"Do you know, Paul," she said, "I can't help wondering whether it's right for Natalie to spend so much time with all this spiritualism and stuff." She still spoke to him as if he were normal, like a mother with an idiot son for whom her love and hopes are one and the same. He looked sombrely at her now, as though he didn't quite take in what she was saying.

"When she and Mrs. Porter get together," Mrs. Fernandez went on, "you can't stop them. She's always going on at me about it—why won't I join them, and all that—but you know I don't quite like it. It doesn't seem right to me somehow. And there they are this afternoon, they've got this Mr. Swanage in again, and Natalie begged me to go in, but I wouldn't. I don't want to talk with the dead any more than I want to be with them."

"Who's Mr. Swanage?"

"Oh, Paul, you must have heard Natalie talking about him. She's always talking about him, and so is Mrs. Porter. He's a medium, and he comes here to make what Natalie calls a home circle."

As soon as she had spoken she wished that she had said nothing, but before her husband could reply, her attention was taken by Rosy, who said:

"Mummy, is Mrs. Porter a witch?"

"Heavens, child! Of course not! Wherever did you get such an idea?"

"Lottie says she's a witch because she rides on a broomstick."

At this Mrs. Fernandez couldn't help bursting out into a merry laugh, but, catching sight of the expression on her husband's face, she stopped abruptly.

"Why, Paul, whatever's the matter?"

Even as she spoke she guessed all too well what was the matter. Fernandez had at once connected her in his imagination with the repeated visits of Swanage to the house.

"Nothing," he said, staring out of the window.

Suddenly she felt a great pity for him. She loved him so much. She had an impulse to go and put her arms round his neck and caress him, but she knew that would be fatal—he would think she was trying to cajole him. So she pretended to be angry instead.

"Oh, Paul, I'm sorry I spoke! It's always the same whenever I talk to you about anything outside ourselves. You always get some strange idea into your head, and then you won't even tell me what it is. But don't think I care about your jealousy!" (It was the first time she had so frankly used this word for his behaviour.) "I don't! I've made up my mind that I won't care any more!" (Which meant, of course, that she was thinking of the very matter she cared most, and would go on caring most, about.) "No, I don't care any longer! I wish now that I'd gone up and joined them in their séance."

"Go, then," he said, with a sneer. "Who's trying to stop you?"

She made no answer, but picked up a bundle of clean linen from the table and went out of the room to put it away. But Fernandez had made up his mind about one thing, and that was that he must at all costs catch a glimpse of this Mr. Swanage, so he stood about near the door, which was slightly open, listening for any sound from upstairs which should suggest that the séance was over. Very soon he heard his wife coming back from the linen cupboard, and, not wishing that she should find him listening at the door, he came back into the room and sat down to play with Rosy. But now and again he would turn his head away and listen intently, and this didn't escape his wife's notice.

When Swanage made up his mind to go, Mrs. Gambitt said she would see him as far as the front door. He said goodbye to Mrs. Porter, came silently downstairs with Mrs. Gambitt, and the two of them were already crossing the hall before Fernandez heard them. He leapt up from his chair, put his head cautiously out, and was just in time to catch a glimpse of Swanage over Mrs. Gambitt's shoulder before she closed the front door. He couldn't see very clearly, as it was just getting dark, but Swanage's face at once struck him as unpleasantly familiar, and he came back into the room looking, in the twilight, even more ashen than usual. His wife noticed that he was trembling violently, that he sank into a chair as if his legs were not strong enough to support him, and that his head sank forward on his breast as it sometimes did when he was greatly upset. She saw, and trembled herself. But she made up her mind not to ask him what was the matter, because she thought she knew. She thought he had simply selected Swanage as the latest victim of his jealousy, and as Mrs. Gambitt came into the room and switched on the light she cast an appealing look at her which Mrs. Gambitt was at a loss to understand. But actually the matter was less simple than she thought.

It may be remembered that Fernandez had once quarrelled with a man who had been his partner in business. He considered that his partner had been at fault, had violated their agreement, and had conspired to defraud him, though none of these things had actually been true. He had made himself impossible, broken the agreement, and by his unreasonable behaviour had prevented any further understanding from being reached, so that the other man was left out of pocket and out of temper, and although he could have sued Fernandez he thought it better to shrug his shoulders and have nothing more to do with him. But for Fernandez that affair hadn't been simply a business difficulty with a certain amount of personal unpleasantness mixed up with it —it had been an emotional crisis of the first magnitude. He had got it into his head that the ex-partner was full of a revengeful spirit (as well he might have been) and was out to "down" him, and for weeks after he had seen him for the last time he had been haunted by the man's face, and was continually looking round corners or over his shoulder to see if he wasn't being watched and followed. Gradually, however, he had forgotten his fears, and in recent months it had only been when he was feeling more than usually ill and idle and depressed that he sometimes thought of his partner again.

But now all the old wounds were opened once more, for in catching that glimpse of Swanage at the front door Fernandez was convinced that he was looking once more at the face of his partner, and a thousand suspicions, like vicious little red ants, had swarmed into his mind, and were stinging and goading him into madness. It was true that in the half-light Swanage's face was not unlike that of Fernandez' late partner. But what seemed to make his identity even more certain was that the partner's name had been Swanwick. This coincidence was to Fernandez a proof. What more likely, he thought, than that Swanwick had changed his name to Swanage (like the swindlers that are shown up in *John Bull*) in order to hide his shady business dealings? And what could be more likely than that Swanwick, or Swanage, as he now called himself, had worked out a fiendish plot to get his own back on Fernandez? Posing as a medium (so Fernandez reasoned) Swanage had not only wormed his way into this very house, but had won the confidence of two of the womenfolk in it. Thus strongly entrenched, what could be more likely than that he would use all his energies to captivate, to seduce and perhaps to run away with Mrs. Fernandez, using Mrs. Gambitt's influence over her as a lever? As he thought over the diabolical ingenuity of this plan, never from that instant in the least doubting that it existed, Fernandez was almost beside himself with helpless rage and fear.

All that the two women noticed that evening was that he was rather more silent than usual, and that he paid a great deal of attention to Rosy, playing with her and generally petting and spoiling her. But at the same time there was a sense of strain, and Mrs. Fernandez felt uneasy. When she went to bed she couldn't get off to sleep. She lay wondering when her husband would come up to bed himself. By the time he arrived, she was just dozing off, but woke up again abruptly.

"Oh, Paul," she said, "here you are at last. Whatever have you been doing all this time?"

"I've been thinking," he said.

"What've you been thinking about?"

"I've been thinking that it would be far better if we could get away from here, if we could live right away from here by ourselves somewhere—in another country——"

"But where? And how?"

"Oh, I know you don't want to go away," he said. "I know you've got good reasons for staying here."

"I don't understand what you mean," she said. "Why don't you come to bed?"

He was standing by the fireplace. Suddenly he turned round and with a deliberate swing of his arm swept everything off the mantelpiece—a vase, a clock, two toys, an apple, letters, matches, a tin box full of buttons, an ashtray, a calendar, two glass ornaments, and some odds and ends. The things fell into the fender with a loud clatter.

"Oh, Paul!" she cried in horror. "Whatever did you do that for? Smashing all those things—the clock——!"

She looked to see if Rosy had been woken up, but by a miracle the child was still sleeping peacefully. Fernandez caught hold of the bed-rail, gripping it tightly with both hands and glaring at his wife.

"Ah, you think I'm a pretty fool, don't you?" he said. "You think I'm blind and deaf and dumb and that I can't read you like a book, but *I* know your plans, *I* know what you want to do! You think you're much too clever for me, but as long as there's a breath in my body you're going to do what I tell you, do you hear?"

And with that he rushed at her and, slipping his hands into her splendid bushy hair, caught hold of it and began to press her head backwards and to shake her frantically. She wanted to scream for help but was afraid of waking the child, and struggled in silence to free herself. When at last he let her go she buried her face in the pillow and wept. Sleep was

P

out of the question, she knew it was useless to argue with him, and in the midst of her fear and excited misery she waited for those tender words and caresses which usually followed quickly upon her husband's outbursts of violence. But to-night none came. He made no sign, but sat smoking and brooding by her side, while her head ached and her heart ached through the long uncertain hours, and she didn't dare to move, but lay in one position till she ached all over.

In the morning she relieved her feelings by weeping on Mrs. Gambitt's shoulder and telling her what had happened. After consoling her Mrs. Gambitt held her at arm's length.

"Look at you, Beryl, you're not fit to be seen, with those great shadows under your eyes and the bruises on your arms. Oh, the brute, if I could only——!"

"No, no, Natalie, he doesn't mean it! It's only because he's ill. Perhaps he's afraid he's going to die. You mustn't blame him, but I couldn't help—I couldn't help—just telling you——"

She broke off with a sob and hid her face against her friend's shoulder. She didn't see the look of grim determination on Mrs. Gambitt's face, but later in the morning Mrs. Gambitt went out shopping and her determination bore fruit. She went up to a policeman.

"Can I have a word with you?" she said.

"Certainly," said the policeman, stooping down with a sympathetic and attentive expression on his face. She told him about Fernandez' behaviour towards his wife, and suggested that he should come and speak to Fernandez about it.

"Well, you see, it's like this," said the policeman, looking very serious, for he was a married man himself, "it's not too easy to interfere between husband and wife. Unless he actually knocks her about——"

"Well, what more do you want than what I've told you?"

"Well, if she likes to come along and lodge a complaint, perhaps something can be done——"

"Oh, she'd never do that," said Mrs. Gambitt, "she'd rather let herself be butchered in cold blood. Then I suppose you'd condescend to act," she added bitterly, and went brusquely away, the policeman staring after her with a puzzled and slightly aggrieved air.

When she got back to the house Mrs. Fernandez took her excitedly aside.

"Natalie, d'you know what it is? I've found out what it is!"

"What *what* is?" said Mrs. Gambitt.

"What's upsetting Paul. It's that Mr. Swanage."

"What! He must be mad."

"Natalie, that's what's troubling him, I'm sure, it's Mr. Swanage. So please, please don't let him come to the house again."

"But it's impossible—he hasn't seen him," Mrs. Gambitt protested.

"Oh yes, he has. He misses nothing."

"But what will Mrs. Porter say? Do you realise that the man has actually put her in touch with her late husband? Do you want to spoil her happiness? Haven't I told you that he's given her a new lease of life? I'm sure if I tell her that Mr. Swanage can't come here she'll want to go somewhere else where she *can* see him."

"Oh no, Natalie, not if you use your influence with her."

"My influence! How can anybody let rooms when no man is to be allowed near the house?"

"I know it's difficult, dear, but think of me. Don't you think some lady medium could take Mr. Swanage's place?"

"Mrs. Porter'd be terribly upset."

"But Paul's terribly upset! He thinks it's a man he used to know, who wronged him, and is persecuting him."

"The same old story!" cried Mrs. Gambitt.

"Oh, Natalie, you've done everything for me. Don't fail me now!" Mrs. Fernandez put her arms round her friend's neck. This was too much for Mrs. Gambitt. There was only one person in the world who loved her at all, and when that person appealed tenderly to her for help all her sternness melted, and she was ready to overcome any difficulty, even though to do so might go against the common sense she had won by hard experience.

"There is a Mrs. Trubshore——" she said in a low voice, and patted Mrs. Fernandez consolingly. Her face was set in a look of fierce determination, and she gazed out at the plane tree without seeing it, for she was struggling to repress her feelings. The look of gratitude with which Mrs. Fernandez at once rewarded her would have given her the strength to drive a hundred Swanages away from the house, and before another day was out she had been to see Swanage himself, had told him that Mrs. Porter would be away for a few weeks, and had also told Mrs. Porter that Swanage had suddenly been called away on business for a similar period. She then telephoned to Mrs. Trubshore, a lady medium who was an old acquaintance of hers, and arranged that she should come and see Mrs. Porter. This arrangement seemed to satisfy everybody.

XIV

As usually happened when he came home, Willy Pascall found himself made much of. On his return from one escapade or another his mother and sister had made no secret of their pleasure at seeing him with them again, and he took their attentions for granted, just as he did the curiosity and admiration of a neighbour here or a young woman there. He always looked forward to meeting old acquaintances at these times, just as they looked forward to seeing him, for he wasn't the kind of person that is quickly forgotten, and being a good talker he amused people. In these intervals he had always quickly found some special companion with whom to spend the greater part of his time—he needed an audience, he needed admiration, he didn't like being alone. Sometimes a young woman had taken his fancy, sometimes a young man of his own age, sometimes both, but never had he found such an audience, such admiration, or any companion who pleased him so much as Alston.

"You two seem just made for each other," said Mrs. Pascall, beaming on the two of them sitting by her fireside while she laid the table for their supper.

"We are," said her son.

Amy, at first delighted that her brother and her sweetheart should get on so well together, began to feel a little piqued at the way they monopolised each other. She had to wait nearly a fortnight for the chance of seeing Alston alone for any length of time. It was a fine warm evening for the time of year and they wandered into Hyde Park. He was talking about Cambodia Crescent and he told her for the first time about Mrs. Rudd. Amy had some very plain words to say about that lady, and it was some time before she would leave the subject.

"I don't think it's right for you to go on living in a house like that," she said. "You know I never wanted you to go there. . . . You'll be telling me the same about that Miss Brixworth soon, I bet she's up to no good——"

Alston laughed.

"Eric, what's happened to that fellow that was trying to increase his height to get into the police?"

"Carol, you mean? Oh, he's too busy nowadays to have any time for stretching himself. Besides, Lottie takes up most of his spare time——"

"Who's Lottie?"

"Oh, she's a girl that comes in to help with the work."

"What's she like? You've never told me a word about her. That house is just like a harem, it seems to me. And one thing I do know, you've never got any time for me nowadays——"

"Oh, Amy——"

"No, you haven't!"

"Well, if Willy hadn't come back——"

"Oh, I wish Willy never *had* come back, he just makes you forget all about me. I don't know what you see in him that makes you think such a lot of him."

"Oh yes, you do," he said, "you know you just worship him yourself."

"I don't worship him! Of course I *like* him, but that's only natural, isn't it, seeing that he's my brother?"

"Well, how could I help liking anybody that was *your* brother?"

He paid her the compliment with that ironical politeness which is so often natural to the English, and although she saw through it she couldn't help being pleased by it.

"Oh, go on," she replied, and slipped her arm into his, complaining that she couldn't see the way properly, for they had taken a very dark path. They reached a heavily shadowed spot from which the Serpentine could be seen, glimmering beyond the trees.

"Let's stop here," he said, leaning against a railing, "I want a smoke."

He lighted a cigarette, and as the match was struck she gave a quick glance at his face as if to read his thoughts. He mischievously decided to go on talking about her brother in order to tease her.

"What I like about Willy," he said, "is that he really makes you feel that life's worth living—here, you're not listening to me," he added, catching hold of her and drawing her towards him in such a close embrace that she could smell the brilliantine on his hair and was aware of the beating of his heart.

"No, I'm not," she said, pretending to struggle.

"Why not?" he said, still holding her tightly with one hand while the other began to explore.

"I don't want to hear about Willy now," she said.

"Then what do you want to hear?" he said, looking close into her upturned face, which he could scarcely see in the dark. "I know," he said, "you don't want to hear anything at all, do you?"

Leaning against him now in soft surrender, her breath coming and going against his cheek, she wondered at his purposefulness, and then gave up wondering, for he kissed her as though something long lost were restored to him, and almost crushed her in his arms, squeezing her flesh in his hands as one squeezes a fruit from which every drop of sweetness must be wrung. And all round them was the deep and soothing evening murmur of the Park, like the very sound of life itself, an immense murmur made up of the traffic of human beings going about their business and pleasure, a rich and subtle and continuous sound which it takes more than motor-cars to make, for it must contain as well the cries of infants, the ranting of demagogues, the tapping of the blind man's stick, the happy laughter of young girls, the vomiting of drunkards, the stirring of squirrels in their sleep, the fall of leaves, the growth of trees, the threats of blackmailers, the solicitations of whores,

the shuffling steps of lecherous old men, the banter
of soldiers, the coy shrieks of housemaids, the shy
kisses of young lovers, the worm in the bud, and the
millionaire's last words. . . .

Amy was brought in touch with two mysteries that
night. First that love, the best and most unattainable
goal of all longing, can never be fully realised in experience.   Second, that Alston loved her, in a sense,
for her brother's sake, and that this had been so even
before he had met Willy, that it had always been so,
in fact.

When you looked at Willy Pascall's face, and especially his eyes, you could see that he was hiding nothing.
His frank and open expression (the exact reverse of
Fernandez') was haunted by nothing much more
sinister than a kind of light mockery. He had a charm
which women often found irresistible, but with his
power over women and his appetite for them went an
unmistakable contempt. Their admiration for him
united to his own self-esteem wasn't enough for him
—there was always this need of being admired and
respected by and intimate with other men. And now,
in his friendship with Alston, he was beginning to
enjoy in his own way one of the greatest of all
pleasures, the power of influencing an immature
person to make him appreciate what one believes to
be good or right or agreeable. He was in the way of
becoming a Hercules to the younger man's Hylas,
"that the lad might be fashioned to his mind, and
might drive a straight furrow, and come to the true

measure of man." And Pascall's code of life was a simple and reasonable one, not too common among the English. He believed that what was most vital, healthy and pleasant was right, so his life was unusually free from the Gothic drabness that troubles the spirit of our race. To see him striding along with his cap on one side, his hair curling and a cigarette stuck behind his ear, to hear him singing as he walked, you might have thought him, but for an obvious Englishness about him, a native of some sunnier country than ours.

Under the influence of this being, it wasn't surprising that Alston became more cheerful and talkative than usual, began to find life more enjoyable than he had realised hitherto, and to get more confidence in himself. Pascall talked incessantly whether they were at his home or out together. He was full of anecdotes of the Navy, of foreign countries and odd events in which he had played a part. His talk was highly seasoned and in certain ways sophisticated, and he wasn't without an eye for effect—everything he said was designed to produce a certain image of himself and a certain view of life in Alston's mind. They went swimming together, they went to the dog races, they met various kinds of people that were new to Alston. Pascall had an interest in physical culture and was an expert in muscle control, and the sight of his firm and supple body, with its movements so easy, confident and splendid, and its tattooed symbols of experience on the white skin, began to teach

Alston to take pride in his own body, which, with Pascall's help, he began to exercise and develop.

One evening, when they were walking past one of the largest and most expensive hotels in London, Pascall said, "I used to work there as a cellar porter once." His experiences there had given him his first view of the lives of the rich. He described the behaviour of a well-known politician, who had risen from nothing to a suite of rooms at this very hotel, where he had given himself up to self-indulgence in the intervals of "leading" the suffering poor. There figured in the story a fat tart who tried to get the hotel servants to call her "my lady," a page-boy remarkable for a pretty face and a cheeky manner, and a long succession of bottles. In contrast to this, Pascall was able to describe the conditions under which the dirty work of this celebrated hotel was done. When not otherwise occupied, he was sometimes put on to cutting up large old potatoes into the shapes of small new potatoes, for which they were made to pass. The parings were all cooked up together for the servants.

"It's bloody hot in those kitchens," he said, "and I could tell you a story about that. One day an order came down for a very special kind of omelette. Well, the fellow that had to make it, a French fellow he was, was as hot as hell. In the middle of the summer it was, and he was just sweating like a pig. You could see the sweat just running down his face into the omelette. 'Here, what d'you call that,' I said, 'an omelette à la sweat?' But he didn't take no notice. He just went on beating it up, and the sweat just pouring off him. I should say there was more sweat in that omelette than anything else. And the beauty of it was, that the people that ordered it sent down a message of congratulation to the chef!"

When he heard this story Alston was rather proud of knowing what an omelette was, and he didn't forget that it was Miss Brixworth who had taught him. At the same time he couldn't understand how he had been content to live so quietly when the whole world lay round him to be tasted. Pascall's influence made him realise how airless and unhealthy life was at 45 Cambodia Crescent, and in consequence made him discontented. He entered the house now with a certain swagger, but the atmosphere inside was not encouraging. Vague rumours, fragments of gossip, suspicion, superstition, and a faint but pervasive odour of decay seemed to glide with the freedom of ghosts through closed doors and solid walls into the troubled breasts of the inhabitants, each of whom seemed to live in a shadow—Mrs. Fernandez in the shadow of her husband, Carol in the shadow of over-work, Miss Brixworth in the shadow of the past, Mrs. Porter in the shadow of the Hereafter, and so on.

Everybody knew that séances had been held in Mrs. Porter's room. Mrs. Rudd was curious, Miss Brixworth still shocked and disapproving, and in the kitchen Carol delighted to give Lottie the most hair-raising accounts of what happened at those meetings, telling her the wildest lies with such a serious air that she gradually got worked up into a kind of hysteria, terrified by the knowledge that these tales, being based on actual happenings, might be true, and fascinated by the relish with which Carol told them, licking his red lips and pushing his lank black hair back from his forehead. Everybody knew that Swanage had been forbidden the house, and everybody knew that Fernandez had threatened to do violence to his wife if he caught her exchanging a word with Swanage, whether by word of mouth or by letter. And more than one person in the house was worried about Mrs. Fernandez. Miss Brixworth, for example, had noticed, or thought she had noticed, that the position was getting worse.

"Mrs. Fernandez looks frightened," she said to Carol.

"She *is* frightened, Miss Brixworth."

"I'm so afraid Fernandez may do somebody an injury, Carol."

"Oh, sure, and he will. It's only a matter of time. If he sees that Swanage again, now——"

"She's not getting mixed up in all this spirit business, is she?"

"Mrs. Fernandez, you mean? No, not yet," said Carol, "but she will. She can't help it. Mrs. Gambitt's always on at her about it. And they've got a new woman at it now. Oh, she's a terror. A fat one with a rolling eye. Mrs. Trubshore they call her, and she'd give you the creeps before you'd time to darken the room, I should say. Wait till Fernandez gets in with them—I expect he'll think the spooks are all after his wife.''

Miss Brixworth had a feeling that Mrs. Fernandez was, if not in danger, at least in a very uncertain position, and she longed to do something about it. But all she could do was to discuss the matter for the hundredth time with Miss Haymer. She found her friend gouty and nervous, in an aggressive, talkative sort of mood, a mood which made her impatient of argument—except where Empringham was concerned. Miss Brixworth had been secretly amused to notice how the manservant was beginning to command the mistress. He even ordered Miss Haymer now to do this or do that, where Miss Brixworth would never have dared to order her, and what was curious was that the dictatorial Miss Haymer, who would never have obeyed anybody else, obeyed him. It was clear that Empringham's inlaid fittings would never be used for their original purpose. They would just stay where they were, for their maker had at last become, in the space of two or three months, what his character had long destined him for—an "old retainer." No actor could have played the part better and more unobtrusively than he did, and of course he was exactly the kind of servant that Miss Haymer needed. "I can't think why I put up with maids for so long," she said. And Miss Brixworth, while she found a certain comedy in the position, was a little jealous.

"Oh, that old house of yours!" Miss Haymer exclaimed impatiently when Miss Brixworth began talking about Cambodia Crescent. "You ought to get out more."

"So ought Mrs. Fernandez, Fanny."

"Why, what's wrong with her now?"

"I don't like the look of things at all," said Miss Brixworth.

"Nonsense. Why don't you mind your own business?"

"I like her, Fanny. I'm sorry for her."

"Well, you can't just go round being sorry for everybody. What's up? Has he begun to knock her about, or what?"

"No, not exactly, but he might at any time. Meanwhile he must be driving her to distraction with his frightful jealousy."

"Nonsense, Connie, he won't hurt her."

"But I'm afraid he will. Or what's much more likely, he'll attack one of these men suddenly. Supposing he were to lie in wait for Carol, or that nice young Alston, or Rudd, who looks to me the meekest sort of creature. How awful it would be!"

"Yes," said Miss Haymer. "But just a minute. You haven't told me much about Alston lately. Do you still see him nowadays?"

"Yes, he still comes and has tea with me sometimes. Such a nice boy! And he seems to have woken up a lot lately, and to enjoy life much more than he did."

"Really? 'The awakening of spring,' I suppose, in

spite of the autumn, or your influence, Connie, perhaps? But to return to Fernandez. What you don't understand is that he won't hurt anybody. What, a man who's as fond of his child as you say he is? The idea's absurd. Don't try and make him out a villain. Human beings, you know, are much less dangerous than they seem—especially men. Haven't you found that out yourself? I remember once, near Jannina, an age ago it seems, a really awkward moment, not to say an ugly one, when I was for an instant very much at a loss, but although I had the wind up I managed not to show it, and knowing it was useless to storm or threaten or get worked up at all, for I was in fact absolutely helpless, I had the sense to turn sentimental, and luckily it worked, for my Greek took me just far enough for that, aided by a modest *œillade*, and the man simply turned out a lamb. You can imagine the headlines—*Adventurous Englishwoman Disappears ; Balkan Tragedy Suspected*— 'Miss Frances Haymer, the well-known traveller, has failed to return from an expedition, says a Reuter message from Athens—remote region—dangerous without adequate protection—known to have been unaccompanied — infested with brigands — rocky ravines — search party's failure — Miss Haymer, daughter of—and author of several—has lectured—' and so on, and so on. Instead of which, Connie, that dagger which hangs over the writing-table, the one with the chased silverwork on the handle, was actually his. . . . And I never even asked for it. He gave it me

Q

when I went away, just to remember him by, he said. Anything might have happened, and nothing did happen—at least, nothing unpleasant. . . . As for your Fernandez, he's not such a brigand as he's made out to be, either. He's just got a bee in his bonnet. Tell her to humour him a bit. Flattery'll do it. No man's worth worrying too much about. And don't be afraid of his knocking her about. He won't hurt her."

"But, Fanny——"

"Oh, a little of the rough stuff won't matter. I expect she enjoys it."

"Fanny! But suppose something *did* happen?"

"Well, she mustn't go against him, she must humour him, and nothing *will* happen."

"Oh, Fanny, you don't understand——"

"That's right, call me a fool. Have I lived all these years for nothing?"

"But, you see——"

"Oh, I see very clearly, I assure you, and what I see is this, that these two people are passionately fond of each other, and that's just where you fail, you're so English that you can't see that a really grand passion can be anything but wicked. You can't see that pleasure can be glorious. No, if it's pleasant it's wrong, that's what the English always think, and it's a dreary, wretched, mean, pinched, puritanical way of looking at things."

"It may be," said Miss Brixworth, "but if to be foreign is to be mad, I think I'd rather be English."

"There!" cried Miss Haymer. "That's typical!

Pure jingoism, Connie! You can't maffick under *my* roof! 'The mad foreigner'! Let me tell you, Connie, I long ago came to the conclusion that it's far better to be a mad foreigner than a cold egg. And what if this man *does* sock somebody in the jaw? Won't that add to the gaiety of Cambodia Crescent? God knows it must need a little gaiety. Is life lived so fully and richly and dangerously in your street that a little display of feeling—emotion—guts—wouldn't come as a welcome change?"

"I'm sorry, Fanny," said Miss Brixworth, who, though feeling browbeaten and rather terrified at her friend's energy and slanginess, was trying to stick to her guns, "but I can't see why love can't be a matter of gentleness instead of what you call a display of guts."

"And I can't see why there shouldn't be both, and I dare say there *are* both in this case, and I think you're making a terrific fuss about nothing. It all comes from that kind heart of yours, but I'm sure Mrs. Fernandez can very well take care of herself."

"Well, Fanny, I only hope you're right."

"And now, my dear, let's change the subject. . . . I meant to ask you, did you see that the member for this division has died suddenly, and we're to have a bye-election. The conservative candidate, so the papers say, will be Sir Herbert Fogg."

"He'll certainly get *my* vote," said Miss Brixworth. "He's sure to be one of the Wiltshire Foggs, who were friends of my great-aunt Ada's."

"I'm afraid he's only a London Fogg, my dear—

one of those dense ones that obscure everything. And you'll find that this election will be the usual absurd affair. There'll be what they call a three-cornered fight. That is to say, there'll be a conservative, a liberal and a labour man—all conservatives really, though the liberal man'll be neither one thing nor the other nor anything else. And the *most* conservative of the three will of course be elected. What on earth we want to go on with parliamentary government for, I can't imagine."

"But, Fanny, what could we have instead?"

"A soviet, I suppose. Or at any rate some business-like way of running the country for the benefit of the inhabitants."

Miss Brixworth was rather afraid to enter on a discussion of politics, but the mention of the word "soviet" gave her courage, for she believed what she read in the *Morning Post* about Russia, and what was more, she still wanted to believe that England under Edward VII. was all that a country ought to be.

"Fanny, when you talk like that about soviets and such things," she said, "you know I can't take you very seriously."

"Then you ought to," said Miss Haymer. "I'm all for the Reds myself."

Miss Brixworth made up her mind that she must pray to God to regulate her friend's political views as well as her health.

"But, Fanny," she said, "they're the enemies of religion."

"They've made politics their religion and the cinemas their churches," said Miss Haymer.

"And you want everybody to be exactly like everybody else, like ants or bees?"

"Connie, to tell you the truth, I don't think much of the use human beings have made of their freedom. All these liberal ideas just led to the War and financial and social chaos. And all this wasteful and sterile self-seeking! Look at your fellow-inmates at Cambodia Crescent. How do they use their precious freedom? Are they beautiful or useful? Do they enjoy themselves? How do they spend their time? In abortive attempts at witchcraft. Are any of them in the least interested in anything beyond their own petty affairs? Not they! No, my experience has taught me that most, probably all, human beings are only fit to be ordered about for the common good. This old-fashioned English idea of democracy is just a fancy that ends in slaughter. Let's have nice, useful ants and bees rather than Mrs. Gambitts, Mrs. Porters or Mrs. Rudds, or men like Fernandez who have thought so much about themselves that their egoism has become a mania. Let's have a humane system where each gives according to his ability and gets according to his needs. Let's put an end to wasteful competition, to war, and peace, too, if it means having half a generation growing up on the dole and the other half on the gossip columns. My idea is an aristocracy which shall include everybody."

"You're even more of an idealist than I am, Fanny. And you think that Russia——"

"I'm not talking about Russia. I'm talking about England. We aren't Russians, and we shall have to work things out in our own way, and it could never be exactly the same way the Russians have taken. But I wish they'd stop teaching children to say 'I'm British, and proud of it.' When people have nothing else to be proud of, they say 'I'm proud to be British or French or American' or whatever it is. Why don't they say 'I'm proud to be healthy, or intelligent, or hard-working, or a human being'? What on earth is the point of nationalism? Some day it will seem as ridiculous as the narrow-mindedness of colonials or provincials. To be a nationalist to-day is to be definitely provincial."

"But, Fanny, you don't really think that you and I would make very good communists, do you?"

"Of course I don't. How could we? We're the products of a different age and a different way of thinking. We're of about as much importance in the world to-day as the bones of our grandmothers. But if we can't *do* anything, let's at any rate try and *think* a little, and make things easier for the people who come after us, the people who are growing up now. You see, to-day it's like this, business means more than culture and the flesh is honoured more than the spirit. Well, before we can get on (not get *back*, everybody talks about getting *back*), before we can get *on* to a world where a new culture can appear, we've got to have a gigantic spring-cleaning. And that's communism. People say that they're afraid of being standardised. Well, what about it? Are they so damned original to-day? Of course not, they're all pretty well standardised as it is, only while they're about it they might as well do it systematically. . . . As for you and I, Connie, as I was saying, we're just a couple of old women of no importance, and it's no good pretending we can move with the times. We can't. But we needn't try and act as a brake on the wheel, for all that, and I tell you, if there were a communist candidate standing in this election, I'd vote for him."

"Then I think you're inconsistent," said Miss Brixworth, "for if the communists were to get into power, which I hope and believe they won't, at any rate in our lifetimes, you'd lose your income and be turned into the gutter and probably get shot or starved."

"Well, Connie, of what conceivable interest could that be to anybody but me? Millions of better people than me were shot in the War, and millions have starved since."

Before Miss Brixworth could answer, Empringham came into the room and addressing himself to Miss Haymer said:

"Excuse me interrupting, madam, but if you don't have a bit of a rest now you know you won't sleep a wink to-night."

"I'm afraid he's right, Connie——"

"My dear, it's really time I was going. It was only that we were having such an interesting discussion——"

"I hate allowing you to go, my dear, but I know Empringham's right, I really ought to rest. And don't worry too much about Red Ruin, Connie. I'm not a real Bolshevik, am I, Empringham?"

"I'm sure I shouldn't have thought you was, madam," said Empringham, and as he showed Miss Brixworth out of the flat he said:

"You remember we spoke about this that day I met you in the street, madam? You see how excited she gets? I don't always agree with her myself, but it's no good going against her too much. You want to 'umour her a bit, you know, and let her think she's right. She likes to let off steam a bit, doesn't she?'

"Ah, well, Empringham, people never agree about politics, do they?"

Miss Brixworth made her way slowly back to Cambodia Crescent through the autumn afternoon sunshine. She felt very tired after so much argument, and depressed by the turn it had taken. It made her despair, it made her feel such a back number, so useless, for Fanny was a clever woman, and although she mightn't be altogether right, there must be a good deal in what she said. . . . Pale sunlight lay tranquilly upon the town, on towers and trees and on the shabby-genteel Victorian streets through which she passed. The houses were large, but most of them had been divided into flats, and many were in need of a coat of paint. There was a wintry chill in the air, and the distant strains of a barrel-organ added more than a touch of melancholy to the moment. People occasionally turned to look at Miss Brixworth, or nudged each other at sight of her, for she cut rather a strange figure—at once benevolent and rather odd, she seemed and felt very much what she was, a survivor from a lost or losing world, trying to behave as it had behaved, to believe what it had believed, and apparently bearing no relation whatever to a world that contained communism or Willy Pascall or that car which had so often caught Alston's eye and which was now standing, as it so often did, opposite 45 Cambodia Crescent. Miss Brixworth noticed neither the car nor the people who noticed her, for she was deep in thought.

When she reached her room she got out her work-basket. Such was her poverty that she was now reduced to the possession of only one hat, and she felt that the time had come to adapt it to the season. All through the summer it had been trimmed with a cluster of four pink roses. They had been good roses, and considering how long they had been exposed to the London air, had kept their freshness remarkably well—no doubt they would see her through another summer, Miss Brixworth reflected, as she took them off and began to replace them with an ornament more suitable for the winter months. This was a band of dark wine-coloured velvet with a narrow edging of dark-brown fur. As she bent over the work, and paused to thread her needle, she was still thoughtful, and with very good reason, for she was faced with the prospect of obtaining and spending a sum of money she could at the moment only get with difficulty and could ill afford to spend. Had it been simply a matter of money she needed for herself she would probably have contrived to do without it, but it was for Rosy she wanted the money. She had never been able to resist Rosy, and although Mrs. Fernandez said she was spoiling the child, the mother could never help being pleased at the attention paid to her offspring. And only recently Rosy had again reminded Miss Brixworth of her longing to possess a rocking-horse, and Miss Brixworth had determined that she should have one.

After turning the matter over in her mind, she hit on the only possible plan. It happened that not very far from Cambodia Crescent—in Parthenon Street, in fact—there was a furniture depository, with salerooms attached, which belonged to one of the big department stores, and she had stored there some few odds and ends of her old belongings. Among them was a small mahogany bureau which she could very easily get rid of, for she knew that she would never be likely to be in a position to furnish rooms for herself again, and although she valued it as one of her few remaining treasures, she reminded herself that she was getting old, and that it might just as well be turned into money and into joy for some young and budding life. After all, Rosy would soon be grown up. She didn't have much of a life, poor child. Let her enjoy things while she could. Besides, by making this little sacrifice Miss Brixworth felt that she would not only please herself as well as Rosy, but she would be doing something to justify her existence and to show that not everybody at Cambodia Crescent was exclusively self-centred or what Fanny Haymer chose to call individualistic. So without telling anybody, she went quietly off next morning and made arrangements for her bureau to be sold at one of the weekly auctions held by the firm with which it had been stored.

And on the day of the sale she went in person to attend the proceedings. The atmosphere of the salerooms was extremely depressing. To begin with, it was a wet day, so the light was dim and greyish, and people came in with wet mackintoshes and dripping umbrellas. There were very few people, however, and a great many things to be sold. And such things! The rooms were packed with cast-off furniture and bric-à-brac, mostly rubbish, though here and there could be seen something good, antique, or solidly made. Miss Brixworth was not usually much given to self-pity, but on this occasion she couldn't help remembering how Fanny Haymer had pointed out to her what a useless old survival she was, and she couldn't help feeling a little sorry for herself and for other people, especially those of her own class, who had lost their possessions and whatever social standing they might formerly have had.

When the auctioneer appeared, he turned out to be an elderly individual with a seedy moustache and a complete lack of enthusiasm. He indulged in none of those humorous sallies which are so important a part of an auctioneer's technique, and did nothing whatever to put his audience in a good temper. It was true that nothing on earth could have made them into reckless spendthrifts, least of all the goods that were set out before them, but still, thought Miss Brixworth, he might have made *some* effort. And after stifling a yawn, she began to try and calculate how long it would be before her bureau was put up to the bidding of these bedraggled-looking buyers. She opened the catalogue and began to read:

LOT 47.—*19 pieces of tea ware, 3 cloisonné vases, a brass fitting, 5 tumblers, bed pan, a small tray, 2 hand mirrors, a scent spray, a pair of horns, 2 cushions.*

And she began to imagine the household that had contained these things — a domineering invalid mother-in-law—frequent scenes—a smell of bad cooking. . . .

LOT 48.—*A plated toaster, an oxidized biscuit box, a pair of female figures, a gent's free wheel bicycle, a plated tantalus.*

A plated tantalus! Oh, this must be a more pretentious sort of household. Perhaps they were also the owners of

LOT 49.—*A very handsome Double Walnut Bedstead and bedding.*   (Special.)

Special, perhaps, but it only fetched two pounds, and Miss Brixworth's heart sank. What came next?

Lot 50.—*A trunk containing a pair of shoes, a collar box with 11 collars, a pair lady's stockings, a bundle of roller blinds, sundry pieces of wireless, and 50 magazines* (approx.).

Surely there must be people even more hard up than she was herself if they could be reduced to selling an old trunk, with frayed collars and tattered magazines!

Lot 51.—*A coal vase, an ebonized overmantel, a child's wicker easy chair, the Holy Bible in 4 vols., a smoker's companion, a milking stool, a deal jardinière.*

Poor child, what a dreadfully dull family it must have grown up in, standing on its creaking wicker chair on wet Sunday afternoons to get down a volume of the Holy Bible in hopes of amusement while mother went out in her old mackintosh to feed the chickens, and father, stupefied with overeating, snored in a cloud of stinking tobacco smoke.

Lot 52.—*Picture in oak frame, "The Death of the Fox"; a ditto, "Dawn of Love"; a ditto, "The Snake Charmer"; a ditto, "Lady Blessington."*

It was all very well to smile, but here was:

Lot 53.—*A lady's small Mahogany Bureau.* (Special.)

Miss Brixworth shivered with nervous anticipation. What would it fetch? Who would be likely to bid for it? She had wanted at first to put a reserve of five pounds on it, but the man she saw about it thought that in such hard times that would be too high a figure, so she had consented to reduce the reserve to two pounds. And now her eye, peering through a lorgnon, rested on the small crowd, or rather group of people before her—the lady who kept a boarding-house, whose false teeth didn't fit, and who had a weary feather in her hat; the other lady with long, cheap earrings and muddied snake-skin shoes; the old man with a wen; the youth with spots and spectacles; the young married couple, she with fair hair, he rather dark, looking out for bargains—yes, perhaps they were the likeliest bidders. But what about those two murmuring, middle-aged men with long, drab moustaches? They looked like dealers. Yes, even while she was looking at them, they moved over to where her precious old bureau stood, and muttering together, pulled out the drawers in turn. How she had loved that piece of furniture, and how high a polish it had kept! Well, it was no good being senti-mental about it. If she hadn't got rid of it now it would have had to go sooner or later. And what was the good of having possessions when you had nowhere to put them and nobody to enjoy them with?

The bidding actually began at thirty shillings, and just as she had foreseen, the young married couple and one of the supposed dealers bid against each other. The bureau was knocked down for three pounds seventeen and six. Miss Brixworth turned away. At the entrance, as she paused to open her long, slender umbrella, a man said, "Bad weather, lady. Nine months winter and three months bad weather." She smiled and nodded, and as she went out said to herself, "Ah, well, I'm lucky. Lots of people have got nothing left to sell." But somehow she couldn't help thinking again of that fine, dark, gleaming, polished piece of mahogany, as it had stood in its old place in her house in the country, with the French windows open, and the warm and scented summer breeze lightly ruffling the curtains. . . .

Two days later a crate was delivered at 45 Cambodia Crescent addressed to Miss Rosy Fernandez.

"There must be some mistake," said Mrs. Gambitt, who answered the door.

"No, lady," said the carman. "Maybe it's a surprise packet."

Mrs. Gambitt bent down and broke the paper that covered the crate and its contents.

"Oh!" she cried, had it carried into the hall, and ran to call the family. When Rosy understood that this huge case contained something for her, she went nearly mad with excitement, and danced round her father while he tried to prise it open with a claw-hammer.

"Who could have sent it to her?" he said, suspecting that some man, Swanage perhaps, was trying to win his wife's favour by giving elaborate presents to her child.

"Miss Brixworth, of course!" cried Rosy, and she

and her mother ran upstairs together to overwhelm that person with thanks and embraces.

"Oh, you shouldn't have done it, you shouldn't, really!" cried Mrs. Fernandez, and being rather overwrought, burst into tears, so that Miss Brixworth, grateful for gratitude and pleased at the pleasure of others, felt quite embarrassed, and more than a little afraid, so demonstrative was Rosy, that the complicated structure of her coiffure might be disarranged —you don't want your hair to come down when it isn't entirely your own.

A little later the toy was moved into the office, where it was put before the window, and after Rosy had had her first enchanting ride on it, she got off, and looked it over carefully. It was a beautiful and spirited rocking-horse, painted a battleship grey, and dappled like a fallow deer, with a mane and tail of real horsehair. The tuft of hair which protruded between its ears was particularly pleasing, and had just proved itself very handy to hold on to while you were actually rocking. The nostrils, widely distended, were painted scarlet inside, while the eyes were large, bold and a trifle bloodshot.

"Mummy, why is it frightened?" Rosy asked.

"It isn't frightened, dear."

"Then why does it stare?"

"Nice horses have big eyes, darling."

"What kind of horse is it?"

"An Arab, sweet."

"And is it a mare?"

"Yes, dear."

"Mummy, are all horses mares?"

"No, dear."

"Then what are the ones that aren't mares called?"

"Just horses, dear."

"But aren't mares horses too?"

"Oh, don't ask so many questions, Rosy; you make me feel quite giddy."

"Mummy, do nice people have big eyes?"

"Yes, sometimes, dear."

"And is the Lord Mayor a horse?"

"Of course not, dear. He's just a mayor."

"But how can a man be a mare, mummy?"

"When he's the greatest man in a town, then he has a gold chain and is very rich and is called the mayor."

"But *my* mare hasn't got a gold chain, so I suppose it isn't a Lord Mayor," said Rosy conclusively.

"Heavens, child, what *are* you talking about?"

Rosy began licking the paint on the horse's neck to see if it would come off. It had a very peculiar smell, and it tasted very much as it smelt, but rather stickier, for in places it wasn't thoroughly dry.

"And what are you going to call him, Rosy?" Mrs. Gambitt asked, pointing to the rocking-horse.

"The Lord Mayor, of course," said Rosy, re-mounting.

R

XV

THE arrival of Mrs. Trubshore, the lady medium, "the fat one with the rolling eye," as Carol called her, not only served to console Mrs. Porter for the absence of Mr. Swanage, but even increased her enthusiasm for spiritualism.

"Now that we have established a home circle," said Mrs. Porter, "why don't we try and get others to join it? Mrs. Trubshore was asking me only yesterday if there weren't any other ladies in the house who might like to join us."

"Well," said Mrs. Gambitt, "there's Beryl, there's Mrs. Rudd, and there's Miss Brixworth."

"Oh, not Miss Brixworth!" said Mrs. Porter. "You remember how rude she was when I sent her the Seer's advertisement."

"I've often spoken to Beryl, but it's no good; she says she won't join us."

"Poor unbeliever! But what about Mrs. Rudd? She must be lonely, with her husband out at work all day."

"Ah, that's just it," said Mrs. Gambitt. "I'll speak to her, and I'm sure she'll be ready to join us as soon as I ask her."

"Get her to come up and have tea with us, Natalie, then she can get used to the idea."

Mrs. Rudd responded as readily as they could have wished. The afternoons had been dragging lately, and she often felt desperately bored. This new idea seemed to her to be just what she wanted—it promised a thrill, a slightly illicit thrill, for Mrs. Rudd had been brought up to think spiritualism wicked. Besides, she had heard vaguely of the magnetic Mr. Swanage, and hoped to make his acquaintance. But the invitation from Mrs. Gambitt and Mrs. Porter, besides offering her an escape from boredom, was the means of opening a safety valve, for she had a grievance. She was discontented with her life and dissatisfied with her husband, but with Alston she was enraged. She had never set eyes on him since the morning when she had tried to seduce him, and brooding over his behaviour she had allowed her mind to become quite poisoned. When there is some check to what she wishes a woman is apt to become not only quite uncritical but to lose all touch with reality. The trouble with Mrs. Rudd, as with some other women, was that she didn't require virtue in a man—she was only looking for a sexual monopoly. And although common sense might still have told her that Alston was a decent young man, and that she had gone quite the wrong way about trying to win his affection, she had become quite unbalanced where he was concerned, and common sense had long since given way to hysteria. So in the course of the tea with Mrs. Porter and Mrs. Gambitt, when the conversation happened to return from the Great

Beyond to the Here and Now, and the house and its inhabitants were spoken of, and Alston's name cropped up, all Mrs. Rudd's accumulated feelings came to a head and burst out, with a wild story, incoherent and made up of hints rather than direct statements, that she herself had actually been the shocked, the chaste, the innocent, the unwilling victim of amorous approaches on the part of Alston. The astonishment and excitement of Mrs. Porter and Mrs. Gambitt when they heard this knew no bounds.

"But please, please," cried Mrs. Rudd, realising that she had gone a little far, "please don't say a word of this to anyone! I put him in his place, I can assure you, and I don't think he'd ever dare to behave like that to anybody again. Of course, I didn't say a word to my husband. I don't know what Mr. Rudd would do if he heard. Oh, nobody must hear of this at all! I only tell you in confidence!"

"It's most shocking," said Mrs. Gambitt.

"Most dreadful," said Mrs. Porter.

"And I'm not at all sure," said Mrs. Gambitt, "that he ought to be allowed to stay in the house. Why, not one of us may be safe." She looked at herself in the glass and patted her hair as she said this.

"And supposing Mr. Fernandez were to hear of it," suggested Mrs. Porter.

"Oh, he'd murder him," said Mrs. Gambitt. "There'd just be murder done, that's all."

"Oh, I wish I'd said nothing about it!" exclaimed Mrs. Rudd, wringing her hands.

"Never mind, dear," said Mrs. Porter. "We won't say anything about it. We'll all keep our doors locked. And I think, Natalie, you'd better just warn Beryl Fernandez about him."

"If it wasn't for the sake of the money being needed, I'd turn him out lock, stock and barrel," said Mrs. Gambitt. Alston had never been a favourite of hers.

After this, Mrs. Porter carefully steered the conversation back into supernatural channels, and by the time Mrs. Rudd left she had quite got over her indignation for the time being, and was beginning to kindle with "psychic" enthusiasm.

"Heard the latest?" she said to her husband when he came back from work. Her manner at once made it clear to him that she was going to tell him something she knew he would disapprove of.

"No," he said. He was washing his hands, and didn't look up.

"I've joined Mrs. Petherham-Porter's home circle!" she declared, dabbing at her nose with a powder puff.

"What on earth's that?" said Rudd, who took the least possible interest in other people's business at 45 Cambodia Crescent, and knew very little of what was going on there.

"Spiritualism," she said.

"What!"

"I said, spiritualism."

"Now you take my advice, dear, and leave all that stuff alone. It's a nasty business."

"Take your advice! Why should I take your advice? What do you know about it? Do you expect me to sit up here from morning till night doing nothing but wait for your lordship to return? Don't you see that I want a little amusement in my life?"

"Oh, you're doing it for amusement, are you?"

"Yes, I am."

"Oh, I thought it was a kind of religion."

"Well, it may be for some people," she said, "but it isn't for me."

"Well, dear, I'm sorry you're going in for it at all. I'm afraid it might upset you."

"All right, you stick to your crossword puzzles," she said. "I can take care of myself."

He didn't care to argue with her, for he was tired, and wanted some peace, his tea, the fire and the evening paper. But the difference of opinion remained, and while Rudd sat on one side of the fire and read the *Evening News* she sat on the other and read an article by the Seer, which had been given to her by Mrs. Porter. Her imagination at once became excited by remarks about the religion of love, the secret of the universe, life force, the lifting of the veil, the piercing of the veil, urges, auras, earth planes and the direct voice. "Procure an aluminium trumpet," the Seer advised, "and paint the base of it with luminous paint. Then stand the trumpet on the floor in the centre of the circle. Open with prayer and a hymn. Then start a conversation, but avoid anything of an unpleasant nature. Talking helps the vibrations, and encourages the unseen guests. You may see spirit lights, you may get a whisper, a voice, a tapping on the trumpet, within a short time. . . ." When Mrs. Rudd went to bed after reading this, she was too excited to sleep. If all else had failed, that magic trumpet would certainly have succeeded in summoning her to the next séance upstairs.

The house had become the theatre of a deep psychic disturbance. It was a house divided against itself. It would hardly be too much to say that some of the inhabitants were on the side of the powers of light, and that some were surrendering themselves to the powers of darkness. One thing was becoming certain, that these deliberate attempts to disturb and excite and explain what should be left mysterious, these attempts to overdraw, as it were, on the supernatural, occurring in surroundings where there was such a fatal dislocation of spirit as that which afflicted Fernandez, would culminate in some frightful catastrophe.

The tension was not lessened by the arrival next day of Alston's double bed, sent round by his uncle. It came on a lorry in the morning, and it was Mrs. Gambitt who opened the door.

"A double bed!" she exclaimed. "What next!"

The workmen exchanged winks. Fernandez, opening the office door just two inches, watched them carrying it upstairs.

"I'm going to keep my eye on that young man," said Mrs. Gambitt, closing the front door after the workmen had left. "I suppose he thinks he can bring some street woman in here."

"Natalie!" cried Mrs. Fernandez. "He told me it belonged to his uncle, who offered to let him have it——"

"Oh, that's what he *told* you. I tell you, I mean to watch him."

"Oh, Natalie," Mrs. Fernandez whispered, glancing fearfully round, "don't tell Paul. You never know, it might upset him."

"It'd upset him more if he was left to find it out for himself, which he certainly will sooner or later."

"Natalie, please, please don't tell him! It'd only make him get ideas into his head."

"Have it your own way, Beryl."

At lunch Fernandez waited and waited for them to begin talking about the bed. He was so agitated he could scarcely eat.

"Why, Paul, whatever's the matter? You're eating nothing at all. Don't look at me like that, dear. What's the matter?"

"Not hungry," said Fernandez. Ah, he thought, she's deliberately trying to hide it from me. That's what the bed's for. I've caught her this time.

He was very silent all the afternoon. His suspicions had now definitely fastened upon Alston, and he gave him credit—as with all his previous imaginary rivals —for all sorts of dangerously fascinating qualities and advantages, many of which Alston didn't possess.

Because Rosy was fond of the young man and because he sometimes paid attention to the child Fernandez was more than annoyed, and one day when he found her eating some sweets that Alston had given her he was tempted to snatch them from her and throw them on the fire. He was ready to believe anything. He wondered if perhaps Alston hadn't means of his own and only worked in the fruit shop as a blind. Further, his fanatical eye had detected Alston's interest in motor-cars, and he tried to persuade himself that Alston actually had a car of his own hidden away somewhere, and meant to use it to carry off Mrs. Fernandez. If he had been able to preserve an air of calm indifference or if he had openly terrified Alston, the matter might have been settled. But he couldn't keep his ideas to himself and complained vaguely of Alston to his wife, who told him to shut up and stop being a fool. She repeated what he had said to Mrs. Gambitt, who looked sour, and said:

"For once, I should say, there's some reason in what he thinks."

"Natalie! What do you mean? Do you mean that I——?"

"Of course not, dear! Don't be so silly. But I've some reason to think that Master Alston fancies himself as a lady-killer." She put one hand on Mrs. Fernandez' shoulder and with the other pushed back Mrs. Fernandez' hair and whispered in her ear.

"Oh, Natalie, I don't believe it!"

"She told me herself."

"It can't be true! You can see he's not that sort of person."

"There's no smoke without fire," said Mrs. Gambitt. "Though if he thinks that any woman could see anything in *him*——"

"Well, *I* can, anyway!"

"Oh? So there is something in what Paul's thinking? That's just it——"

"Natalie, you know what I mean. Of course I've never thought of him in that way. I mean I think he's as decent a young man as you could expect to find. And do you know what I think? I think Mrs. Rudd just made that up because she sees that Alston's much more of a man than her husband, and she just wished he'd take some notice of her. But Alston goes out with a young woman of his own, as you perfectly well know, a young woman that works at Pélagie's. I never did like that Mrs. Rudd, nasty, vain little thing, lying in bed half the day, while her husband works his fingers to the bone for her. . . ."

It was from the well-informed Carol that Alston first heard of the direction which Fernandez' thoughts had taken, and he was more disturbed by the news than could have been guessed from his manner.

"I thought he'd get his knife into you sooner or later," said Carol, finding the new turn of events pleasantly exciting. "What'll you do about it?"

"Nothing," said Alston. "What would you expect me to do? Leave the house, or what? Does he think he's just going to frighten me away, as he did the Indian? He's got a hope. He won't get *me* out of the house so easily. Here I am and here I'm going to stay. *I'm* not afraid of him, though I don't know why Mrs. Fernandez sticks to him, I'm sure."

"That's what Mrs. Gambitt's always on at her about," said Carol. "She won't leave him, and 'I can't turn him out in the street,' she always says. No, you know what it is, a woman's glad to have a husband that's so jealous of her."

"She's got that all right."

"Oh, sure, and she has," said Carol. Returning to the kitchen, he told Lottie he shouldn't be surprised if there was trouble ahead.

Alston was at the Pascalls' that evening, as he was almost every evening nowadays, and although he felt very happy and was as lively as he always was in the presence of Willy Pascall, yet Amy noticed him once or twice looking rather thoughtful. She wondered what was the matter, but decided to say nothing until they next had some time alone together, and contented herself with wishing him the tenderest of good-nights. The truth was, he was worried about Fernandez. But on his way home he spent a few minutes at the coffee stall where he had first met Willy Pascall, and the thought of Willy's friendship and Amy's love gave him courage. He told himself that he wasn't really afraid of Fernandez. . . .

As he passed Pélagie's he noticed how deserted it

looked, and wondered idly if there was a night watch-
man in the building. A belated taxi went hurrying
into the distance, leaving a trail of fading sound
along the air. As for Cambodia Crescent, it was quite
deserted, except for two policemen at the far end,
who stood talking under one of the street lamps. The
autumn night was mild and clear, and the moon
appeared to be sailing through the clouds, which
were transparent and wavelike.

Alston let himself in at the front door as quietly as
possible, and fumbled in his pocket for matches, but
he could find none, so he began to make his way upstairs as best he could without them. He made no
noise, his feet sinking into the thick stair-carpet. He
could have found his way blindfold, he knew it so
well, but in any case a dim light was provided by
the reflected glimmer of the moon. Just as he was
approaching the landing, he had the uncomfortable
feeling that there was someone about. He paused for
a moment, his hand on the banisters, to listen. There
seemed to be no sound. When he reached the top
stair he paused and looked back. The moon, invisible from where he stood, had suddenly come out
from behind a cloud, making the window on the
stairs a livid rectangle, and there, against that rectangle, he could distinctly see the outline of a man's
head and shoulders. It was Fernandez. He had been
standing there, with his back pressed against the
wall, and had held his breath as Alston passed him.
He imagined that Alston hadn't yet seen him, and

he didn't make the slightest movement, but listened, with every nerve strained, to discover whether Alston was going upstairs to his own room on the floor above or not. He heard Alston go slowly upstairs. He heard Alston's door close behind him.

Fernandez began to breathe freely again, but rapidly, with short, husky, feverish breaths, and then broke into a subdued spasm of coughing, leaning against the wall with his hand pressed to his side, which pained him. The faint moonlight shone upon his face, a grey mask of physical and mental disorder, which there was nobody to see. When his coughing ceased, he spat on the stair carpet, and then stood quite motionless and silent again, listening intently for any sign of life either from his wife's room just behind him or from Alston's above. He stood like that for nearly half an hour, but as he had long since lost all sense of time, it seemed to him like five minutes. At one moment he distinctly heard Alston brushing his teeth, and a grim, ironical smile spread over his lean jaws. "I'm not such a fool," he muttered to himself; "it's only bluff, it's only a trick to make me think he's going to bed." After a long time he crept upstairs as far as Alston's door and put his ear to the keyhole. He could hear the sound of regular breathing, for Alston was fast asleep. Again the smile returned to his face. If anybody had seen it, they would have noticed that now it was almost a kindly, pitying kind of smile. "Poor fool," it seemed to say, "as if I didn't know that he's only *pretending* to be asleep!" And he stood a little back from the door, waiting. . . .

The patches of moonlight on the walls of the staircase slowly changed their shape and their position. Somewhere a clock struck three. Out in the garden two cats were making the most frightful noise. Perhaps they were making love, but to a curious human ear it would have seemed that love among cats must be a cruel affair, in which the intensity of animal passion was mingled with frenzies of hate and anger and jealousy. But to the ear of Fernandez the cats were just an annoyance, a tiresome interruption which might prevent him from catching the sound he was waiting to hear.

Some time after the silence had returned, a deep and prolonged silence this time, Fernandez began to feel cold, with that subtle, penetrating coldness of the very early morning which creeps into the bones and the vitals. Partly from the cold and partly in reaction from his long vigil, which had kept his nerves and muscles tense, he suddenly began to tremble violently, not simply at the knees, but from head to foot, for he was chilled to the marrow. His hands shook like the hands of a corpse suddenly galvanised into violent activity by an electric current, and his teeth chattered together, but where anybody else would in such circumstances have felt discomfort he only felt annoyance. Supposing that which he expected to happen *did* suddenly happen, and caught him not sufficiently master of himself to remain silent and self-possessed!

The thought troubled him more and more, and he struggled to control his twitching limbs. For a moment or two he would manage to remain quite still, and then the shivering would break out again all over him more uncontrollably than ever.

At last he put his hand into his coat pocket and took out a piece of string which he had put there in readiness the day before, and with this in his hand approached the door of his own room, where his wife and child lay asleep. There was no moon now, and it was very dark on the landing, but he knelt down and began groping at the side of the door until his hand encountered a tack which he had previously driven into the woodwork at a time when there was nobody about to watch him. To this he firmly attached one end of the string, and then tied the other end to another tack on the opposite side. The string was thus stretched across the threshold at the height of about a foot from the ground, so that anybody trying unawares either to enter or leave the room would be tripped up. Satisfied with his handiwork, Fernandez stepped carefully over it and entered his own room.

The night light, which was usually kept burning at his side of the bed, had long since gone out, but the room was now filled with the first vague greyness of the dawn. The child was asleep, and Mrs. Fernandez was asleep, lying on her side, with her dark hair spread out fanwise on the pillow. Fernandez, still shivering, got into bed without taking off his clothes, and pulled the blankets over him, lying close to his wife for warmth.   When he had stopped shivering he sat up and looked down at her.   In the twilight he could just see the outline of her forehead and eyebrow, and with an infinite tenderness, of a kind which he seldom showed in the daytime, he bent and touched the depression at the temple, so smooth and white, with his lips. But immediately his expression changed, an extraordinary emotion akin to anger took hold of his heart, and he put out a shaking hand for a cigarette, one of his strong and stinking cigarettes, which he lighted, sitting upright against his pillow and inhaling the foul smoke into the innermost recesses of his lungs. As soon as it was nearly finished he lighted another from the stump, and went on smoking till he had a fit of coughing which disturbed his wife, causing her to turn over uneasily, without actually waking her. By this time it was getting light, so he slipped out of bed, opened the door, and removed the piece of string.   At about a quarter to six, just when Carol in the basement was beginning to wonder about getting up, Fernandez fell into a doze. . . .

The following evening, which happened to be a Friday, Alston spent with Pascall, who took him to see some speedway racing in the suburbs, where an acquaintance of his was one of the performers. Afterwards, when they were alone together, they went into a public-house for a drink, and Alston began describing how Fernandez had behaved the night before.

"By God, it's not safe for you to stay in that house," said Pascall.

"Oh, I'm not afraid of him, Willy. Anyway, I'm going home this week-end."

"You are?"

"Yes, to mother's, at Crotchester. They're expecting me. It's a good time since I went down. . . . Fernandez'll have calmed down by Monday, I expect. If he doesn't I'll just shut him up like a halfpenny book."

"And what about to-night? What if he knifes you in your sleep?"

"Well, what about it? Wouldn't worry me much, would it?"

He laughed, but Pascall said nothing.

They were late, and caught the last train back.

"Look here," said Pascall, when they got out of it, "do you know what I'm going to do?"

"What?"

"I'm coming along with you."

"What do you mean?"

"What I say. I'm coming along with you to-night. You oughtn't to be alone to-night with that Fernandez about. . . . You can put me up, can't you? You've still got that bed, haven't you?"

"Yes, but——"

"Now don't argue with me."

"I'll be all right, Willy. I can look after myself."

"Of course you can, but I can look after you better, see? . . . Anyway, it's late for me to get home now. Your place is nearer. You don't *mind* putting me up, I suppose?"

s

"After all you've done for me? I should say not."

They went back together to Cambodia Crescent. Alston opened the front door quietly.

"I'll turn on the light over the stairs this time," he said.

He turned it on, and they went up. There was no sign of Fernandez, and before they reached Alston's room they turned the light off again.

"I don't know why you've never asked me to come and see you here before," said Pascall, looking round the room.

"Well, it's not much of a place to ask anybody to. . . . Of course I'd have asked you before, only I didn't quite know how they'd take it."

"Who's 'they'?"

"The people in the house."

"Oh, to hell with them. An Englishman's home is his castle. Don't they ever have visitors to see them? Don't you pay rent like the best of them?"

Half undressed, Pascall looked at himself in the glass, stretched his arms, and yawned. The light fell upon his curly hair and the gleaming whiteness of his muscular back and arms.

"But don't you lock your door?" he said, seeing that Alston was already in bed.

"Can't, Willy. The key's lost."

"Well, I don't know how you can sleep in peace with the door not locked and that Fernandez perhaps roaming about and thirsting for your blood."

"I tell you, I'm not afraid of him."

"Oh yes, you are," said Pascall, putting out the light. "Anybody would be," he said, getting into bed. "There's nothing to be ashamed of in that, so you may as well admit it."

Alston laughed in the dark.

"All right, I'll admit it," he said, "and I'll admit I'm not sorry you're here to-night."

As he spoke he was surprised, but not unpleasantly surprised, to feel Pascall's arm slip affectionately round him. It gave him a feeling of comradeship and safety.

"This is something like a bed," said Pascall. "I wouldn't call the king my uncle now. . . ."

In the morning Alston was the first to wake. A delicious and unfamiliar happiness had taken hold of him, and seemed to flow calmly through his veins, as though he had taken some drug which was only good in its effects. And when he looked at his bedfellow, sleeping so peacefully by his side, he couldn't have put his feelings into words, but for the moment he was utterly content. He loved Amy and she had made it plain from the first that she needed him; he cherished her trust in him; and now he enjoyed the warm, protective affection and companionship of her brother; he was just off home for the week-end; there was even some prospect of his wages being raised at the shop—everything seemed to have come together to bring him good luck. . . .

"Hullo, boy," said Pascall, opening his eyes, yawning luxuriously, and smiling. "I suppose I must get up, because if I don't get home in time for breakfast they may be worrying about me."

Alston wanted him to stay and share his breakfast, but he got up and began washing himself. When he was dressed, Alston, still lying in bed, offered to get up and show him downstairs.

"Don't get up, boy," said Pascall, "I can let myself out."

And after saying a more than friendly good-bye, he went quietly out of the room and noiselessly down the stairs. But when he got to the front door, he found, after fumbling with the catch, that he couldn't open it. It was still very early, and he doubted whether anybody would be about, and was just thinking of going back upstairs to get Alston's help, when he heard sounds from the kitchen, so he went to see who was there. It was Carol. Pascall explained amiably that Alston had put him up for the night, that he had to leave early, and hadn't been able to open the catch on the front door.

"Oh, I'll come and do it for you," said Carol, as soon as he had got over the surprise of seeing a stranger in the house so early in the morning.

It took several seconds to get to the door and open it. And it just happened that Fernandez, having heard something of Pascall's movements, had come out on to the landing and was looking over the banisters, expecting to see Alston. Pascall didn't see him, but he saw Pascall just as he was going out, and heard the front door close behind him. Alston was

instantly forgotten. And the strange thing was that
although Fernandez had spent the entire night in
bed with his wife, he was convinced that the retreating figure of the stranger was a lover of hers who had
not only had free access to the house but had perhaps
actually passed part of this very night with her,
probably while he himself was asleep. He tried to go
over the whole course of the night again in his
memory, butt here had been little to mark the passage of the hours. Even the little alarm clock which
usually stood on the mantelpiece had for once been
left downstairs in the office. The more Fernandez
tried to think the more confused he became. The
night had been so timeless! He couldn't even remember the beginning of it. Everything seemed to be
slipping from him. He felt as helpless as one who
drowns with no hope of rescue. A heaviness seemed
to be closing in on him like a cloud, and he didn't
know how to escape from it. A spiritual suffocation
was gradually overpowering him. And then suddenly his imagination began to work with great
power and brilliance, and a complete hallucination
became more true and real to him at every moment.
. . . He could see the office in the small hours of the
morning. The sofa that stood there was faintly outlined against the darkness by the glow from a few
dying embers in the grate, and in the background
could be seen the head of the rampant "Lord Mayor"
against the window-curtains. There were soft footsteps outside, and then his wife came in laughing

softly and followed by the stranger, who was Pascall. The stranger's hands (in Fernandez' imagination) were large, strong and muscular; his face had been carefully shaven, and his smooth cheeks and chin and his supple white neck still smelt of talcum powder; a red-hot coal fell into the fender; a long conversation took place, in which Fernandez was laughed at; and then, every word and intonation appallingly clear, the conversation became more intimate and amorous, until the two mouths closed in a kiss. . . .

Shivering with cold, Fernandez went downstairs to the office in order that he might see by morning light the scene of these imaginary events which were far more real to him than anything that had actually happened.

"You're down early this morning, Mr. Fernandez," said Carol. "Shall I bring you a cup of tea?"

"Please, Carol."

When he was drinking his tea he said:

"Carol, who was that stranger that you let out at the front door this morning?"

My word, he's sharp, thought Carol, he misses nothing.

"Oh, that was a friend of Mr. Alston's," he said. "Put him up for the night, I believe, as he missed his last bus home, or something."

"Oh," said Fernandez, quite casually.

"I suppose it worried you," said Carol, "seeing a stranger about at that time of the morning. You might have thought it was a burglar or something."

Fernandez smiled.

He was very quiet all day, uncomfortably so, but in the afternoon Mrs. Gambitt heard him muttering something about a stranger at the front door. She found out the facts from Carol, and complained to Mrs. Porter.

"From all accounts he was just a common working man," she said contemptuously. "He might be a thief or anything. I shall have to speak to Beryl about it. Looks strange to me that Alston should have him in to stay the night like that. You never know what that young man'll be up to next. The day he leaves this house I shall be downright glad, and we'll get some decent young business girl in instead."

XVI

VERY early on the Sunday morning Mrs. Fernandez was awakened by the sound of her husband stropping his razor. She was awake instantly, and felt certain that something was wrong, but was determined not to show it, and pretending to be very sleepy, said in a drowsy voice:

"Oh, is that you, Paul?"

Fernandez turned sharply round, and his eyes gleamed fanatically in the light of the solitary candle. Behind him his shadow, like some dark and menacing phantom, seemed to be watching and waiting.

"You're awake, are you?" he said.

"Yes. . . . What's the time?"

"It's about two."

"Well, I can look forward to a nice long sleep, then. But what are you doing, Paul? Surely you're not going to start shaving yourself at this time of the morning?"

He didn't answer, and her heart began to beat quickly with fear.

"What did you mean just now," he asked, "when you said, 'Is that you, Paul?' Who did you think it was?"

"I thought I must be dreaming," she said, affecting a yawn.

"You weren't dreaming of anybody but me, I suppose?"

"I don't mean I was actually dreaming. I was fast asleep, and then I heard you moving about, and as I was still half asleep I wondered what it was."

"You mean, you wondered *who* it was?"

"Why, Paul, who else could it be?"

"You ought to know that better than me."

"Oh, Paul," she cried impulsively, giving up all pretence of sleepiness, "isn't it time you stopped all these fancies? You can't really believe that I ever give a thought to any man but you!"

She had grown so used to his tyranny, had for so long meekly submitted to it, that she could hardly believe her own voice as it uttered these words. Her husband looked piercingly at her, and then turned away without a word and went on sharpening his razor.

"Come back to bed," she murmured, "or you'll be waking Rosy. The child looked so tired last night, with dark rings under her eyes."

"It's not the child I'm thinking about," he said, without turning round, "it's you."

"Paul——"

"You, woman!"

"Paul, if you won't come back to bed, I shall have to go up to Natalie's room for the rest of the night. You're disturbing me."

"You'd like to leave this room, wouldn't you? But

it wouldn't be Natalie, perhaps, that you'd like to sleep with."

"You go too far," she said. "You'll have to get some light work to do, something to occupy your mind. But if you go on like this, you'll just make a scandal and a nuisance. Everybody's talking about you, as it is."

"And who is everybody? And where did you hear anyone talking about me? Ah, you think I don't know, you think you can fool me, because I'm sick and can't work, but I'm not blind yet, or deaf, or dumb!"

"I can't argue with you now, dear. Please let me sleep," she said, and she turned away from him, laid her head on the pillow, lay on her side, drew the bed-clothes up to her nose, closed her eyes, and pretended to be going off to sleep again. But her heart was beating fast and loud with fear, and she was as far from sleep as one can be. With all her senses on the alert, and a sense almost of suffocation, she began to breathe deeply and regularly as if she were asleep. Between her breaths she could hear near her head the light and untroubled breathing of Rosy, asleep in her little bed. She timed her breathing by the child's, making a slow and tranquil pattern of sound, so soothing that she was on the verge of beginning to feel calm again, when she became acutely and uncomfortably aware of the silence in the room. Her husband had stopped sharpening the razor, but he hadn't come back to bed. What on earth could he be doing? He must be standing quite, quite still, brooding, as he did sometimes, with an inscrutable expression on his face. Had he folded up the razor and put it down somewhere, or was it still in his hand? Perhaps he really meant to shave himself, for his habits had been erratic lately, and one could scarcely be surprised at anything he did. Or was he perhaps trying to frighten her? If so, he had certainly succeeded. Poor Paul, he had got so much into the habit of acting the jealous husband that there was no knowing what he would do next. It was his hobby, you might say, and it no doubt excited him to see other people's concern about it. . . .

She had lost all sense of time. Her breath rose and fell, rose and fell, in the intervals of the child's, and she could hear the alarm clock ticking quietly away on the mantelpiece. But what of her husband? Not a sound. Not even a floor board creaked. What was he doing there? He must be just standing sunk in a kind of trance. The night was very quiet. If only Natalie were here, she'd soon put a stop to his nonsense. . . . Beryl Fernandez felt an overwhelming wish to look at her husband. She felt that she knew exactly how he was standing, but still she wanted to look at him. Very slowly, very cautiously, she opened one eye a little. But she saw little except the biscuit-coloured rectangle of the blind between dark curtains, the top of the wash-stand, the back of a chair, and the end of Rosy's bed, for everything that mattered was behind her—the candle, her husband himself, and that

enormous shadow. If only she could have seen the
shadow now, or even a part of it! For the shadow
would have told her what he was going to do; it
seemed like a sort of dark angel that anticipated his
movements instead of following them. . . .

She lay wondering for a long time whether she
would dare to turn over. But was it really a long time?
Perhaps it was only a few minutes, perhaps it was
years. She didn't feel so frightened now. Paul would
soon get tired of standing there, would wake up from
his reverie, would come back to bed. She missed the
nearness of his body, lean, warm, bony, in the cheap
poplin pyjamas with the wide lavender stripes, his
breath smelling of cigarettes, his hands with their
hairy backs. It wasn't when he was near her that she
feared him. His nearness was comforting, reassuring,
delightful. But when he was aloof like this, just out
of touch, out of reach of her encircling arm, when
he was unmovable by reason, self-sufficient like this,
wrapped up in his own mad thoughts, two yards
away but infinitely alone and independent, this was
when she feared him.

All her fear suddenly came back upon her with
redoubled force, and with it her curiosity, and she
could no longer resist the inclination to look at him.
But nothing must be done suddenly. She would turn
vaguely over, as if in sleep, and then, after lying still
for a few more minutes, would take a glance at him.
But probably before those few minutes were over, he
would return quietly to bed. She turned over with

a dreamy sigh, and lay still, aware of the candle-light shining directly on her face. And she composed her features so that they should seem as innocent, as helpless, as gentle, as attractive as possible, raising her eyebrows very, very slightly, and allowing her lips to pout a little, so that they almost suggested the hint of a ghost of a smile. She hoped to appeal to his better nature, for a mild woman in a dangerous pre-dicament will if possible exploit her mildness to the utmost in the hope that it will save her without there being any necessity to resort to that firm courage, decision and initiative which she conceals only just below the surface of her apparent tenderness and helplessness.

Fernandez stood looking down at her, and al-though his soul was balanced on the very edge of chaos, he couldn't help being stirred, as he had always been stirred, by her youthful beauty. She had never looked more beautiful than she did now, young wife, young mother, asleep in candle-light. For an instant the impression he had that she lay there thus at peace, loving and especially trusting him, was stronger than the intoxicating knowledge that he had her in his power, and the faint trembling which had for some minutes shaken his whole body suddenly ceased. But then she made a fatal, an irrevocable mistake. Instead of opening one eye the tiniest frac-tion of an inch and glancing at him through her thick and fringy lashes—a movement which he couldn't have detected—she suddenly opened her black eyes wide, as a baby does, and stared at him. He started perceptibly, and in the same instant she realised her blunder. She saw him start, she saw the razor still in his hand, she saw the expression on his face, and lay there motionless, staring at him, her heart beating rapidly.

"You were pretending to be asleep," he said. "D'you think I didn't know it all the time?"

"Oh, Paul," she said, again pretending to be sleepy, "are you still there? The light must have woken me up again. Aren't you coming back to bed, dear? Is anything the matter?"

"You'll never deceive me again," he said. All his better feelings had vanished the moment she opened her eyes. He had only one thought now, and she guessed what it was. She lay as if turned to stone, and said nothing. He took a step towards her, a fiendish step. She could bear the suspense no longer and sat bolt upright in bed, patting her hair into shape with her hand.

"We can't go on like this," she said. "If you want to prowl about all night you'll have to do it by yourself. I shall go up and sleep with Natalie."

She threw back the clothes and sat up on the edge of the bed, her pretty bare feet groping for her slippers.

"Oh, mummy, what are you doing?" It was Rosy's voice.

"There, you see," said Mrs. Fernandez, "you've woken the child up. I hope you're satisfied. Well, I

shall take her up with me. She'll never go to sleep
again with you walking about the room. Rosy, put
on your dressing-gown, dear. We're going upstairs."

"Why, mummy?"

"You stay where you are!" cried Fernandez, as his
wife rose to her feet.

"Don't touch me, Paul!"

He flung his arms round her and tried to kiss her,
but she turned her head away, to the left, to the
right, and struggled in his embrace. In a moment she
had managed to free herself, and stepped back, leaning against the chest of drawers, her bosom heaving.
Fernandez stood facing her. He was holding on to the
bed-post with his left hand. In his right he held the
razor, which he slowly opened.

"Are you mad?" she cried, seeing the gleam of the
blade. "Leave me alone! Think of the child! Shut
your eyes, Rosy!"

But Rosy, crouching on her little bed, clutching
a doll against her childish breast, couldn't move,
didn't understand what her mother had said to her,
couldn't take her eyes off her father. The expression
on Fernandez' face was intense and powerful and
utterly inhuman. He advanced towards his wife, and
she retreated slowly, catching hold of a chair to
protect herself with. A moment later, and she was
again struggling to free herself from his embrace.
A vase fell off the mantelpiece, and smashed on
the edge of the fender. In the struggle Fernandez
caught a glimpse of his wife's throat, white in the

candle-light, and it was too much for him. He hacked at it with the razor. But the blow glanced aside, and cut her in the neck. The blood spurted out, and she screamed.

"What are you doing to mummy?" cried the child.

"Oh, Paul—I've loved you so much—and is this how you thank me?"

He made no answer, but she could hear his breath come panting huskily from his labouring lungs.

"Think of the child!" she cried, as she found herself struggling with him again.

But he had gone mad, and had only one idea—to cut her throat. When she put out her hands to defend herself, he slashed wildly at them, and she screamed again and again, throwing herself down by the side of Rosy in the hope of protecting her and vainly hoping that the sight of wife and child together might soften the murderer's rage. Then she rushed to the door and tried to open it, but he stood with his back to it and prevented her getting near it. Then he caught her by the hair, dragged her on to the bed, and kneeling on her, cut her throat. Again she struggled free, and fearfully disfigured, stood facing him, sobbing with pain and terror.

For long he had domineered over her with his male arrogance, his fierce and ever-watchful protection, but now there arose in her all that concentrated, emotional courage which women may keep in reserve for years, but which, at a moment of stress, enables them to triumph where men might fail. It was as if she knew that she, the victim, was really the victor. All her pride and energy thrilled through her quivering nerves, and the grandeur of her appearance at this moment was not lost even upon her demented husband. Stretching out her lacerated hands she caught hold of the terrified child and lifted her from her cot, and the child was at once stained with the gushing of the mother's wounds. She staggered back towards the door, where her husband still stood, and raised the terrified child up at arms' length before his eyes. He made no movement. Then, with an effort, feeling her strength ebbing, she cried in a terrible, choked voice the one word, "Open!" Overcome by her authority, Fernandez turned and unlocked the door and opened it, and as he did so the razor fell from his hand with a clatter on the floor, and his head sank on his breast. Without turning aside to look at him, the woman, her child in her arms, stepped wildly but firmly through on the last ourney she was destined to make in this world.

She had one thought only, and that was that there should be a witness to her awful fate before it was too late, a witness to whom she could confide the child. She had one witness in view, and that was Mrs. Gambitt. But to reach Mrs. Gambitt it would be necessary to climb a double flight of stairs. Like a Magdalen who has repented too late, she took one, two, three, four laboured and unsteady steps across the landing, moving as though all the sins of all the women in the world were on her back. Scarcely able

T

to stand, feeling that every gurgling breath was her last, too faint and stifled to cry out, too set on the task of climbing those precipitous stairs, she was yet aware of the child's body clasped in her arms, clasped tightly, unnaturally tightly, the child's body gone all stiff with fear like an animal's, so that the child too could neither stir nor cry out—the child, her last and only earthly treasure. At the foot of the stairs she stumbled and fell. The child was still folded against her breast, as though she would carry it safe through all the fires of hell, and there she lay an instant with her head bowed down till it touched the very path she must tread. Her breathing became faster, hoarser, thicker, more confused with liquid, bubbling sounds, and then she put out a hand, of which the palm was one wound, gripped with it a banister-rail, and dragged herself up a stair or two on her knees, her hair hanging like a curtain over her tortured eyes and over the stark white face of the child.

What an ascent! A martyred saint, a martyr to love, ascending to heaven in a robe of blood! Every footstep was as sharp as a blade, every breath taken more difficult than all the concentrated pains of a lifetime; the martyrdom was gradual, not yet accomplished, and purgatory would only end at the very door of heaven. A ghastly progress through a sleeping world, and she had no voice to waken the sleepers. Drops of blood fell silently on the stair carpet, audibly on the inch or two of woodwork on either

ide of it. The right arm stretched out and the flayed
and at the end of it gripped first this banister-rail,
hen that one, two or three steps higher, and gripping,
ightened all along its length, raising two lives, one
almost over, one scarcely begun, up their twilight
path.

It was no longer with the strength of her muscles
or what was left of the warm vigour of her body that
he moved. It was solely her will, her courage and
her nerves that forced her onwards and upwards. It
was as if some invisible guardian angel had arrived,
not to make the last stages of her ascent easier, but to
make them possible, and as if it were assisting her
with a powerful hand under each armpit, heaving
her fast-weakening body forward. There was no fear
of pursuit (she knew he wouldn't follow her), no
fear even of failure; there was only effort, a prolonged, agonised effort.

Ah, if only she could cry out to Natalie! But it was
all she could do to draw breath; she felt she would
never be able to form the word. It was the idea of
Natalie that filled her whole soul; that idea was the
guardian angel which drew her powerfully, painfully upwards. The idea of Natalie drove her on as
surely as a wind filling the sails of a ship drives it
directly homeward through the roughest and most
maddened sea; she made for Natalie as instinctively
as a lost, a frightened, or a wounded child makes for
its mother; as a hunted beast makes for its lair; as
earth is drawn to earth.

And now Natalie's door was in sight. If only tha
door had been open, that trap-door into peace! Bu
it was shut, looming infinitely high and grey abov
the stairs in the half light. How would she ever reacl
it or get it open? The handle was very high abov
the floor, and where would the strength come fron
to enable her to knock on those lower panels? Alread
her strength had ebbed so far that a deliciou
drowsiness was beginning to enfold her. She wantec
to sleep. . . .

Reaching the top stair, she tried to stand, anc
collapsed on the floor, making little noise, however
for the stair carpet was thick. She knew now that shc
would never have the strength to knock. A deliciou
warmth was beginning to fill her veins, bringing witl
it, as wine does, a complete indifference to the world
But there loomed the grey panel of the door, and
rising on her knees, she lurched heavily against it
. . . Mrs. Gambitt woke abruptly, sat up in bed
turned on the electric light, leapt out of bed, and wen
boldly barefoot towards the door, pausing only tc
listen for any possible sound. The door opened in
wards. She threw it open without a moment's hesita
tion, and as she did so stepped bravely backward
as if to face at a proper distance the intruder, whethe
it was a burglar or Carol drunk—for these alterna
tives had already flashed through her sleep-ridder
mind. As she stepped back, Mrs. Fernandez, witl
Rosy all blood-bedabbled clasped in her arms, fel
face forward on the threshold.

"Beryl!"

That delightful feeling of indifference and warmth and calm, that supreme pleasure which is experienced by persons about to be frozen to death or those mauled by a lion, now overtook the prostrate woman, but she raised her head, and, turning her great eyes, black and dazzling, upon her friend, she managed, though there was so much she knew now, to utter only a few words:

"Natalie—I knew—this would—happen——"

And with that she fell dead across the living body of her child.

XVII

THE next few minutes were mainly remarkable fo
the courage shown by Mrs. Gambitt. With the chil
in her arms she rushed all the way down to the base
ment and pulled Carol out of bed. "Run, run for th
police!" she cried, and Carol ran, barefooted an
with a mackintosh hastily thrown over his pyjama
Mrs. Gambitt then ran to the door of the Rudd
room and hammered on it until Rudd came with
poker in his hand and took a cautious peep at her.

"Something terrible's happened," she said. "Here
take the child and tell your wife to keep her safely
Then come with me, quick!"

Rudd did as he was told.

"Where's Fernandez?" he said.

"You find him! Go and find him and watch hir
till the police come! They'll be here any minut
now."

"What has he——?"

"Go on!"

And with that she hurried upstairs in extrem
anguish of soul to spend the last minutes she woul
ever spend with the body of her dead friend.

Rudd, with the poker still in his hand, and his thi
legs shaking in his shrunken cotton pyjamas, then s
out to find Fernandez. But he had hardly taken

step when Carol burst into the house with two policemen, so he was relieved of the danger and responsibility of capturing Fernandez. That person was found in the office, smoking a cigarette and coughing slightly. He looked a trifle dazed. When asked if he had anything to say, he said no, he had nothing to say. One of the policemen took charge of him while the other went to the telephone, and before very long some sort of order was restored. Mrs. Gambitt made a long statement with surprising calmness, and she was supported by Carol and Rudd, who then retired. Fernandez was seen to smile: he pointed to his feet, which were in slippers, and asked that his boots might be brought to him. The body and the criminal were taken to their different destinations, and the house then grew quiet again. Mrs. Rudd, after washing Rosy, had managed to get her off to sleep, and was now listening horror-stricken to her husband's whispered account of what had happened.

It was just when the first light was beginning to show in the sky that Mrs. Gambitt found herself alone in the office. She sank exhausted into a chair. But she forced herself to stand up again, and went to the door. An awful, haunted silence had settled on the house and it seemed hard to believe that at any moment she might not hear Fernandez shuffling along the passage from the kitchen or see his ashy face looking suspiciously, ghoulishly down over the banisters. And then suddenly in the room above, the Fernandez' room, the alarm clock went off, and the metallic whirring sound of the alarm could be distinctly heard by Mrs. Gambitt where she sat. She jumped when she heard it, and then immediately reflected that it had been set to wake Mrs. Fernandez at this hour, that it was ringing in vain in that silent room, that it couldn't wake the dead. . . . She hid her face in her hands, and her sorrow might have overwhelmed her had it not been displaced by the thought of Fernandez. No, she wasn't afraid of him. She had never been afraid of him. She had always put up with him, but now she couldn't bear even the thought of him, she couldn't bear to remain a moment longer in the office, the room he had last been in. She was cold, she was alone, she was frantic. She couldn't bear to go back to her own room. She had a vague feeling that something was incomplete, something was lacking, that there was something she had meant to do and had forgotten . . . ah yes, she had forgotten to tell Mrs. Porter—but perhaps, but surely Mrs. Porter knew already, for her room was next to the Fernandez' bedroom.

Mrs. Gambitt went up and knocked on the door. There was no answer. An awful suspicion struck her. Was it possible that Fernandez had also——? With a palpitating heart, she hammered again at the door. Again there was no answer. And she called to Mrs. Porter by name, in a desperate, pleading voice.

"Who's there?" she heard from within.

"It's me—Natalie—open the door! Please open the door!"

"Oh, Natalie, is anything the matter?" cried Mrs. Porter timidly, as she hastened to open it.

"What, have you heard nothing? Nothing through that wall? Is it possible? To-night's been like the end of the world, it's the end of the world for me, and you've heard nothing!"

Mrs. Gambitt laughed harshly, with a touch, but only a touch, of hysteria in her laughter.

"Why, Natalie, what is it? Is it Beryl? Has something happened to Beryl? I'm sure it's Beryl!"

"She was murdered hours ago."

"Murdered!"

"And you heard nothing!"

"But tell me!"

Mrs. Gambitt was only too ready to tell her, and she stood there pouring out the whole story, refusing to sit down, while the older woman crouched on the bed, looking fragile and terrified, which indeed she was. When Mrs. Porter had heard it all, Mrs. Gambitt began to repeat herself, for she couldn't bear to be silent, as that might oblige her to think, and she couldn't bear to think just now, and indeed the sound of her own voice was all that kept her anything like steady.

"But I can't understand how you heard nothing," she said again.

"Of course the walls of this house are thick, Natalie, and I never was a light sleeper. But I must say I had an extraordinary dream, a very nasty dream. I can't quite recollect the details, but I know it was something about Beryl."

In actual fact, the old girl had been wide awake when the struggle was going on in the next room, and although she didn't realise at the time that it was a matter of life and death, had been frightened out of her wits. Prudently enough, she had simply put her head under the bedclothes and kept it there, thanking God that she always kept her door locked at night. When at last some sort of silence seemed to return, she had felt very much tempted to unlock the door and peep out, but as it was known that she seldom left her room, she saw no reason to correct her habits at such an unpropitious moment. So she had returned to bed, and at last had fallen into a light doze, in which condition she was when Mrs. Gambitt began knocking at her door.

She now began to try and make amends for her prudence by cherishing Mrs. Gambitt. She lighted the fire and made her sit by it, brewed some tea and made her drink it, and gave her an impulsive kiss on the forehead.

It was getting quite light now, and downstairs in the Rudds' room little Rosy was sitting on Mrs. Rudd's knee. Mrs. Rudd chatted away to her and told her stories—anything, anything, to avoid the fatal subject. She helped her to dress herself and gave her some things to play with. Then looking up suddenly she saw that the child had thrust her fingers into her ears and had a strange, wild look in her eyes.

"Why, whatever's the matter?" she cried, thinking that perhaps the child was going mad.

Rosy shook her head, and kept her fingers in her ears.

"Can't hear, can't hear!" she said.

The church bells were ringing for the early service, and although the sound came faintly enough through the still morning air the child had heard it at once, and as always it maddened her. (These same bells were making Miss Brixworth upstairs hurry through the last details of her toilet, for fear that she should be late for the early service—these same bells that spoke to her of duty and reverence and holiness only enraged the child Rosy, destined to godlessness). When Mrs. Rudd realised what was the matter and tried to console the child, Rosy only stamped her little foot and cried for Mrs. Gambitt.

"All right, then," said Mrs. Rudd, "run along to Mrs. Gambitt for a bit."

Rosy went upstairs, and hearing voices in Mrs. Porter's room, thought she would go in there. The two women were still deep in conversation, and didn't hear the child slip into the room. Suddenly Mrs. Porter caught sight of her.

"Oh, you poor little orphan!" she cried impulsively, stretching out her arms to the child.

"Shshsh!" said Mrs. Gambitt, but it was too late.

"What's an orphan?" said Rosy, looking from one to the other.

The two women looked at each other in consternation—Mrs. Gambitt looked reproachful, Mrs. Porter repentant.

"Now, Rosy, don't talk so much," said Mrs. Gambitt, "you'd better run along back downstairs to Mrs. Rudd."

Rosy sidled thoughtfully out of the room with a finger in her mouth. Mrs. Rudd was surprised to see her back so soon.

"Well, you haven't been gone long," she said, "Didn't Mrs. Gambitt want you, my little duck?"

"I'm not a little duck," said Rosy.

"Oh yes, you are!"

"Oh no, I'm not!"

"Then what are you?"

"I'm an orphan," said Rosy very proudly.

"Oh! . . . Who told you that?"

"Mrs. Porter."

"Oh, well, she's made a mistake."

"Why?"

"Never mind why."

"What is an orphan?"

"Now, Rosy, I haven't got time to talk, so run and play by the window there, like a good little girl."

But Rosy had just thought of somebody who would answer her question instead of putting her off as everybody else did when she wanted to find out anything interesting.

"Where's my daddy?" she said.

Mrs. Rudd was startled.

"He's not very well just now, Rosy."

"Can I go and play in the kitchen?"

"All right, then," said Mrs. Rudd, hoping to avoid

having to answer any more awkward questions, "but don't be long."

"Carol," said Rosy, going into the kitchen, and giving herself airs, "I'm an orphan."

But Carol was no more sympathetic than the others had been.

"You're a bloody little know-all," he said.

And just then the front-door bell began ringing. It was a detective to see Mrs. Gambitt. A few minutes later the police came again, then two reporters and a camera man arrived together, and then Mrs. Fernandez' next-of-kin, who had been telephoned to, came and took Rosy away with him.

The only person in the house who had remained ignorant of what had happened (not counting Alston, who was away) was Miss Brixworth, and somehow nobody had thought of telling her. On her way downstairs there had been nobody about, but she felt somehow that there was something strange in the atmosphere, and when she came back from church she heard voices in the office which sounded unfamiliar. Then Carol was very late bringing her breakfast. . . . When he came he told her the news.

The effect of the news on Miss Brixworth was considerable. She was not an insensitive person. Carol was surprised at the calm way in which she *appeared* to take the news, but even he could guess how extremely agitated she must be at heart. Besides, his account of the murder had added to the effect. He had given it with gusto, he had enjoyed the telling, the excitement of the whole affair gave him far more pleasure than pain—he was sorry that Mrs. Fernandez was dead, he was ready to agree that her husband's behaviour had been horrible, but a murder in the house! He was just longing to tell Lottie the news. He felt quite a hero after leaving Miss Brixworth's room, and would have whistled on his way down-stairs had not his sense of good behaviour checked him.

Miss Brixworth had no appetite for her breakfast. She made up her mind to go at once and see Fanny Haymer. That was the only possible thing to do. But first of all she thought it her duty to see Mrs. Gambitt, whom she so much disliked. She thought she ought to sympathise with her, and ask if she could help her in any way. Mrs. Gambitt of course took the chance of telling the whole story over again in the fullest detail, with all the latest developments, and Miss Brixworth, by the time she got away, felt thoroughly shaken.

Directly she got out of the house all her strength seemed to leave her. Miss Haymer's dwelling seemed infinitely far away, and she didn't know how she would ever get there. When she came down the steps, very erectly, a group of people hanging about outside the house stared at her much more curiously than people usually did (the news had already got about the neighbourhood), and it was more than she could bear. So she did something she hadn't done for many months—she raised her long, slender, old-fashioned umbrella into the air and signalled to a passing taxi.

As she got in and settled herself down she felt none of that pleasant and slightly illicit thrill which sometimes comes from spending money on something one cannot afford. She felt much too battered for that, and simply leant back and closed her eyes. Inside her gloves her hands felt icy, and she felt faint, in reaction from the shock she had received. When she opened her eyes she caught sight of herself in a narrow looking-glass opposite and was surprised to see that she was very pale, so while the taxi rattled along she fumbled in her bag for some rouge and began rubbing it on to her faded cheeks. After all, one must keep up appearances.

How would Fanny take the news? Probably the only possible way she could have learnt it was by reading the paper, but would it be in the Sunday papers? Hardly. In any case Fanny had funny ideas; she had "views" about newspapers as about everything else. . . .

"My dear Connie, you've come upstairs much too quickly," said Miss Haymer as soon as she saw her friend. "Now sit down in that chair at once and behave reasonably and get your breath back before you utter a word."

Glancing at Miss Brixworth's pale and agitated face, she pressed her down into a chair, but even as she did so she realised that there was something wrong.

"Connie, what's the matter? Are you ill? Are you feeling all right this morning?"

"I'm all right," said Miss Brixworth, forcing a very wintry smile. "But I've got rather bad news. Mrs. Fernandez has been murdered by her husband."

"Murdered!" cried Miss Haymer, sinking into a chair, and putting her handkerchief up to her mouth. "That *is* nice."

With a shrivelled hand, large and arthritic and full of character, she groped for her stick, that familiar support.

"I hope you weren't mixed up in it at all?" she said.

"No, Fanny, fortunately not. I've only just heard of it."

She related what Carol had told her.

"I'm glad you were well out of it," said Miss Haymer. "I must insist on your taking a glass of sherry."

"Oh no, Fanny——"

"Now do as I tell you——"

Miss Haymer rang for Empringham.

"We won't tell him now," she said. "He'd be so fascinated we should be cruel to send him away. I'll tell him later. . . . Some sherry, Empringham, please, for Miss Brixworth."

When Empringham had brought the sherry and had gone again, Miss Haymer's expression changed, and although her nose was too heavily powdered this morning, and her wig awry, the sombre look in her old eyes made her appear ghastly rather than absurd.

"It's not a very nice thing to have to face," she said, "but I'm partly responsible for this woman's death."

"Fanny! What on earth do you mean?"

"I mean exactly what I say. Haven't you come to me again and again and said that something like this might happen?"

"I never thought anything so awful as this——"

"And haven't I lectured you again and again and said that the man and the woman ought to be allowed to work out their own salvation? I see now how wrong I was——"

"But, Fanny, perhaps you were right after all. How can we understand these mysteries. If God——"

"Oh my God, my good intentions! When I look back at my life and see the harm they've done!"

Miss Brixworth was afraid and unable to answer this.

"It's always the same story!" Miss Haymer went on. "It's the young and good and healthy and fresh and cheerful who suffer and are taken, and the old and ill and evil and useless who are left. . . . Will they hang him?"

"They say not, Fanny. They say he's mad."

"Love's always mad. . . . And yet perhaps this could have been prevented. . . . And the child was in the room? Where is she now?"

"She doesn't seem to have understood what has

U

happened, and has been asking for both her father and her mother as though they had only quarrelled. She has been taken away by a relation of her mother's, who will take care of her."

"I was going to say I might have tried to make amends by doing something for the child."

"There's nothing to make amends for, Fanny."

There was silence for a moment, except for the quiet muttering of the fire.

"Well," said Miss Haymer at last, "you'd better get out of that house as soon as you can and come and stay here for a bit until you find a new abode."

"Thank you, Fanny, but I don't see any reason for leaving *now*. If I had left *before*—but never mind. Besides you haven't really got room for me here."

"I'll make room."

"Well, I might perhaps come for a couple of nights," said Miss Brixworth. And remembering how she used to go and stay with her friend years before, in the country, in the days when there was money and safety and peace and people believed in the British Empire and Mr. Kipling, when the nectarines ripened quietly on the wall and the petals fell quietly from the roses, when there was honey for tea and the gardener touched his hat, and the drawing-room was full of furniture and ornaments which had been in the same positions for years and years, the chintz, the Dresden, the satinwood, the miniatures, all embalmed in a faint sweet odour of pot-pourri, while the shadows lengthened on the lawn, and the parlour-maid, her apron rustling with starch, came in with the tea things—remembering all this, Miss Brixworth added, with an attempt at gaiety, "It'll be just like old times!"

"H'm," said Miss Haymer, who knew it wouldn't be in the least like old times. "I should say the case is rather altered."

XVIII

On the Monday morning, which was cold and wet
and miserable, Alston returned to London. The air
was full of the sound of rubber tyres moving over wet
asphalt, the jolts and warnings and the roar of traffic.
The wet, grey pavements reflected the wet, grey
landscape. The bus on which he was riding stopped
before a hoarding covered with huge posters. Each
of them showed a gigantic human figure, and each
figure seemed to live in a strange world of the
imagination. A giantess in evening dress was in raptures at having discovered a new tooth paste to apply
to a set of teeth that looked like the keys of a piano.
A young man in ballooning plus fours was bursting
with health over a tankard of beer outside a Tudor
inn in a sun-drenched landscape. Next to him a
superman with a neat moustache was laughing triumphantly at his own underwear, which fitted him
like a glove. And then a whole group of heads could
be seen grinning from ear to ear with pleasure at the
privilege of acting in a new musical comedy. But
below this Utopian fresco was an old man selling
newspapers, and near him was a newsbill which said
SHOCKING LONDON TRAGEDY. Alston wondered idly
what it was, and just then the bus moved on.

He felt far removed from tragedy himself. Coming

back to London this wretched November morning, when people huddled in overcoats put up their umbrellas and stepped over puddles, he felt as calm and cheerful and happy as he had ever felt in his life. He had enjoyed a good idle week-end at home, lying in bed till the middle of the day with a packet of cigarettes and the *News of the World*. His mother had not only been overjoyed to see him, she had been fascinated by the change that had come over him. She said she had never seen him looking so well, and had made a great fuss of him, taking special pains to give him plenty to eat. His stepfather had been easy to get on with, and on both evenings he had had plenty to drink with old acquaintances. His enjoyment of his week-end at Crotchester had been based on the contentment of one who finds the deepest needs of his nature appeased. Pascall, who had swum far into the cave of experience, had brought him a handful of jewels, and his heart was comforted. And yet, as the bus went rushing now towards his lodging, he had a vague feeling of discomfort, for after all it was cold and wet, it was November in London, and Monday morning at that, and the shop, with its dreary routine, was waiting for him.

The front of 45 Cambodia Crescent didn't look particularly inviting, and two or three people stared at him in an inquisitive way as he went up the steps. He wondered why. He let himself in as usual with his latchkey, and on opening the door felt at once something of the strain in the atmosphere. He found himself face to face with Mrs. Gambitt. She still looked quite green, and her face seemed to have contracted in an odd sort of way, making her seem thinner than ever.

"Ah, it's you," she said in a low, difficult voice, pressing one hand to her breast. "I thought it was another reporter. I was wondering when you were coming back. Of course you know what's happened?"

"No."

"Will you come in here?"

She led the way into the office, where she stood facing the light. Her face looked ghastly, her eyes were those of someone greatly overwrought, and her hair was disarranged.

"Mrs. Fernandez has been murdered," she said.

"What?" said Alston. "Oh, no. . . . She's *dead*?"

He looked at Mrs. Gambitt as though he expected her to contradict him.

"Yes, dead. He cut her throat. You were lucky to be away. The worst's over now."

Alston grew quite pale. He felt cold, terrified, and began to shiver. His knees seemed to give way. He felt winded.

"If you don't mind," he said, "I think I'll sit down."

The woman remained standing and he felt a little ashamed before her courage and firmness. She began telling him the story. She had already told it again and again, to the police, to the pressmen, to Mrs. Porter, to Carol, to Mrs. Porter again, to Mrs. Trubshore. The telling and re-telling of it seemed to be necessary to her nerves, as one squeezes a festered place again and again to get rid of the poison. With every detail Alston's horror increased.

"It was your bringing in that bed of yours," she said, "which was the last straw. And didn't a man, a stranger, leave your room early on Saturday morning? Fernandez saw him fumbling at the front door, and of course he thought that Mrs. Fernandez—you understand? . . . *That*, you see, and that double bed of yours——"

"By gum!" said Alston, "but that was just a friend of mine that I put up for the night——"

To his other emotions was now added something like a feeling of guilt. He didn't know what to say, and hid his face in his hands, as if to hide the nakedness of his feelings—the hatred he felt for Fernandez, the regret he felt for the death of Mrs. Fernandez, and stronger than either the fear that he himself might be called up in court, might be called to account for his deepest feelings—which would be made shamefully public—and held somehow responsible in part for the crime. Worst of all, suppose, he thought, that Willy Pascall's name came up. Ah, but they couldn't touch Willy! Alston felt sure of himself, felt sure that he could and would do anything to keep Willy out of it. . . . But his mouth had gone dry, and his hands were as cold as ice.

"I suppose I shan't have to appear?" he said in quite a casual voice. His love for Pascall gave him the power to act, which wasn't otherwise in his nature; it gave him the power to put a bold face on any situation for fear that he might disgrace himself. He stood up.

"At the inquest, you mean?" said Mrs. Gambitt. "No, I don't think so."

He felt much relieved, but his relief was short-lived.

"But at the trial," she went on, "perhaps you might have to appear. I don't really know. But no, I think not; the police asked about you, and I told them, and they seemed satisfied."

She didn't say whether the police had asked who the stranger was who went away early in the morning, and he decided to say nothing on that point until obliged to.

"Ah, you were lucky to be away," said Mrs. Gambitt. Her face looked quite haggard as she turned to the light. "But perhaps if you'd been here you might have heard, you might have been able to do something to prevent it. . . . Well, it's no good talking, it's too late now. . . . Please come upstairs with me and I'll show you the room. It's been locked since—then. I can't face it myself."

He didn't say that he didn't want to see the room. A fearful fascination drew him upstairs after Mrs. Gambitt—an unconscious wish, perhaps, to have a vivid, first-hand story to tell to Willy and Amy Pascall later.

Outside the door of the room where the Fernandezes had lived there was a dark stain on the stair carpet— the carpet Mrs. Fernandez had so lately bought and had been so proud of. Mrs. Gambitt opened the door and then stood back with averted eyes. Alston looked in.

It was the first time, of course, that he had ever seen the interior of the room, and before he noticed anything definite he was overcome by a feeling of intruding on something private and intimate. He had admired Mrs. Fernandez and had been fond of her, and in a small way his feelings now were comparable to those of a penurious young lover who penetrates at last into the most private retreat of an adored mistress, rich, powerful, exotic, and far above him, only to find that she has gone for ever, and to find himself not only alone, but alone with the things that she has touched, used and worn, the bed that has held her sleeping form, the looking-glasses that have reflected her in all her splendid, her vanished, her irrevocable moods.

The first thing he saw was the child's cot, with a teddy bear and a doll sitting on it side by side, disfigured with brownish stains. The room was a shambles. Fruit was trodden into the rugs, furniture was upset, a candle had burnt out in its socket, and everything bore traces. On one wall, near the door, the paper was sprayed with rhythmical dark lines.

Coming out a shade paler than he went in, Alston caught Mrs. Gambitt's eye, and an electric flash of sympathetic understanding seemed to pass between them, but, fearful lest she should try and read the secrets in his eyes, he said hurriedly:

"It can't be left like this, can it? The police aren't coming again, I suppose?"

"No, they saw all they wanted to, and I locked it up."

"Then it had better be cleaned up at once."

"Mr. Rudd said this morning that he would do it," she replied, "but I told him then that I thought the police hadn't quite finished with it and might come back again. He's at his office now, of course. And Carol can't possibly do it yet. He's got so much to do——"

"Then I'll do it."

"Will you? Carol could perhaps help you a bit. I can't."

She turned away, and Alston went down to the kitchen.

"Ah, you're back," said Carol, tired, excited, and overworked. "She's told you everything, I suppose? Ah, you were well out of it. 'Nastiest business ever I saw,' one of the policemen said to me. . . . How could he do it? That's what I can't understand yet. How could he? I know I couldn't do anything like that. I wonder he didn't go and put his head in the gas oven at the end. But I must say I wouldn't have the heart to do meself in."

"No," said Alston vaguely. "Will you give us a hand to clean it up?"

They got together a bucket of hot water, some soap, disinfectant and a scrubbing brush.

"I'll do this part of it," said Alston. "You light a

fire in the back garden. Call up to the window, will you, when you've got it going, and I'll chuck out the things that have to be burnt."

"Right-o," said Carol.

Back in the bedroom for his task of cleansing it, Alston was at first aware of little but the smell of blood, stale, sweetish, sickly, all-pervading, and a slight nausea overcame him. As he began peeling off the stained wallpaper in long strips he began to turn the whole affair over in his mind. The blood that had at first rushed to his heart was now flowing back to his brain and warming it into thought. He understood clearly that Fernandez had been just like a child saying, "I'll pick this flower because it's pretty, because I want it badly, and so that nobody else can have it. . . ." Vaguely he picked up the doll from Rosy's cot, and was wiping the blood away from its bright, stupid, china face when he heard his name called, and glancing up, saw through the window a line of blue smoke ascending through the now nearly leafless branches of the plane tree in the back garden. Carol had lighted a fire. Alston opened the window as wide as he could and threw down the doll. In falling it looked like a human being falling from a cliff. Then he bundled out all the bedclothes, the mattresses, some clothes and other tainted movables, and watched Carol piling them on the fire. As the smoke thickened in the rainy air he felt that thrill of pleasure which destruction always gave him. Then he turned to scrub.

It was only after half an hour's work that the room seemed fairly clean again. But although the job was done he felt little easier in mind. His task had been a sickening one. When he left the room he went and washed his hands and forearms, and although they were soon spotless, he had the feeling of having absorbed some uncleanness into himself. He felt in some degree what a murderer himself may feel—a deep need of lustral rites, of a religious purification. The best he could do was to go off and take a strongly disinfected bath. Afterwards he emptied over his hands, head and shoulders more than half a bottle of eau-de-cologne which Amy had once given him, but which up to now he had scarcely made use of at all. When he was drying himself Mrs. Gambitt knocked at the door and said she had luncheon ready downstairs—would he care to come and join them as soon as he was ready? He said he would.

A large room on the ground floor, which had stood empty ever since the house had been taken over, had now been provided with a table and chairs. And there all the women of the house were assembled, besides Mrs. Trubshore, whom Alston had never seen before. His eye met Mrs. Rudd's for a second, and she gave him a fierce look.

"Mrs. Trubshore is very psychic," said Mrs. Gambitt, as she introduced him.

"Oh, yes," said Alston politely, and saw before him that stout motherly party with her rolling eye and her hands folded across her stomach. She was trying to look otherworldly, but only succeeded in looking well-nourished.

At this moment Carol came in with a dish of Irish stew, and went out with a wink, and they all sat down to lunch. Mrs. Gambitt helped them to stew, and there was rather an awkward silence broken only by remarks like "May I trouble you for the salt?" The way these people ate their food was fussy without being fastidious. Every detail of their behaviour was in fact characteristic of that vast bourgeois convention which has choked so much heartiness out of our race.

Alston shifted uneasily in his chair, stole a glance at Mrs. Gambitt, and then looked down at his plate again, wondering who would be the first to speak.

Not once, since the death of Mrs. Fernandez, had Mrs. Gambitt said anything at all direct about her feelings. The shock of her friend's death seemed to continue to affect her very much as it had affected her at first, but instead of allowing herself to break down, to put her head on the nearest shoulder, burst into tears and cry, "Oh, how I loved her!" (which was the truth) she had kept on repeating over and over again the same details of the weeks before the murder and of that event itself. The nearest she could get to proclaiming her love for Mrs. Fernandez, who had for long been the whole centre of her existence, was to curse Fernandez. "Oh, if I could just get hold of him now," she would say, grinding her teeth together, "I'd just scratch his eyes out!" This failure to give way to her deepest impulses had long since embittered her, and now it was making her hysterical and unbalanced. What she wanted was a good cry, but all she had to indulge in were the dubious thrills of suburban witchcraft.

No doubt she had largely been drawn to Mrs. Fernandez by seeing in her so many of the qualities that she herself lacked—youth, beauty, health, improvidence, and especially frankness. What in others might have seemed almost too much frankness was in Mrs. Fernandez a giving of confidence, and when people used to see those pretty eyes fill with those extraordinary tears which were distilled from a mingled fear and excitement, their hearts at once went out to her. And afterwards, when they asked themselves, "But why should she tell *me* all that?" they could find no reason, but felt flattered. Actually her free ways had much to do with her being a Jewess—an unconfined Jewish vitality just sprang freely out of her as a branch springs out of a tree, shaking all its flowers and leaves in the sun and the rain. . . .

It was certainly rather a paradox that all this should have enchanted Mrs. Gambitt, who had tried to set such careful standards in the house. But after all, nobody had lived up to them, no, not a soul. Under a thin crust of genteel behaviour, and behind those dark curtains of secrecy which veil every human heart, the house had been the scene, in the course of a few short months, of the most powerful emotions and the most extravagant behaviour. The mud and the crystal had welled up together from the springs of human nature, while Mrs. Gambitt, widow, spinster, disappointed woman or whatever you like to call her, stood firmly for canons of behaviour which are utterly futile.

"You've seen the cousin again, Natalie?" said Mrs. Porter suddenly.

"Yes, he came again this morning, and I had a long talk with him," said Mrs. Gambitt in a firm tone of voice. "And there's something I think I ought to say. He tells me that Beryl wasn't really married to Fernandez, and his name isn't really Fernandez at all."

A scandalised silence followed this.

"Ah, they weren't married," said Mrs. Trubshore, as if she had suspected it all the time. "No wonder he was so jealous of her. You see, he had no legal hold over her. He thought if *he* could win her, somebody younger and richer could easily have got her away from him."

"Ah, it explains a lot," said Mrs. Porter, shaking her head significantly.

"Yes, if she'd been tied to him she wouldn't have been so easy and care-free in her manners," said Mrs. Rudd.

Mrs. Gambitt at once came to the defence of her dead friend.

"Of course it was wrong of her," she said, "but she hadn't so much happiness in her life that she can be blamed for taking the little that seemed to offer. It wasn't her fault, poor thing."

"No, it mayn't have been altogether her fault," Mrs. Trubshore conceded. Claiming divine inspiration, or at least an insight into what is hidden from ordinary eyes, she was determined to give her ruling on every topic discussed.

"And anyway it's all over now," said Mrs. Porter.

"Poor dear!" said Mrs. Rudd. She had absolutely ignored Alston from the moment she saw him when he first entered the room.

None of them seemed to feel that Mrs. Fernandez had been wrong to persist in living with Fernandez, who was neither sane nor her husband, but when people refuse to blame the folly of a member of their own sex it is generally because they are indirectly excusing their own. Besides, Mrs. Fernandez was dead, and that made it easy to be charitable about her. After speaking her praises they began to abuse Fernandez. They felt a real horror at his behaviour, but they wouldn't have been quite so savage in speaking about him now if he had ever shown the slightest interest in them, if there had been any other woman in the world for him besides the one he loved.

"Mrs. Trubshore will hold a sea-ants this afternoon," said Mrs. Gambitt, turning to Alston. "Perhaps you would like to be present?"

All the women glanced deferentially at Mrs. Trubshore.

"Well, I'm sorry, I'm afraid I have to go back to

work this afternoon," said Alston, who was due back at the shop by two o'clock.

All the women glanced at him reproachfully—except Mrs. Rudd, who stared deliberately out of the window.

"I see you're a sceptic," said Mrs. Trubshore clairvoyantly, but with a slight Australian accent. (She pronounced the word "septic".) "But may you be led to the light, may you cease to be earth-bound!" She spoke these words as if they were a kind of incantation.

"Hear, hear," said Mrs. Porter.

"We hope this afternoon," said Mrs. Trubshore, and she lowered her voice impressively, "to get into communication with one who has lately left us."

Alston felt a little shocked by this, but the women looked at her with a hint of greedy anticipation in their faces, like so many old Zulu hags assembled by moonlight to "smell out" some previously chosen victim.

"This has seemed to us a terrible happening," Mrs. Trubshore went on, "but it had to be. Yes, it had to be. We, on this earth-plane, cannot *vistualise* the reason why. We only know it had to be."

"Yes," said Alston, as she seemed to intend the remark for his special benefit. Was she trying to convert him?

"But of course," said Mrs. Trubshore in what was meant to be a dreamy voice, "it all happened millions of years ago." And she uttered a deep sigh.

x

This was too much for Alston. His native straight-forwardness overcame his reserve and youthful diffi-dence. But more, the thought of Willy Pascall im-pelled him to speak. He already foresaw himself repeating this conversation to Pascall, and the idea gave him courage.

"You may be right," he said bluntly, "but I was under the impression that it happened early on Sunday morning."

There was a fearful silence, as there would be in a church if anybody lifted up the altar hangings and pointed out that there was nothing but a table underneath.

Then Mrs. Gambitt, turning coldly away from Alston, addressed herself to Mrs. Trubshore and said:

"The Seer will be with us this afternoon?"

"Yes, presently," said Mrs. Trubshore.

The individual in question had taken immediate advantage of the recent happenings at 45 Cambodia Crescent to reassert his influence there.

"You've heard of the Seer, Mr. Alston?" said Mrs. Porter severely.

"Yes," said Alston.

"A *wonderful* man!"

"Wonderfully psychic," Mrs. Trubshore amended. "You know he psychometrised something of Mrs. Fernandez' only last week."

"Pardon?" said Alston.

"Psychometrised, I said. That means he took an object, clasped it in his hand, closed his eyes, made his mind a blank, pressed the object to his forehead, went into trance, and saw the future of its owner without knowing who the owner was. An inkpot, wasn't it, Mrs. Gambitt? Mr. Swanage said her future looked very dark."

Blue-black, thought Alston, glancing at his watch, but he said nothing. It was ten minutes to two, and he took advantage of the arrival of Carol with some tea to excuse himself and leave the table. As he went out of the room, Mrs. Trubshore shook her head and said in an undertone, "He's just *frivolious*!"

"They give me the creeps, these women," he said to Carol just outside the door.

"Och, they'll be the death of me yet!" said Carol. "With their sea-antses and their psychic this and their psychic that. You know what they want? What they want is——! . . . And this Seer of theirs. Coming this afternoon, isn't he? Well, the baker's brother-in-law knows all about *him*. And do you know what he says? He says Swanage keeps a mummy in his bedroom and kisses it. Yes, one of these Egyptian mummies. And that's not all, either . . ."

XIX

In the course of the afternoon Carol went out for a few minutes to buy some cigarettes. Outside the fishmonger's he saw the familiar figure of Lottie, who hadn't been near the house since the murder. She happened to be talking to the fishmonger's boy about that very subject—she was just telling how she had seen Fernandez standing over her after she had cut herself in the bathroom. With a wink to the boy Carol went softly up behind her and put his hands over her eyes. The poor girl, whose nerves were all on edge with the fear that she might sooner or later be called upon to give evidence, let out a shriek and struggled to turn round. When she saw Carol, hatless, with his lank black hair falling over one side of his face, and his red lips parted in a laugh which showed his bad teeth, she gave him a hearty scolding. But in a few minutes they were reconciled (she found it impossible to be angry with Carol) and all three of them went on talking about the murder.

"Oo, what a lovely murder!" said the fishmonger's boy with a wink to Carol.

"How can you!" cried Lottie indignantly.

At 45 Cambodia Crescent there was a continual coming and going. The Rudds were moving immediately, and the men had come to take their

324

things. Mrs. Porter was busy packing. Then two relations of the dead woman arrived to argue with each other and with Mrs. Gambitt about the belongings she had left. They had so disapproved of the "marriage" of Mrs. Fernandez that they had taken no notice of her whatever since it had occurred some years previously, but they now saw fit to spend an hour and a half disputing the possession of a fur coat which had been found among her things. It eventually came in half during a tug-of-war, for, although a relic of better times, it was somewhat moth-eaten, and in any case hardly made to stand this strain put upon it at last by the ties of kinship.

Mrs. Gambitt was very worried about the money that was owing here, there and everywhere. A man called from the electric light company to say that the current would be cut off within two days if the arrears weren't at once paid, but Mrs. Gambitt didn't mind this, because she meant to close the house and leave it on the following day at latest—Mrs. Trubshore had offered her a temporary refuge. Then the gas-man came with a similar threat, although he was very civil in the way he delivered it. "I'm glad *he*'s out of the way," he said with a smile as he was going away, "never liked me, he didn't." Then Mrs. Gambitt remembered that this was the very gas-man who had been driven off by Fernandez soon after they first settled in the house, and thinking of those early days and of her dead friend's gaiety and sweetness she felt almost inclined to weep. But there was no time to weep, for the hire-purchase people had just arrived to take away the stair-carpet, on which only a very small instalment had ever been paid. They too were polite, but firm. Mrs. Gambitt couldn't bear to see them taking up that carpet which for her had something almost sacred about it, like a relic. Not only had Beryl's feet pressed it a thousand times, but it was actually (if they only knew) stained with her very blood—and now strangers would use it, in a strange house.

The front door bell rang again, and, snatching up her little dog in her arms to console her, Mrs. Gambitt reluctantly hurried to open it. She found herself facing a tall and smartly dressed young woman in tweeds and with a fresh face, a confident manner, and an upper-class accent. Mrs. Gambitt stiffened.

"Can I speak to the lady of the house?" said the young woman, who wasn't very bright in the head.

Mrs. Gambitt started as if she had been stung, but as she said afterwards in telling the story, "I didn't move a muscle of my face."

"I am the lady of the house," she said grimly.

"Oh, I beg your pardon!" said the young woman, giggling, and giving off a whiff of expensive but not obtrusive scent. "I hope you're not too busy for me to see you just for a moment or two, but I'm doing some last-minute canvassing for Sir Herbert Fogg, the Conservative candidate, you know——"

"You don't know what you're doing," said Mrs. Gambitt, and there was a dignity that was almost grandeur in her bearing. "A lady has been murdered in this house."

And pointing to a notice on the area railings which said:

NO ORGANS, NO HAWKERS, NO CANVASSERS

she closed the door before the young woman had time to answer. Later there were calls from persons interested in the claims of rival candidates and parties, but Carol answered the door in each case and drove them all away.

Tea time came, and still Swanage hadn't put in an appearance.

"I can't make out what can have happened to him," said Mrs. Porter.

"There's many a slip," said Mrs. Trubshore, rolling her eyes. "I foresaw trouble in a dream."

"What kind of trouble?" said Mrs. Porter.

But before she got an answer the front-door bell rang.

"Oh, that bell!" said Mrs. Gambitt. "I suppose I'd better go this time. Carol's been answering it all the afternoon."

"That's probably him," said Mrs. Porter as Mrs. Gambitt went out of the room.

"I can tell you one thing," said Mrs. Trubshore enigmatically. "Whoever it is, it's not the Seer."

A moment later Mrs. Gambitt came back. She was agitated.

"I can't make it out at all," she said. "A man at the

door asked for Mr. Swanage. 'He doesn't live here,' I
said. 'No,' he said, 'but he's in the habit of coming
here, isn't he?' "Not at all,' I said, 'he hasn't been here
for a long time. What was it you wanted him for?'
'He's *wanted*,' he said. Now what did he mean by that?
'You're sure he's not here?' he said. 'Positive,' I said,
'I'd tell you if he was.' He looked a bit doubtful, but
he seemed to believe me, and went away. Oh, I'm
sure something's wrong!"

"I knew it," said Mrs. Trubshore.

"I'll go and ring Mr. Swanage up right away," said
Mrs. Gambitt, going out of the room again.

"She won't get him," said Mrs. Trubshore. "Listen."
She and Mrs. Porter listened.

"Hullo," they heard Mrs. Gambitt say. "Can I
speak to Mr. Swanage, please? What? . . . Oh, when
will he be in, do you know? What? . . . Oh no, it's
impossible! . . . Oh, he *hasn't*! . . . I can't understand
it at all, I was expecting him this afternoon. . . ."

She came back.

"Well, this is nice," she said. "He's just gone,
vanished into thin air. With rent owing, too, and not
a word. And he hasn't left a thing behind him but
a mummy, an Egyptian mummy! Oh, I just can't
believe it!"

She and Mrs. Porter looked at each other in dis-
may. That doubts should be cast upon the Seer, and
such very equivocal doubts, was almost, if not quite,
enough to shake their belief in the Hereafter. But
Mrs. Trubshore wore a sly smile on her face, the smile

of one who is in the happy position of being able to say, "I told you so. . . ."

"VOTE FOR FOGG, VOTE FOR FOGG, VOTE FOR FOGG, VOTE FOR FOGG, VOTE FOR FOGG——" shouted a passing election-van, and a few moments later Alston heard it passing the shop where he worked.

When his work was over, he went straight to his aunt's. He was full of the murder and had news from Crotchester as well. Both his uncle and aunt tried to make him stay the night, saying they didn't like the idea of his going back to 45 Cambodia Crescent for another night when it was so much on his nerves, but he would only agree to come to them on the following night and stay with them until he could find new lodgings. He left them late and went to the Pascalls', where he was very disappointed to hear that Willy was out and not expected back till late. Yes, of course, they had all heard of the murder, and weren't they just thankful that he was right out of London when it happened! Willy wanted to see him the following evening, said Mrs. Pascall, and was dying to hear all about the murder. . . . Alone with Amy, Alston gave her a description of what had happened, and she was so thankful for his safety that she couldn't utter a word, but just hid her face against his shoulder.

It was unpleasant returning to Cambodia Crescent. A stillness that seemed uncanny filled the house, and it was a long time before he could get to sleep. When he slept, his sleep was full of dreams.

He dreamt that he and Amy were standing in

Y

Parthenon Street and waiting for a bus. Bus after bus arrived, but none of them was the right one. And then he suddenly caught sight of Willy, who was walking slowly up and down on the opposite side of the road, and smiling at him. His first impulse was to cross the road and speak to him, but then, remembering that he was with Amy and that they were going out together, he forced himself to look away instead of smiling back at Willy, and gazed fixedly up the road to see if a bus was coming. When he looked at Willy again he saw him still standing there with an expectant smile. And he was wondering whether he shouldn't say something to Amy about her brother (of whose presence she was plainly unaware) when the bus drew up at the kerb, and he reluctantly climbed on to it after Amy and followed her up the stairs. When he was half way up the bus started and he looked back to see what Willy was doing. Willy had begun walking slowly away, but he turned and smiled rather sadly over his shoulder, as though he still half hoped that Alston might change his mind. With his heart torn between the brother and the sister, he thought he should at least make some sign of courtesy to Willy. So he waved his hand and smiled. Willy saw him, and stood quite still as if he still expected Alston to get off the bus and come to him. But alas, it was now moving very quickly, and in a moment it turned a corner and Willy was hidden from sight. A fearful regret overcame him as the bus sped away, and Amy seemed to understand that something was the matter and tried to console him. But he was inconsolable, and the bus rushed on and on, gaining speed at every moment, through street after street, and at last over some open fields, where it rushed right over the edge of a cliff—and with an awful sensation of falling, he woke up in a cold sweat, overwhelmed by regret—until he understood that his fears were only those of a dream.

There was a yellowish, wintry moon that night. It lighted with a ghostly radiance the gaunt plane tree in the back garden, from which the last leaves had already fallen, it shone faintly through a window upon the once more uncarpeted stairs and through another window into the room where the Fernandezes had lived; it shone likewise through the "office" window, touching with a dull gold the prancing silhouette of the "Lord Mayor", the wooden horse which (it had been decided) was never going to be restored to its owner, for fear it should "remind" her.

The whole house was silent, except that Mrs. Gambitt in the depth of the night and in her own room had completely broken down under the motherly influence of Mrs. Trubshore, who was taking care of her. She was shaken with wild sobs and could not be consoled, and the sound of her weeping was terrible, as if her spirit was trying to leave her body, and the body, with animal rage, was trying to prevent it. The sound of her weeping was far more terrible and unearthly than any of Mrs. Trubshore's "psychic" experiences, and as that stout and not easily upset woman said afterwards, she feared that Natalie would never stop, that she would have a fit or a stroke; she said she had feared for her reason, and had had to *wrestle* with Natalie's spirit in order to calm it. . . . But nobody else heard a sound, and it was only noticed in the morning that Mrs. Gambitt looked very pale and tired and was more placid than she had been since the fearful event.

Miss Brixworth was up early, preparing to leave the house for good, and on the stairs encountered Alston, who felt a little ashamed, while she felt a little sad, at the small response he had made to her kindness. But how could she understand a young fellow like that, and the feelings that governed his life?

"I'm so glad you weren't mixed up in all this," she said, shaking his warm hand with her cold one, "and I'm sorry we have to part. I hope you'll have very good luck, and perhaps we may meet again some day."

He hardly knew how to answer her, feeling ashamed before the open generosity of her nature, and as she turned away she felt sorry that she could have no place whatever in his life, that she could obviously be of no help to him at all, and that she would never see him again.

It is a strange fact that when he left the house for the last time he didn't even notice that the car was standing on the opposite side of the road, that very car which had once seemed like a symbol of life itself to him. Yet there it stood, looking as new and

powerful as ever, and all ready to be driven away. . . .
He had come nearer to life lately, and had other
things to think about.

As far as Fernandez was concerned there is little
more to tell. He was committed for trial, and when
he came up very little light was shed upon his past,
except that he had had something to do with a
theatre in Mexico, that he was supposed to have been
once employed for a time by a rubber company in
the East Indies, and that there was some reason to
believe him to be partly Swiss. Mrs. Gambitt felt
strengthened by the presence in court of Mrs. Trubshore, Mrs. Porter and Mrs. Rudd, and enjoyed
being for once in her life a centre of interest, a
heroine—a sergeant of police had been among the
first to congratulate her on her plucky behaviour.
She gave her evidence with firmness and courage,
and Fernandez was found guilty but insane, ordered
"to be detained during His Majesty's pleasure," and
removed to an asylum for criminal lunatics.

"I don't know whether capital punishment *can* be
right," said Miss Brixworth when she heard of the
sentence, "but I can't help thinking that he'd be
better dead."

"I should call the sentence very reasonable," said
Miss Haymer. "After all, a good many people, dead
and living, were responsible for the death of Mrs.
Fernandez. If disease and poverty and fear and love
are crimes, then Fernandez is a criminal. And he *is* a
criminal, there's no doubt of that. Fernandez,

whether mad or not, is responsible for what he did, but the community is responsible too, and it's only right that each should help to pay for the consequences—he by losing his liberty, and the community by undertaking to control the rest of his life."

"I don't see why the community should be held partly responsible."

"Well, he was a member of it, wasn't he? And still is."

"But does the community care, Fanny, what happens to the child?"

"No, but it ought to."

"Poor little Rosy, what a lot she'll miss!"

"And what a lot she'll gain! She'll escape, at any rate, the horrors of family life."

"I never can understand," said Miss Brixworth, "why you hate the idea of family life so much. I adored my parents, and they adored me. They did everything they could to make my childhood happy, and it *was* happy."

"You argue from your own case, Connie, and I argue from mine, so, although we differ, we're both of course right. I thought family life a perfect hell. It's not that our parents weren't fond of us and we of them—indeed, they were much too fond of us; that was just the trouble. They completely poisoned my sister Agnes's life with their wretched love. She was naturally an affectionate child and a docile one, and they brought her up to love and obey them. And when she began to grow up and they began to grow old the worst happened. They tried to bring her out and push her out a bit into the world, but it was already too late. They'd got their hooks into her by then and got them in deep. As their own world began to crumble (ill health kept them at home, and with advancing age their friends began to die off) they didn't try to make the best of the ruins. Oh, no. What did they do? They clung to Agnes. They were just like two huge parasites on the poor child. They just poisoned her existence with their beastly love, and because she was fond of them and sorry for them she just allowed them to go on with their "Aggie darling" here and their "Aggie darling" there until she woke up, and found that she was as old as they had been when she first started being the faithful daughter. All the love and pity she felt for them, or most of it, should have been turned on to a man and children, and instead of that it all turned sour. And to-day, conscious of duty done, she sits up and moulders on twopence a year with nothing to look back on and nothing to look forward to, and without the power to earn a living. It isn't as if our parents couldn't have done perfectly well without her (for nobody's indispensable in this world), they just made her think and made themselves think that they couldn't do without her. . . . Oh, family life can be a bitter business, Connie! And that's why I don't in the least mind the idea of the world having a dose of communism (if it's going to). No more helping mother for a bit! No more nursing father! No more ingrowing affection!

No more sexual atrophy! Let's think of the community for a change instead of the family—it'll be kinder to the individual in the long run."

"Well, I think it's just inhuman," said Miss Brixworth simply and boldly. "If you're going to take away the love of parents for children and children for parents and brotherly and sisterly love as well, it seems to me there might just as well be no life at all."

"It's not so much a question of taking away," said Miss Haymer, "as of ordering and controlling——"

"Anyway, I think it's horrible and unnatural. And what's more I don't believe human beings would ever submit to it."

"Human beings will submit to anything," said Miss Haymer, "if they're told to. They submitted to the War. . . . Anyway, we shall see——"

Miss Brixworth felt that it was no good arguing, but Miss Haymer returned to the attack.

"Look at the way those two awful women behaved," she said, holding up a large, claw-like hand, "the two you told me about, that wanted the fur coat."

"It's certainly rather an awful way to behave," Miss Brixworth agreed, "considering they're supposed to be her relations."

"Relations!" said Miss Haymer scornfully. "Relations are always rather awful."

"*My* relations were very kind to me, Fanny."

"So you say. *My* idea of relations is evidently not yours. *I*'ve found that if they're rich they despise you for being poor, and live in perpetual fear that you may ask them for help; if they're poor, they most unreasonably expect you to help them, are ungrateful if you do, and resentful if you don't. If they're neither richer nor poorer, they'll in any case treat you in a way they'd never dare to treat anybody else. Relations always obey that mysterious law, that people are hardest on their own kind. Set a servant to rule servants and see what happens—think of Mrs. Gambitt and Empringham. . . . And then try and do business with relations. They're sure to swindle you, or you'll swindle them, because one party'll conclude that the other's too nice to protest against its faults. No, my dear, that's an advantage of communism as I imagine it; it'll kill the family, at least for a time, and with it all its creaking machinery of odious cant and humbug, all the legacy-hunting, the dictatorships and useless sacrifices. Of course, it won't last. I'm not expecting a utopia on earth. In any case I shan't live to see some of the things I should like to see."

"I suppose not," said Miss Brixworth.

"And now," said Miss Haymer, "as I think I see a pale and watery gleam of sunshine—the only sort we can expect, I suppose, at the end of the year—let's put on our things and go out for half an hour before tea. Also, I think I'll just tell Empringham to pop out and get some flowers. It makes him feel important to order tradespeople about, and a breath of fresh air'll do him good."

I don't see anything very communistic in *that*, thought Miss Brixworth, but she said nothing. Perhaps she understood that Miss Haymer's enthusiasm for a cause so alien to the system she had been brought up to believe in was nothing but a kind of ironical courage—Fanny Haymer loved life, and would keep hold of it as long as she could, putting a good face on impossible conditions, and not only a good face, but a face at once cheerful, sophisticated, sceptical and painted.

A few minutes later the two of them might have been seen promenading slowly along the street, Miss Haymer leaning with one hand on her friend's arm and with the other on her rubber-ended stick, Miss Brixworth carrying that long, slender umbrella of hers with the curved silver handle, and both of them obvious survivals of an age that is past. And so we may leave them, Miss Haymer, with her raddled face, baroque jewellery and old-fashioned furs, a hard, shrewd, sentimental old English eccentric, holding forth in a rich, cracked voice, while her friend Miss Brixworth, rather shabby and rather unwilling to attract attention, now and then protested against her arguments in tones that were mild and pleading, in a gentle, cultivated voice that seemed, in this harsh and grinding world, almost the voice of a ghost. And indeed, as the sun was now setting, and the winter afternoon fading into a whitish, frosty fog, the two women, tottering slowly out of sight, seemed to dissolve into some other element than that in which ordinary people must live. . . .

How different their world to that of Pascall and

Alston! Imagine these two, a few days after the
murder, driving off with Amy into the country in a
little old two-seater car which Alston had borrowed
from somebody, the three of them wedged in together, Amy in her little red hat with the swallow
ornament, Pascall at the wheel with his curls blowing about, and Alston between them, enjoying some
of the best moments of his life, while the leafless
woods flew past and the speedometer needle, pointing to the highest figure it could reach, trembled as
if it were pointing to the magnetic pole of joy. Many
a moment now told how things were—Alston pushing
away his plate in the middle of a meal and lighting
a cigarette; Amy fingering her cotton-gloved left
hand with her right, touching the third finger to feel
the little ring he had given her; or the expression on
Pascall's face as he came out of the water at the
swimming baths. . . . Oh, and then there was the bye-
election. Not that it was so different from others. The
voters were as usual bamboozled by worthless pro-
mises and silly lies to vote for one or other of a batch
of harmless self-seeking windbags to represent them
in the grandmother of parliaments, but there was a
good deal of fuss in the press; indeed the more Conservative papers had much to say about "organised
rowdyism" and "communism," by which they meant
that the candidate they supported was so dull that
only a donkey could have listened to him patiently,
and that a crowd of workless louts enjoyed making a
fool of him and a nuisance of themselves at every

one of his meetings. Sir Herbert Fogg was a pompous bore who was trying to get into Parliament mainly because his wife knew that some of his investments were in danger and vainly imagined that he could use some power to save them—he was one of those elderly men who forget to cut the hair out of their ears, whose eyebrows look like moustaches, who read *Punch* every week and admire themselves enormously.

Alston and Pascall were present at his last meeting, which was certainly a lively one. Every time the old buffer tried to speak there was a mocking roar and a chorus of catcalls from the yahoos. A rotten tomato caught him on the jaw and oozed down between his tall collar and his puffy neck, and in the end there was a general scrum and stampede, together with a terrific din of shouting and struggling. Alston and Pascall were both mixed up in the free fight (not, of course, as Conservative supporters) and Pascall got a nasty cut on the hand from a piece of glass falling from a broken window. Alston managed to fight a way through the crowd and get him outside, where he produced a handkerchief and tied up the place as carefully as he could. In his eyes there shone something like the bright, fanatical devotion of the beardless Achilles kneeling to bind up the wounded arm of Patroclus, who, seated on the ground and in pain, clenches his white teeth between his bearded lips (eager that no complaint shall escape from them) and turns away his graceful head, the two men forming, for an instant of time and for ever, an image of courage, beauty and love.

Seeing them together one might have regarded them as one little sign among many of approaching changes. We know we are nearing the end of the long Gothic age of chivalry and mariolatry—individualistic, commercial, "Christian" and bankrupt—and if society returns (as Miss Frances Haymer half jokingly and half seriously anticipated) to more communistic forms at all comparable to those of the early world, perhaps it will be rediscovered that friendship can be a noble passion, no enemy to good government and good taste, but something that can be made (as in the past) to serve the State directly, turning those who share it into good citizens, temperate, unselfish and resourceful.

THE END